SHOULD THIS BOOK BE BANNED?
An Anthology

Published by:
Ohio Writers' Group
DBA Ohio Writers' Association
838 Campbell Avenue
Columbus, OH 43223 USA

Editors: Brienne Daugherty & Travis Ray
Concept: Jim Hodnett
Typesetting & Cover Design: Joe Graves

Special thanks to all of our judges and editors who made this anthology possible.

Print ISBN – 13: 979-8-9870174-7-0
eBook ISBN – 13: 979-8-9870174-8-7

Printed in USA.

SHOULD THIS BOOK BE BANNED?
An Anthology

Presented by
The Ohio Writers' Association

"Any book worth banning is a book worth reading."
- Isaac Asimov

CONTENTS

PREFACE

We were all set to begin work on our 2024 anthology. The theme was nearly finalized, the team was built, and we were in the final stages before announcing it publicly. That's when the Ohio Writers' Board met and discussed the onslaught of banned book debates happening in our country. As a literary and writing organization committed to championing diverse stories, we felt responsible for responding. So, we shifted the focus of our anthology and went back to the drawing board—even building a new team from scratch. I'm glad we did.

I am particularly grateful to Jim Hodnett for contributing and campaigning this idea. His story, "Trophy Husband," is an excellent example of the kind of narratives we hoped to amplify in this collection. None of this would have been possible without the tireless efforts of Brienne Daugherty and Travis Ray, who poured countless hours into making this anthology a reality.

The authors of this anthology bring together diverse perspectives, including LGBTQ+ and straight individuals, allies and critics, atheists and clergy, Black and white voices, psychologists and neuroscientists, college students, and retired professors. What follows is a deeply human collection of stories—honest, authentic, and moving. Within these pages, you will encounter narratives that wrestle with religion, the LGBTQ+ community, race, immigration, and the tangled realities of privilege and hypocrisy. The topics explored range from sex, money, and power to their often devastating impact on the most vulnerable among us. These characters embody the courage to embrace their true selves and the struggle to do what's right in a world that often pushes back. Alongside these themes, you'll find examinations of capitalism, toxic family dynamics, abuse, resilience, and even a touch of science fiction and horror—and these themes only scratch the surface of what this anthology has to offer.

The beauty of reading stories is that you don't need to agree with a narrative to understand it. In this understanding, empathy sneaks in quietly and transforms us for the better.

Joe Graves
President, Ohio Writers' Association

INTRODUCTION

I once heard it said that coming out is an act of survival.

The more people who know they have an LGBTQ+ family member, neighbor, co-worker, or friend, the less likely they are to view the community as a threat. The same goes for any other marginalized group. The more visible its members and their perspectives, the more clearly they can be seen in the fullness of their humanity.

Storytelling can play a vital role in this process of fostering understanding and appreciation of those different from us. Numerous studies have shown that readers of fiction, particularly literary fiction, tend to exhibit more empathy toward others, especially others in stigmatized groups. (Check out the Aug. 28, 2020, issue of Discover magazine for more information on this topic.) With fiction, readers enter the lives of characters and learn what makes them tick, what their struggles are, and how they view the world. We are presented with opportunities to challenge preconceived or outdated ideas, including hateful ones. When readers are members of one or more privileged groups, they can grow to understand how those who are marginalized view them and what they can do to foster equity. An additional benefit, of course, is that representation of marginalized groups in literature can lead to fewer feelings of isolation and more empowerment for members of those groups.

As a writers' organization, we encourage creators of all sorts to speak truth to power, whether those truths are difficult, joyful, or boundary-pushing. All of us are enriched when someone shines a light on a difficult topic like capitalism, religion, racism, or mental health. But it is important to remember that the truths we speak to power may not always be blatantly political or polemical. There is value in simply sharing one's experience of life in, for instance, a black body, a fat body, or a trans body. Some of the stories in this anthology do just that.

In embracing the humanity of people and ideas less familiar to us we leave ourselves open to a fuller understanding of the world and how we fit into it. Authentic, honest stories written by and about marginalized communities have the power to save lives. This is our goal with Should This Book Be Banned?

Jim Hodnett
Ohio Writers' Association Board Member

MONTAG, READ ON
by John P. Michael

We stand in praise of Ulysses and in
wariness of the firemen who would
burn Mann, Steiner, Jung and Locke.
Let evil sit down away, away as a
forgotten rock.

For knowledge bears hate kindly and
calls forth fruitful thoughts, pushing aside
simplicity, darkened lights and imagined
naughts.

We will bear as a monk
hunched, determined and aflame
for intellect will not
be a blackened effect made.
Press on and defy at the embattled hour
no moth will eat the script so painfully laid.

Take the books, burn them, we watch the
immolation
of your minds papered with godly
righteousness.

John Michael (he/him) is the author of numerous poems published in literary journals. A new collection of poetry is to be published in Autumn 2025. He is a member of the Cincinnati Writers Project and Greater Cincinnati Writers League. He resides in Cincinnati with his wife and her vegetable garden.

HER EYES AND MINE
by Austen Masters

I'm still not happy when I see my reflection. Last night I almost cried when I saw her, even though I knew she didn't do anything wrong. I was just having a bad day, which to be fair is most of them. I couldn't be her yesterday, and I don't know if I can be her today either, but maybe I'm a bit closer.

She doesn't have a name, not yet. She's me, but I'm not truly her. She has had many temporary names but none of them stuck. The last time I bothered to give her a name she was 'Erica', but that didn't last longer than a day. Other names have been Julie, Carmen, Kassie, Abigail, Nora, Olivia, Isobelle, Evelyn, Megan, Ivy, Sophie, and Rebecca. None of the names I have chosen feel right.

So I kept the name I was given at birth, even if it felt like a cold mesh covering my skin. Every time I'm called that it feels suffocating. I strike different poses in the mirror. If I stretch out my neck it looks a bit thinner, then if I push my shoulders back I feel just a touch more elegant, more refined. I place my hand on my chest, imagining my nails manicured, but I don't like the length of my fingers. They're too thick, too masculine.

I'm brought out of the trance my reflection has placed on me by the sound of my phone ringing. The default jingle that could mean anyone was calling. I'm surprised to see my brother, Stephen, appear in the image of his contact photo. His photo smiles at me; a moment captured when we went to the county fair together. The last time we ever had fun before I told him the truth. When I answer the phone he calls me by that horrible name, but I don't fault him for it.

"I have some bad news," he says, his voice soft.

"Is she gone?" I ask, a bit quicker than I intend to. I know I sound uncaring, but we all know it was only a matter of time before Mom died.

He is quiet for a moment, but confirms my suspicion with a quiet 'yes'.

"How's Dad handling it?" I ask. I can easily envision what he looks like right now. His pinkish skin turned a darker shade of red, his lips formed into a tight line as he tries to hold back his tears despite them slowly falling down his face.

"Not good," Stephen says. "Normally he only cries this hard when he's chopping onions for dinner."

Stephen lets out a weak laugh that I don't return. I know he's only trying to lighten the mood, but not even he expects humor to work at a time like this. The crack in his voice gives him away. He's broken up by this but doesn't want to show it.

"Thank you for letting me know," I say, unsure of what to do in this situation. Perhaps it's because I knew it was only a matter of time, but instead of sadness, I don't feel much of anything. I'm numb.

"There's something else," Stephen says, his words slow and careful. "Dad says because of everything you have…going on, that you shouldn't come to the funeral. He says it would be too much."

"I can still go," I say. "I'll keep to myself if that would make things easier."

"No," Stephen says firmly. "You know we don't live in the safest place for people like…you. We can't keep you safe."

He's right. Dad nor Stephen have ever been good at confrontation, so I don't say anything as I hang up the phone. The silence of the room, of my mind, and of my heart feels empty yet overwhelming.

This isn't right. I just found out my mother died, and I can't even go to her funeral yet I feel nothing. I had heard that sometimes numbness was an early sign of a panic attack; the calm before the storm. I go to the kitchen to make myself some tea. I pick black chai tea, a personal favorite of mine. I think that if I can become calm before I become sad it will be easier for me.

I feel my heart rate slowly go up as I wait for the water to boil, and even more when I steep the bag. I don't bother to add anything to it, and I burn my tongue on the hot tea. I barely register the pain of the scalding liquid going down my throat until I begin to cough. The tea erupts from my throat and onto the table, splattering on the hardwood and dripping onto my pants and carpet below it. It still burns through the fabric of my jeans, and I hiss at the heat.

My heart rate is only going faster, and I feel my breath quicken despite my coughing fit almost making breathing impossible. My mother's face flashes through my mind. I remember when I was sitting on her bed before she got ready to go on a date with Father. I was perhaps 5 or 6, young enough for my interest in her jewelry and makeup to be seen as a childlike curiosity. She asked for my help picking out her earrings, no doubt just finding it cute that I wanted to help her get ready. I remember she smelled nice that night, and I was mesmerized by how different she looked with makeup on. Her pale skin almost seemed to glow when she stepped outside into the moonlight with Father. I wanted to look like that, I wanted to look like my mother. Her slim frame and delicate hands, her sharp eyes, and a wide smile.

I run back to the bathroom, almost slipping on the tile floor as I look into the mirror. I don't have any of her features except for her brown eyes. My shoulders are too wide, my hands too large. My eyes are round like Father's, and I can't even bring myself to smile to see if I see her in it.

The only other similarity I see in myself is the anger in my face, the same anger I saw in hers when I visited her in the hospital. The anger she felt as she screamed at me to get out of her sight. She knew she was going to die, we all did, and yet she couldn't embrace me. She couldn't set aside her pride to embrace me, her child one last time before the end. I won't even get the closure of seeing her before her burial. I won't be protected by my father or brother. I've been abandoned by them too when all she had to do was embrace me!

I look into my mother's eyes as I rear back my fist and punch the mirror, cracks forming a large web around it. Blood slowly trickles down my trembling fist as I pull it back. There is no sound other than my ragged breaths and the gentle trickle of blood hitting the bathroom tiles. The mirror distorts my reflection. I don't recognize myself. I look better this way.

Austen Masters (he/him) Austen is a grad student from Kent State University currently enrolled in the NEOMFA program and attends classes at Kent State, Akron University, and Cleveland State. He is known for having several writing projects in the works at any given time because only having one to focus on isn't exciting enough. He lives with his husband, his best friend, and their dog and cat in Cuyahoga Falls, Ohio.

ROSE GARDEN
by Lois Spencer

"I know what you and Dad should do for your silver anniversary," April announces this morning as soon as her father leaves the table. She drops her half-eaten muffin on a napkin and focuses her attention on the business at hand: "Repeat your wedding vows right here in your own rose garden."

My roses will be in full bloom by then, she says, and the new arbor finished—no surprises there. Then she says all I need to do is make a few decisions; she will handle the rest. She reels off bakeries I could count on and local musicians—including a stringed quartet she had probably never heard of—much like a server regurgitating the day's specials they have yet to sample. Oh, she has been coached all right, and by an expert. She winds down as a heavy rumble advances up the driveway, her fiancé Mark's pick-up. "And you won't have to do a thing, Mom, I promise." She vanishes through the door like the ethereal ribbon of steam wafting up from the coffee carafe.

Through the window above the sink, I watch April bombard Mark as he alights from his truck, but her topic is certainly no longer my anniversary, but details of her own wedding in August. My husband Daniel leans against the fender of his vintage Stingray, arms and ankles crossed, waiting. Then April, clinging to Mark's side, gives her father a thumbs up: Message delivered.

I've seen enough. I grab a sweater and slip outside, avoiding the threesome by way of the gentle rise leading to my rose garden, the yellow tabby Fitz at my heels. I imagine my sister Marian's reaction when I tell her about April's announcement: "That's a mighty big offer, what with her own wedding coming right up." We both know whose Huckleberry April is.

The breeze barely moves the chimes on the patio this morning, but the morning Daniel and I first stood here viewing the brand-new house and uncultivated grounds, a March gale whipped through our hair, bearing traces of snow. After years of hard work and setbacks, Daniel's chain of auto parts and service stores had finally taken off, and a showcase house in a swanky neighborhood was next on his agenda. The evening before, I'd discovered that a fine-looking wife was another essential, and April, a toothy thirteen-year-old, had been put in charge of Mom's wardrobe.

"You can't wear that old thing to a big company dinner," she said as I laid out my go-to gray suit. Her solution: an emergency run to Belle Toi, the one posh ladies' shop in Bickford, a mid-sized town hugging the banks of the Muskingum River. The female contingent of FFBs, my sister's shorthand for First Families of Bickford, all shopped there. Too bad Polaris Mall in Columbus was so far away; I'd have felt a lot more at ease enveloped by a crowd of strangers. But April got her way, and I met Daniel at the door that evening, decked out in a red taffeta sheath and a pair of large silver earrings. "Perfect," he said, giving me an appreciative kiss and his daughter a high-five.

The next morning, in this windswept spot, he gathered me up tightly, no doubt remembering the heads I'd turned the night before. The rough wool of his jacket and his arms around me took some of the chill out of my bones. "Here's where your rose garden will go—the biggest and the best Bickford has ever seen."

A month later we abandoned the five-room dwelling with my grandmother's tea roses banking the front porch and hauled our meager belongings to this place, as vaulted and echoing as a cathedral. Marian and her husband Carl helped with the move, their twin boys tagging along.

As she climbed out of the pickup, my sister's expression reinforced the stark difference between this dwelling and the doublewide where she, Carl, and the boys lived on the other side of town.

Never unprepared for the moment, Marian gestured toward the tiny rose bushes—stick-like ugly ducklings tethered to their stakes by string and hope—and rendered the first two lines of Lynn Anderson's "I Never Promised You a Rose Garden" slightly off-key. "You picked a winner, Sis. Danny Boy not only promised you one but delivered it too. Never been that lucky myself." Carl's bloodshot eyes registered oblivion at Marian's comments. Not so Daniel, tuned in as he always was to Marian's sarcasm. His fine dark eyebrows met over the bridge of his nose.

"April," I called loud enough to drag her away from her phone and to prevent a verbal slugfest between my sister and my husband. April's blond head caught the morning sun as she appeared on the patio.

"Why don't you give your cousins the grand tour." Then I picked up a box of dishes from Carl's truck bed and handed it to Marian. I slid out another box and led the way to the kitchen. In silence, we unwrapped cups and glasses and placed them on newly papered shelves.

April's tour eventually ended at the sloping backyard where new green shoots had begun to appear beneath the straw. Marian's boys whooped and hollered as they rolled downhill and then staggered back up for another go. Viewing them through the kitchen door, Marian tossed down the dish towel, ready to end their fun, but Carl, jolted out of his hangover by their shouts, got there first. He yanked both boys by the arm and dragged them to the open tailgate of his pick-up where he dropped them with neck-wrenching jolts. Neither boy uttered a peep.

Marian turned away, visibly swallowing her words. The sunlight flooding the kitchen made her pale skin translucent. Along one cheek was the dark shadow of a fading bruise. My finger traced it gently, and she covered her initial flinch with a laugh. "Clumsy me, I slipped on the stairs," she said, pointing to a scuff mark on her arm as further proof. I wondered what else I had been missing.

That evening, I carried a stack of emptied boxes to the garage where Daniel was aligning wrenches in his new tool chest with the same precision as the neckties on their rack upstairs. "Carl's too rough with the boys," I said. "And Marian has a bruise on her face I'm sure Carl put there."

"Those boys are a handful and Marian's got a nasty mouth on her," was all he had to say. So much for that, I thought.

From the day of the move through June, I noticed that Marian's normal bravado and cryptic commentary remained subdued. But I was so busy minding my roses with what I dared not admit was a love-hate relationship and creating a home in Daniel's showplace that concern about my sister received short shrift. Then, in September, came a 911 call from the doublewide that put Marian in the hospital, the boys into foster care, and Carl into police custody. The last thing Daniel needed was the notoriety of association, so—coward that I've always been—I limited contact with my sister to phone calls and texts.

By Thanksgiving, Marian had rebounded with a vengeance. She retrieved her boys, and all three moved to a women's shelter, its location she couldn't disclose even to me. By the time I was hanging festive lights and garlands on a massive spruce, Daniel had placed at the two-story window, Marian had landed a job and found an apartment for her and the boys, the date for her divorce hearing already set.

***

Walking through the stake-marked area in the rose garden this morning, I spray glossy dark leaves and tight buds with a gentle mist, keeping one eye on the driveway where the trio is gathered around the raised hood of Mark's truck. He's come to the right place for help; Daniel has never lost his love of working on engines and such. When we were dating, I hung around the garage at his parents' house many evenings at his insistence while he tinkered on a '69 Camaro, his long torso stretched across the nose or booted feet sticking out from beneath the chassis. By the time he walked me home, I was scented with gasoline and motor oil too.

As Daniel reaches deeper into the engine compartment, Mark's arm drops from April's shoulder, nudging her aside without so much as a pause. Her chatter stops and she steps back in silence. The morning sun is warm on my back, but a chill runs up my spine. How many times has she observed Daniel's nudges—physical and verbal—and my compliance?

They say girls marry men like their fathers and if anyone proves the adage true in my family, it's my sister, because Daniel has never raised a hand to me. But then, neither had Dad. When he showed up rotten drunk and mean and took his misery out on Mom, I cowered under the quilt fearful of my fate if I ran into the fray. Marian, though, waded right in, learning all about bruises and bloody noses long before she met Carl.

By comparison, Daniel was a saint, and I had no trouble believing that he was. When we were first married, I'd come in from closing out JC Penney's to find his face lit by a computer screen filled with spreadsheets, dark hair falling across his forehead. I'd plant a few kisses along the back of his neck, across the stubble on his jawline, and by the time I reached his mouth, nothing in his world mattered but me, and I felt wholly cherished. And that was enough, it seemed at the time, to make up for abandoning my hopes for college and career. But once Daniel found his sweet spot in the business world, my job as a manager at Penney's became an embarrassment, and he made sure I was too preoccupied to focus on college classes even when we could afford them. A growing daughter and a rapidly changing lifestyle overrode my regrets for a time.

***

Following Marian's divorce and establishment of life on her own, she and I got together now and then for a girls' day out, something that would never have happened when Carl ruled the roost. Those days weren't high on Daniel's list, either; unless they included a stop at Belle Toi, the dress shop on Front Street where April had dragged me to buy the red taffeta. Since then, rag-tag had been out and high-end in.

It was Marian who spied the "Position Open" notice in the display window a couple of years later as we strolled casually toward the door. "Hey, Sis, you should apply."

"Me? Why?"

"To get you out of that mausoleum before you go stir crazy for one thing." She grabbed my arm and practically shoved me inside.

Under her steely gaze, I filled out the application, feeling like Alice tumbling headlong into the rabbit hole. Knowing me as a steady customer, the manager, Helen, hired me on the spot. Marian and I were back in the car with a folder full of new employee information. Marian was exuberant and so was I for about five seconds. As usual, Marian read my mind.

"He'll get over it," she said. "Don't take him so seriously."

Back home, though, I was tempted to call Helen and say an emergency had come up. But wandering through my elegant space, kept spotless by a human dynamo masquerading as a cleaning lady, I realized how much I wanted the job. I'd been great in sales at Penney's. And, as Marian had said, there wasn't much going on here.

I waited until Daniel snapped his laptop shut that evening, ending his business day. He didn't appear surprised at my revelation, but his words were measured and emphatic, exactly what I expected: "April's just starting high school, and you run your wheels off keeping up with her already." I could have said the job was part-time. Or that I really wanted it, but his decisions never changed because of petty excuses.

Later, I kept well to my side of the bed, facing the wall. Daniel's method of reconciliation once we've gone to bed usually begins with an impatient hand on my shoulder, my cue to roll over and initiate amends. If I fail to comply, a lesson in logic is often necessary.

"Can't you see how absurd it would be for you to get a job? If you had a real profession, maybe. But clerking in a store? Anyone can do that."

Anybody but me, it seems. I wish I had the guts to voice my thoughts aloud. When I don't roll over with open arms, he flips onto his other side and gives me the cold shoulder too. Even so, I knew holding out for long would be impossible. Finding an excuse for Helen at Belle Toi might be awkward, but all I could do about Marian was try to avoid her.

***

Over the spray from the garden hose, I hear Mark's truck start.

He backs down the driveway with April beside him gesturing a mile a minute. As soon as Mark gave April her diamond, she dropped out of Ohio University and left everything but her clothes to her dorm mate. I urged her to change her mind: "What if you want a career later on? It never hurts to have choices."

"All I want is Mark and a houseful of babies," she said, leafing through the glossy pages of Modern Bride.

When I mentioned my concern to her father, all I got was a shrug. "April was never a serious student. And it won't be long before Mark can take care of her and all the babies she wants." In the meantime, he gave April a piece-of-cake job in one of his stores.

From the driveway, I hear, "Damn you, cat!" and a prolonged yowl from a yellow streak escaping Daniel's wrath: You'd think that cat would learn to stay off his cars.

"Sounds like you had better call the carpenter and get him busy on the arbor," Daniel says, joining me as the garden hose retracts into its housing and I head back toward the patio.

"April's plans don't sound half bad, do they?"

Despite his effort to mask it, I sometimes see the uncertainty, the ghost of poor-boy-out-to-make-good. It reminds me why his lawn and his house have to outdo all the neighbors. He needs the perfect venue in which to display the crowning accomplishment of the man who has achieved it all: the ideal marriage.

Just then the house phone rings. Daniel crosses the patio and picks up the unit inside the back door. I follow him into the kitchen. "Of course, she's here, Marian. What do you need?"

Although I'm within arm's reach, Daniel turns, keeping the phone to his ear. "I'm sure she would love to go any other time, but we've made plans."

Since this is Saturday, Daniel will wash the Vette, and if he doesn't have a golf game, he may run downtown for car wax. I don't see a "we" in any of that. As I take the phone, my nails rake the back of his hand. "Hi, Marian, what's up?"

"Bet your plans can't beat a girl's day out," she says. A voice I'm not sure is mine responds: "Great, but let's check out the Bridgeport

Mall. I'm tired of the stores here."

At the sink, Daniel runs cold water over the faint pink stripes on his hand. He jerks a dish towel off the rack and dries his hands, then wipes up water spots that have splashed out of the sink. The coffee left in the pot beside us smells bitter and stale.

His words follow me as I head for the stairs: "I can't believe you did that."

I wonder, Is he talking about my scratching his hand or what I told Marian? It really doesn't matter. During the daytime, salvaging his goodwill requires a slightly different process: One, slide my arms around his waist. Two, apologize for my transgression. Three, comply with his wishes. And there he stands, arms folded, with every reason in the world to expect this time to be like all the others.

Again, my thoughts adopt the stranger's voice: Sorry about your luck, Danny-boy. When Marian pulls up in the driveway, the house is silent, and Daniel is nowhere in sight.

My sister and I wander in and out of the Bridgeport shops, small talk covering April's wedding and Marian's boys' latest girlfriends. However brave I'd felt when we left, I know there is no avoiding the imbroglio I'll face upon return.

When we take a break on a bench across from the pet store, Marian confronts me. "What's he done this time? Brought home another car you hate or insisted that you redecorate the living room?"

Marian never forgets. Last year Daniel sent my well-used Impala to auction and brought home a Cadillac Escalade. I'm still trying to figure out all its features. Just last week he informed me that wallpaper in the foyer is yesterday's look. Another task for you-know-who.

I watch the white Norwegian Elkhound leaping ineffectually against the window. "You know about the anniversary bash he's got in mind. The whole idea makes me sick to my stomach. Any ideas how to tell him?"

Marian takes a long swill of Coke through her straw. Since she got away from Carl, she looks more like the sister I grew up with, the one who had spunk enough to challenge Dad and take a licking for her trouble. "Just like you told me. What's hard about that?"

"It's not that simple, Marian." I get up and toss my paper cup into the trash bin and run damp palms down the sides of my capris. "It's never that simple."

My sister's voice is brisk. "Well, Little Sis, it's high time you make it simple. Is this the way you want to spend the rest of your life?"

I wish I could say yes and mean it or no and not feel guilty and thankless. What I really want is a chance to find out what I want. But how do I say that to her? Or to Daniel?

Marian's look is arch and knowing: "Not all bruises are on the outside. But they do make themselves known Evelyn, and yours are screaming loud and clear."

We pull back into my driveway as the spring evening darkens. Daniel has turned on the floodlights to enhance the house and grounds. He is somewhere in that well-appointed structure, hoping I'll get over whatever is bugging me before I mess up his plans for the big day.

Marian reaches across the console and touches my arm. "I want you to listen. There are two reasons I stuck with Carl as long as I did. First, I thought I could keep a lid on things. Play by the rules. I don't open my mouth, and Carl doesn't knock me around. Trouble was—well, you know my mouth, and you know Carl. And as crazy as it sounds, the other reason is even worse. However bad things got, I knew what to expect. Giving up that certainty, twisted as it was, was hard going. And being on my own hasn't been all sunshine and roses either."

Flinching at her reference to roses, I slide from the seat.

She backs out as I walk up the driveway and around to the rear of the house. The disquieting spring evening has grown chilly, and spring peepers have set up their chorus in the marsh below the house. Recovered from his mad chase through the neighborhood, Fitz wraps my ankles, and I gather his damp, furry body close. A deep, rumbling vibrates in my arms.

In a few short weeks, this lawn will overflow with festivity, my roses, a riot of color, just beyond the impressive arbor where Daniel and I stand to cut the tiered cake, the admiration of our guests warming him to the core. No one will notice that my cheeks have begun to cramp, that my smile is as brittle as the rosettes on the cake. April's smile, as she leans on Mark's arm, is radiant. But what happens if fissures mar her storybook marriage? Will she take up the harlequin's mask? And when I see that happen, will I look back at this moment of absolute clarity and regret my silence?

I walk to the outline of stakes that delineates the proposed arbor. Holding a contented Fitz to my side the way April used to carry her Pooh Bear when an extra shot of courage was needed, I pull up the stakes, all eighteen of them, and leave them where they fall, crisscrossed, helter-skelter. A glance toward the kitchen doorway shows a silhouette, unmoving as marble, a man fully convinced that his wife has taken leave of her senses. Once I've said my piece, the tissue-thin mystique of marriage that Daniel prizes for all the wrong reasons will shatter like a champagne flute, and I don't know what will be left.

Lois Spencer (she/her) has taught English at Fort Frye High School, at Washington State Community College and Ohio Valley University, and in the ILR program at Marietta College. Publication credits include OWA's House of Secrets Anthology, Pine Mountain Sand and Gravel, Anthology of Appalachian Writers, Persimmon Tree, The Poorhouse Rag, Change Seven, Women Speak, and Northern Appalachia Review. Her memoir, In the Language of My Country, highlights life in Southeastern Ohio.

BLESSED BE THE PIG
by Christina Moore

My enemy is Porkchop. He's on the other end of the boxcar, as far from me as he can get. Beside him snores Bacon, perfuming the night with his flatulence. Gravy nestles beneath the straw. Despite the oppressive heat, she sleeps peacefully, her round stomach rising and falling with each breath. Picklefoot is fitful, cradled as she is in the back corner. Her breath labors through her snout. Occasionally, she wakes with a snort but settles back again.

I lay awake, feeling the rock and sway of the boxcar. We are on the move again. The mechanical whir of the fan mixes with the clicking of wheels. I'm grateful for the thick straw cushion between me and the metal floor.

Thanks be to the Farmer who comforts us with straw of purest gold.

There are horses in the car ahead of us, massive creatures with heavy hooves and flowing manes. They punctuate the night with stomping and unhappy bellows. In front of them are the sheep and goats bleating in fear as the train lurches and jolts down the track.

As I doze off, I forget where I am. I dream I'm back on the farm huddled against the warm hull of my mother. In sleep, I can see the barn clearly, how its dark interior frames the broad green meadow and deep blue sky. I remember the dew shimmering above the grass and the fireflies mingling with the stars against the purple night. Most of all, I remember the warm milk of our mother.

There are five of us left, all born of the same sow. Even as sucklings, we pushed each other aside scrambling for the same row of teats. Originally we were ten. I don't know what happened to the other five.

We left the farm behind when we were loaded into the Farmer's truck. I watched the barn recede into the distance through wooden slats, inhaling fresh meadow grass as the truck rattled us away toward tar and asphalt.

From there we traveled to a ramshackle house shaded by a giant chestnut tree. Its generous limbs spread out across the entire yard.

We slept beneath the safety of its branches where we wallowed in mud and ate slop straight from the kitchen. We learned to race on a track constructed from bales of hay. There were six of us back then. Five to race, with one to spare. At the end of every race, each pig was rewarded with a carrot pulled from the soil.

It was also there that we discovered the apple and the sweetness of its flesh.

The sunlight in my dream dissolves as the train erupts in a mournful howl. I'm reminded of where I am. My snout is filled with the scent of burning coal. This night has not brought its gift of cooler temperatures. The boxcar has become an oven, its darkness weighing heavy on my chest.

Tomorrow, we'll awaken in a different town, but I'm not worried. My pen will be the same and so too will be the track and all that surrounds it. Dull parking lots will be transformed by rows of garishly painted booths, each selling a minute or two of time. The sky will be blanketed with canvas-striped blue, with lights of every color displacing the stars. All this will be assembled after we reach our destination.

Only then will the faces emerge. Broad faces with narrow snouts appear even more grotesque through the shimmer of heat. Their voices pour together like rushing water until I feel as if I might drown. The sea of faces used to terrify me. Now they are blurs and shadows. They are barely even real.

I drift back to sleep and dream about the apple again. Its sweetness coats my tongue. In my dreams, the apple is mine. But in the real world, it belongs to the quickest pig around the track. Currently, that pig is Porkchop. He is the fastest of us, but I'm more determined. I will get my apple back.

Blessed be the determined pig for the apple shall be his.

I almost got the apple back three races ago, but it was stolen. As I approached the finish line, Porkchop nipped my ear with his sharp incisor, drawing blood and causing me to turn my head. It was just enough for him to get a single trotter across the line before me. Yesterday, Gravy won the apple by stretching her snout across the finish line and beating Porkchop by an inch. The Farmer called it a photo-finish but gave the apple to Gravy. Porkchop nursed his temper for the rest of the morning.

Gravy lost the apple in the afternoon during the second race of the day. Bacon sent her careening into Picklefoot who slammed into me. I tumbled onto the track rolling into the rail. By the time I regained my footing, the apple had already been placed in Porkchop's mouth. After the race, he handed the apple over to Bacon. Such things should never be allowed, but the Farmer turned a blind eye.

When we first started racing, Bacon used to win almost every race, but as his belly grows fatter, he grows slower. He hasn't won a race since three towns ago, back when we were still piglets. He's now twice as large as the rest of us, larger than Gravy and Porkchop combined. Yet, despite his gluttony, the Farmer is pleased with him, often awarding him with treats on the sly for doing nothing other than sleep in the hay.

Only Picklefoot has yet to win, despite starting on the inside track she consistently falls a pig length behind. The problem with Picklefoot is that until recently she's lacked determination. She was never going to win simply by trying her best. I think she must be digging deep inside herself, to find her inner apple, because she's starting to catch up. Soon she'll have an advantage. Unlike the rest of us, she hasn't suffered the loss of speed that comes with bulk. Her body remains as lean as it was when she was a piglet. I sometimes hear her tiny hooves hot on my trotters as she attempts to overtake me from behind. The day will come when she will rush by me, winning the apple for herself.

Picklefoot is not my enemy, I remind myself. *My enemy is Porkchop.*

The next morning, I wake to the sound of rain pounding against the metal roof. It's now comfortable and cool inside the boxcar. The engine has gone silent. The Farmer is busy filling the troughs with our feed, poured forth from a burlap sack. If he's generous, we'll get slop, which he carries in a green bucket. I do not see the green bucket today.

Sing praises to the Farmer who bathes the earth in showers of corn.

I nudge Picklefoot with my snout, but she lays motionless in the ammonia-soaked straw, her eyes staring past me toward the open door.

The Farmer spots her too and knocks me away with a firm kick from his leather boot, "Get away from that Hambone, you vulture!"

I shrink back in deference. He holds a lantern over Picklefoot's prone body, sending shards of flickering light through the shadowed corner of the boxcar. Gravy now stands beside me, her body tense with anticipation. Together, we bear witness to the Farmer whose munificence knows no bounds.

This is the moment when the Farmer will bring Picklefoot back to life, granting her a piece of his own spirit by sending his breath through her inanimate snout. He'll then brush his calloused hand across her forehead in a blessing, and she will rise, ready to race again.

All hail the Farmer who bestows miracles on those who believe.

"Well shit," the Farmer mutters as he crouches above Picklefoot, scrutinizing her through deep-set eyes. When he carries her away by the trotters, I experience a sensation I can't describe. It's like watching the barn disappear over and over again in my sleep. It can't be real, yet the barn is never here when I wake up.

The Farmer stands outside the open door in conversation with the Hand. The Hand is not gentle like the Farmer. His eyes are pale and hard, and his boots have metal studded toes which he uses to make us obey the Farmer's commandments.

"Well, it looks like we'll be down a pig for the rest of the season," the Farmer says, dangling Picklefoot by a single trotter.

"I warned you not to pick the runt," the Hand responds through a cloud of cigarette smoke, "Surprised it lasted this long."

"People like the small ones," the Farmer responds, "gives them an underdog to root for."

"But this one is useless, ain't never won a race." A burst of raspy laughter erupts from the Hand.

"It'll win with the missus," the Farmer responds, "It's practically a suckling. We usually roast one up at the end of the season anyway."

"It'll finally get that apple in the mouth," the Hand's laughter degenerates into a rolling cough. The Farmer rewards the joke with a soft chuckle.

Sing praises to the Farmer and to his Hand, I remind myself reflexively.

I try to shift my focus toward the next race and the anticipation of winning back the apple, but I can't shake the image of Picklefoot's vacant stare.

Is this the fate of all pigs?

If the Farmer is benevolent, why do pigs suffer?

The Farmer is my shepherd. I shall not want.

The rain falls heavy as we're led from the train to our wallowing place. Bacon is coated in a clear glaze of water which he shakes off spraying the Hand with a wet barrage, much to the amusement of the Farmer. Bacon will pay later. He may be favored by the Farmer, but the Hand favors nobody.

While the world is reemerging around us, we are allowed to wallow. I normally enjoy rolling about in the thick, cool mire, but the surrounding mud is mixed with despair. I meditate on my hatred for Porkchop hoping to displace the sadness I feel for Picklefoot.

The generosity of the Farmer knows no bounds. He leads us beside still, muddy waters where he restores our souls.

Bacon and Porkchop have yet to register the absence of Picklefoot. They snort over a pile of rotten carrots softened by time. I try to grab one, but they snarl as I approach. I back down, looking toward Gravy for guidance, but she lays listless in the mire, her snout resting between her two front legs.

For the first time in my life, I'm without allies.

That night, I slept alone in the wet straw seeking solace in the Farmer whose love is eternal. *May I find my strength in the apple,* I tell myself. I wake up to a burst of sharp pain in the ribs, as the Hand lurks above me holding a pail of water.

Glory be to the Farmer who quenches my thirst, and glory be to his own right Hand.

As the morning wears on, it's time for the next race. The rain from the day before has given way to steam rising from the pavement in a misty curtain. The others trot beside me, their hooves clicking across the asphalt, except for Bacon who lumbers behind the pack. We pass through a corridor of people on either side. The women shine like flowers in their calico dresses and silk hats. I try to keep my mind focused on the track but I'm distracted by the swirling lights and the clatter of the carousel nearby.

The Farmer shouts through a bullhorn as the Hand leads me to the outer gate. My position puts me at a disadvantage. I have the furthest to run and must work twice as hard for the apple. I am also the last pig on the track. Bacon now occupies the inner lane next to Gravy. Porkchop will run the center lane while the lane between us stands vacant.

With each pronouncement from the Farmer's booming voice, the crowd roars. "Our next challenger might not be our fastest pig, but he still smokes the competition. Let's hear it for the powerhouse of pork, the elite of meat, let's give a big Iowa welcome to HAAAAAAAAAM BONE!"

The instant the gates open, I surge forward, feeling my trotters slip against the wet pavement. I stumble but manage not to fall. This mistake puts me behind the other three. I'll have to make up ground. I pass Bacon easily as he waddles down the track. When I pass Gravy, I don't give her a second glance. Her body is running down the track, but her heart lies elsewhere, her face blank rather than determined.

Porkchop runs just ahead. Laughter erupts from the crowd as I grab his tail in my teeth to slow him down. The Farmer is right. Porkchop is slightly faster than I am, but I've always been the more ambitious pig. Soon we are neck and neck. As we round the bend, he glares in my direction, hatred flashing through his dark eyes. I push harder, the apple looming large in my mind. I realize now that while I want to win the apple, I want even more to see Porkchop lose.

The final stretch looms before us. It's just Porkchop and me, snarling and snorting, neither yielding so much as an inch. The crowd roars around us. I sense that Porkchop is gearing up for a burst of speed. I do not have it in me to outpace him. I'm running as fast as my trotters will allow. Halfway down the straightaway, I muster my superior bulk. Slamming Porkchop into the wooden railing, I send him crashing onto the track.

I don't look back. Not even to gloat.

I cross the finish line before Porkchop can regain his footing. My heart pounds loudly in my chest, filling my ears with the sound of rushing blood. I squeal victorious.

The Farmer arrives with the apple. "Good boy! That was the best race I've ever seen," he says, holding the apple towards me in his liver-spotted hand. I take it in my muzzle and then spit it to the ground, crushing it with my front trotter. Its sweetness tastes like decay.

For an instant, The Farmer appears stunned, his eyes wide with alarm. I glare at him the same way I glared at Porkchop moments before.

The Farmer smells like Picklefoot.

His eyes grow hard as he regains his composure, returning my stare with a stare of his own. A smile crosses his mouth, a mouth full of autumn pig roasts and Christmas hams. There'll be another Hambone come spring. In the meantime, the pig has learned what the Farmer has known all along.

This pig will never race again.

Blessed be the pig who sees beyond the apple.

Christina Moore (she/her) lives and works in Columbus, Ohio with her two dogs and two cats. She works at the Ohio State University, cataloging library books in Slavic languages. She is an avid cyclist and classically trained soprano, activities which she frequently intermixes.

TROPHY HUSBAND

by Jim Hodnett

The first thing that happened that day was that John came into the study while I was prepping for my certification exam in respiratory therapy. He wasn't wearing anything but a pair of boxer shorts tented with a big old Viagra boner.

So, naturally, I dropped to my knees and did my duty.

And then we went to the bedroom for more fun.

And then he fell asleep.

And then I returned to my desk and studies.

Now, don't think because I said "did my duty," I don't enjoy sex with John. Our sex life was never a string of business fucks where I serviced him in return for rent and designer clothes. Nor was it charity fucks where he serviced me while I rolled my eyes or scrolled on my phone. I liked having sex with John. I'm … versatile, as they say, and, through the miracle of pharmaceuticals, so was he. So, there was never any lack of satisfaction.

And I liked John's looks too. It wasn't just his handsome, lined, gentleman-of-a-certain-age face, which was still topped by thick, wavy hair—silvery as a wedding band. I liked all of him, including the saggy pouches of flesh at his elbows and the gray hairs flecked through his eyebrows and pubes, and also the ones sprouting on his fleshy pecs, which sighed lightly and elegantly with age. And those crepey wrinkles where his ass met his thighs? Perfection! There was a warmth to John's soft, wrinkled body that could also sizzle and a comfort to it that could rev up to sexy in a split second—and stay there a good long time.

And you also don't need to think I didn't have other options. Plenty of young guys—a lot of them hot as hell—head turners—have chatted me up. A few took me to bed. But there was always something missing, no matter how square their jaws were or how hard and bulgy their muscles. They all seemed to be in such a hurry—so angsty—like sex was something taking place in a railway car and had to be finished before the next stop. Sometimes I felt pushed off the train as soon as they were done. But most of the time, I'd hop off on my own. Who needs all that frenzy? All that flexing and posing and attitude?

***

The second thing that happened that day was that Frederick dropped by. Let himself in with his key. Didn't even knock. I was still at my desk in the study but caught up with him in the kitchen. He was standing in front of the refrigerator with the door open. Physically, Frederick is a younger version of John, but without the polish and kindness in his bearing. He was wearing skintight jeans and a tank top. With his muscled body, he might have looked sexy, if only he weren't... well, Frederick.

"Where's Dad?" he demanded, closing the refrigerator door.

"A gracious hello to you, too, Frederick. He's napping."

"Well, wake him up. I need to talk to him." Frederick is eight years older and thinks he can boss me.

"I'm not waking John up from a nap. It's rude." I always said "John" rather than "your father" because I liked to make it clear that John and I had a special relationship that didn't include Frederick.

"It's an emergency!" he insisted.

"What's the emergency?"

"None of your business. Just wake him up. I need to ask him something, I told you!"

"Never mind. I'm awake," said John, walking into the room and tying a robe around his nearly naked body.

That was when I realized I was wearing nothing but boxers and a tee myself. Frederick looked at me, then John, then back at me. "God," he said, scrunching his face like he'd just swallowed some pink stomach medicine, "at three in the afternoon?" He turned back to the refrigerator and re-opened the door. "Got any beer?"

"God," I said. "At three in the afternoon?"

Frederick gave me a glare that could make a wolf whimper, but not me.

"Cool it, boys," said John. John knew to nip things in the bud when it came to Frederick and me. One time, we got up in each other's faces, each of us shouting, "Gold digger!"

"That's fine," I said to John. "I need to get back to studying." I turned my back and sauntered away, calling, "See ya, Freddie," over my shoulder. He hates being called that, and I could feel the heat of his stare on my neck as I left the room.

Turns out Frederick's "emergency," was wanting to borrow John's truck while his Mustang—which John bought for him—was in the shop. John agreed, but why Frederick couldn't borrow his mother's extra car was beyond me. She and her husband are both retired and don't need two vehicles.

Well, now that I think about it, I do get it. Evelyn's cars are not sexy. And looking sexy and getting laid are about the only things Frederick is good at or good for. Not that he doesn't work. He's had a succession of jobs, all of them involving bullshitting: car salesman, time-share salesman, etc. Right now, he's selling sketchy life insurance policies.

***

Frederick isn't the only person who thinks I'm a gold digger. A lot of people have even called me a trophy husband. Not to my face, but I've heard them whisper it behind my back. And I saw more than one person mouth the words after looking at John and me from across a room. They'd smile thinly in our direction with half-closed eyelids and raised brows, like some catty drag queen reading a real woman's bad hair and makeup.

It's not true, though. I was never John's trophy, nor even his husband. Oh, sure, he was old, and I'm young and hot—or so people tell me. Not in that studly-beach-body-in-a-Speedo way, but I'm reasonably tall, with a trim waist and broad-*ish* shoulders. My smile is full of straight, square teeth, and my thick black hair seems incapable of falling on my face and neck in anything other than soft and pleasing ways. And yes, though I don't dress to emphasize it, I do have a… well, let's just say good hair isn't the only way I've been blessed.

Furthermore, I didn't take John away from anyone. He'd been single a year before we met, and it was his ex who dumped him, claiming John was boring, didn't want to do anything but sit in front of a TV and watch Netflix or Hulu every night. "Can't we go out to a movie or concert or something?" Clement would whine. John tried to comply, he said, but then Covid hit, and that was the last straw. Clement, a man John's age, packed up and moved into a place of his own. Said he'd rather be alone by himself than alone with someone else.

It's true that John was a homebody, and didn't care much for parties or bars. But we met friends at restaurants all the time. John had a lot of buddies from all his years in healthcare, and I have friends, too—fellow baristas at the coffee shop where I worked and classmates from my respiratory therapy program at the community college. They were all poor like me, so John graciously picked up the tab, saying our energy enlivened him. Must've been true because he had no problem keeping up with us. Movies and music? He was current. Not so much with social media and influencers, though. But neither am I. Influencers are vapid and chirpy show-offs if you ask me.

But my point is, Clement was not totally off-base. John and I did spend a lot of time sitting on the couch watching television. I didn't mind. When we did, our bodies were always touching: a head on a shoulder, a leg draping over a lap, or our toes tapping and tickling on the ottoman. After the movie or episode was over, we'd talk about the plot and characters and always, always the hot actors.

A lot of those evenings remind me of when I stayed with my grandparents as a kid. Grandpa and I would sit on the sofa and watch a Disney movie. Or rather, I'd watch, and he'd stroke my hair and look at me with a smile on his face like I was the best thing ever to happen to him, a gift from that God he talked about and prayed to so much. Sometimes, when he was saying grace, he ended by thanking God for the "precious gift of our grandson, Joshua." I always had a good appetite at my grandparents' house and slept well, too—sometimes in the middle—and never had nightmares.

Nonetheless, I never took to Grandma and Grandpa's religion, and they were gone before I could come out to them. But I know that they would have still loved me, with all the grace and divinity of a hundred of those guardian angels they claimed were all around.

I feel the same thing with John now—loved, even worshiped, in a way no guy my age has ever offered. And if you think that's not a turn-on in and of itself, you might want to give it a little more thought.

And where are my parents, you might be asking? The answer is that I don't know. I told you how good my grandparents were to me and how I liked staying with them as a kid. That was because Mom and Dad (in name only!) spent most of their time high and living on the street or serving time. They'd drop me off at Grandma and Grandpa's place, then disappear for days or weeks. Eventually, my grandparents got the court to name them my guardians, and thank God for that. I haven't seen my parents in years, but I assume they are still alive, or else someone would have tracked me down and told me.

Yeah, I know what you're thinking. My most loving parent figures, my rescuers, were my grandparents. And then I ended up in a relationship with an older man. Your point being? Love is love is love.

***

The third thing that happened that day was that I asked John to marry me. Not for his money, though. I loved him. And he'd already been plenty generous to me—helping me with car payments and tuition. I kept track of everything and always planned to pay him back once I'd been working as a professional for a while and had saved some money. I know he would've refused to take it, but it would've been a statement.

And I'd always planned to make it a point to hand the check to him in front of Frederick.

All that being said, I kept hesitating to ask John to marry me, even after two and a half years. It just didn't seem right, him being the older one, the man of means. When I finally did ask, we were sitting on the couch. I hadn't planned it out or thought it through, but we'd just finished watching the movie, "All of Us Strangers," and I was breathless with sadness and joy, and transported by love and life and the urgency of them all. The words of proposal left my mouth almost before I knew it.

After I asked, John smiled and reached across my lap to grab my hand. He took it to his lips and kissed it. "I love you," he said, "but no."

A weight pushed down on my neck and shoulders. I could feel my tear ducts sting. "Why not?"

"I've done it before, and it didn't work out. Everyone got burned— Evelyn, Frederick, me. She felt lied to, and she was right, although it was me I lied to first and foremost. And Frederick felt abandoned like he'd lost his dad, even though Evelyn and I shared custody. And when he got into his teens, he got scared that he was gay because I was. I told him not to worry, that things didn't work that way. I said, 'You're attracted to girls, aren't you? Relax.' But he said, 'Yeah, but you thought you were attracted to girls, too, and then you weren't. Is that going to happen to me?' No amount of reassurance seemed to help, even after he had a serious girlfriend or two. I think he's *still* afraid. That's why he won't settle down, why he's on the make with one woman after another. Trying to prove something—to himself or me, his mother, or somebody."

What John said made me understand Frederick better, even empathize with him. And it made me understand John more, too, but still… "John, none of that is going to happen again. It's not like we'll get married and then you'll suddenly figure out you're straight after all. I want to be your husband."

He smiled again. "Now think about it," he said. "You don't want to tie yourself down to an old guy like me. A nursing home and hospice care are not some tiny dots down the road I can barely see. They're right ahead, a block or two away."

"But that could be true of anybody," I countered, "me included. It's only an accident or a diagnosis away."

John touched my cheek with the back of his hand. I could feel the wear and wrinkles on it, also the love. "You'll be well taken care of after I'm gone. I'm making sure of it. Okay?"

"That's not what I'm after."

"Be that as it may, I'll make it happen." He put his arm around me and pulled my head to his shoulder. "My sweet, wonderful young man," he said.

***

When the last thing happened that day, I didn't believe it at first. It was like watching a movie. I thought, *This can't be real. It's too cliché, bad acting.* Isn't it funny how the mind works? I saw him grab at his chest, then watched as his knees buckled and his face contorted. *Did he trip?* I wondered. *Is this a joke?* Everything was happening in slow motion—yet, too fast at the same time.

Then he hit the floor. *Jesus! This is really happening!* In my memory, this is all still surreal. I remember looking for my phone to call 911 but couldn't find it at first. When I did, I thought, *Wait! Should I be doing CPR already?* But I called anyway.

"What's your emergency?" the dispatcher asked in a voice that she probably thought would calm me but just freaked me out more. Somehow, she got the gist of what I was saying—*fell … unconscious … eyes set …* She talked me through the steps: put the phone on speaker, check the carotid for a pulse, check for breathing. Pulse faint! Breathing shallow, very! *Why hadn't I already done those things? Me—a trained respiratory therapist who couldn't remember those things on my own? What a fuckup!*

Then she talked me through CPR: get him on his back, tilt his head, open the airway, thirty chest compressions, two rescue breaths, repeat, repeat, repeat. The dispatcher called the time after each set of compressions. Even though I already had my degree and was a working therapist—as long as my proctor was in the room—I had never administered CPR to an actual person, so I was grateful for her guidance. But after each sequence, his vitals became weaker, not stronger.

When the squad arrived—in a flurry of shouting and (*thank God!*) competence—I stepped back, wringing my hands. I heard the rising tone of the defibrillator, then "Clear!" Then "No pulse." They may have tried again, maybe several more times. I don't remember. When they lifted John onto the gurney and pushed him to the ambulance, their voices became quieter. They were like grim but hurried pallbearers—premature pallbearers, I hoped. The siren blared a mournful howl as the ambulance left for the ER. I followed in my car. After I parked, I ran to the waiting room and sat. It was only a few minutes before the doc came out. He was a young guy, probably a resident—face speckled with that twelve-hour-shift stubble and jaded look ER men can have. Yet his eyes were clear and kind when he told me John had passed. He asked if I was his son. I lied and told him John was my husband because I was afraid he wouldn't let me go see him and say goodbye if I didn't.

After I smoothed John's hair back one last time, kissed him on his cold forehead, and spoke my last words to him, a nurse led me back to the waiting room. I hadn't been able to think of anything profound to say. Just "thank you," and "I love you," and "I'm sorry."

What they say about shock and denial is true. Cool and methodical as a robot, I called Frederick and gave him the news, then waited until he arrived. He brought his mom with him. They both went in to see John before he was taken to the morgue. They didn't invite me to go along.

When they came back, both he and Evelyn were cold to me. Frederick's eyes were moist, but he still had the energy for meanness, "Couldn't you have done something?" he asked. "Aren't you a trained medical professional? What was the point of that fucking degree of yours Dad paid for?"

I was feeling guilty already, so I didn't have the will to say anything, to defend myself. I just shook my head. Maybe he was right. Maybe I did do it wrong. "Just leave then," he said. "We can take it from here."

I did leave. It was one of those drives you know you made because all of a sudden, you find yourself parked in your garage but don't remember how the hell you got there. Could have run a bunch of red lights for all I knew. I unlocked the door and walked in, then looked around my home—if that was what it was anymore.

I sat on the sofa where I had asked John to marry me not three hours before. I could still see the indentations of our bodies on it. I pressed my face to the couch's back where John always sat and tried to take in his clean and minty smell, but it wasn't there. I tried to remember what his touch had felt like that very night, his lips on my hand, his palm caressing my head. And I could remember—but couldn't at the same time, couldn't make it real. I wanted his ghost to appear, like one of those characters in "All of Us Strangers," so I could commit him to memory, stroke his wrinkled face, run my fingers across the parchment skin on his arm—just one more time, so I could savor every detail. Then I would never forget. I knew it. If only I had one more chance.

***

I started packing the day after John died. Frederick had a copy of the will. Maybe John had good intentions about not leaving me high and dry when he died, but he had never gotten around to it. The will had not been revised since before he met me. Everything went to Frederick and Evelyn and some charities.

Frederick told me he'd "give" me a few days to move out. That's all it took me. I couch-surfed with friends for a couple of weeks, then found a place of my own—not so difficult now that I'm pulling in a professional's income.

Frederick had John cremated, according to his father's wishes. The memorial service was not held for more than a month. Frederick wanted to do it right, he said. What he meant was that he wanted to show off, impress everybody. And it *was* a fine affair. Must have been more than a hundred people in that funeral home chapel. John had no particular religious leanings, and neither did the chapel. It was funeral home generic, designed not to offend anyone of any faith, with its dark wood paneling and stained-glass windows depicting nothing but geometric forms. Five or six folks gave echo-y testimonials about John and praised him for his character and compassion, all of which were nice.

But as I sat in the back, motionless and numb, I wished I could stand up and say something about John that was real and intimate, about how his smile could send tingles down my spine, or how the touch of his hand on my thigh could make me want to cry with desire and happiness and fear all at the same time. But Frederick had not invited me to speak and said no when I asked if I could.

At the reception afterward, I found Frederick and asked if I could talk to him alone. He gave me a wary look but nodded. We went into a meditation room near the chapel's entrance.

"Look, Joshua," he said even before I opened my mouth, "you've just got to accept the fact that being a trophy wife didn't pay off for you. I've already told you there isn't anything for you. Everything is set out in the will, and I can't change it. Lawyer says."

I ignored the "trophy wife" comment. "I'm not here to ask for anything. I'm here to give you something."

I pulled an envelope from my coat pocket and handed it to him. He pulled his chin back, suspicion written in his wrinkled brows. "What's this?"

"It's a check for $10,504.22. It's all the money John gave me while I was in school and working at the coffee shop. I kept a record."

"I don't want this," he said. "Keep your fucking money!"

He shoved the envelope toward me, but I threw my hands in the air. "Nope, not taking it."

"I'll tear it up!"

"That's your choice," I said and walked past him toward the door.

"Look! I'm ripping it to shreds!" he yelled from behind my back. I could hear paper tearing, strip by strip.

"Your choice," I repeated as I left the room.

What Frederick—what no one—will ever understand is that I was never John's trophy. He was mine, my prize for loving someone most young gay men can't even see. His gray hair and wrinkles made him invisible, not even worthy of a nod, let alone a passionate kiss.

Thank heavens Frederick tore up that check. It would have bounced higher than an acrobat on a trampoline.

***

I like to remember how John and I met. He was sitting by himself on the patio at Tremont Lounge. I'd been watching him for a while. Two friends—a couple, it seemed—were with him at the table when I first spotted him. The three of them chatted and sipped expensive-looking cocktails for a good hour. After his friends left, with kisses and hugs, he pulled his phone from his pocket and scrolled it like a teenager. Adorable!

"Is this seat taken?" I asked as I approached his table.

He looked startled but said, "Why, no. Please, sit down."

"Thank you. Hi, I'm Joshua," I said and extended my hand.

He shook it. "John," he offered. He smiled and took me in with his eyes, admiring but not lustful. "Joshua, has anyone ever told you that you look like a gift from the gods?"

His question set a pinwheel twirling in my chest, but I didn't let on. I just pursed my lips in mock reproval. "Why, John! How many drinks have you had?"

"Too many," he replied. "Three. But you didn't answer my question. Has anyone ever told you that?"

No more pretending. My heart pried itself open, wider than the gates of heaven. "Yes," I said, "but it was a very long time ago."

Jim Hodnett (he/him) is a retired psychologist and educator. Although he grew up in Arkansas and has spent time in Texas and New York, he has lived in Columbus, Ohio for over thirty years, most of those, happily, with his husband, Joe Heimlich, Ph.D., a researcher and consultant in the area of environmental education. Jim has been writing for twelve years, mostly short stories that focus on the lives, loves, and challenges of gay boys and men. "Trophy Husband" is the third story Jim has published, all three in OWA anthologies.

THE WHITE MINORITY
by Travis Ray

I'm in constant fear for my life. Everywhere I go, I get dirty looks. The saddest part is I have done nothing wrong. I have never drunk alcohol or done drugs, I volunteer once a month at the soup kitchen, and hell; I'm a doctor for Christ's sake! I mean, it's not my fault. I didn't choose the way I look, I was just born this way. But that doesn't matter to the rest of the world. All they see, all they will ever see, is my skin color. The year is 2023, and I am a white man.

It's only been a few months since the shutdown halted the world. I still remember the first time I heard about FS-UP; Fox News reported on an unknown sickness wreaking havoc on England. They stated that scientists were puzzled but were confident they'd have it figured out in no time. This was late 2022, mind you. I can recall feeling sorry for the British people, but also, remaining upbeat. It's not gonna make it to America, I thought. How could it?

I remember the progression just like it was yesterday, almost like a slow burn. From the point it first emerged it began to slowly migrate East. In February, it finally hit the US. I remember the health department saying just stay inside, maybe wear a mask, and we should be through this in no time. I recall the feeling of being torn as I, a medical professional, considered this to be a serious matter. On the other hand, I really wanted to go watch the game with my friends.

I couldn't believe it when I first heard it. The first breakthrough in research for this new illness would be announced later that day. As a doctor, I was thrilled! As a person, I was more so. Perhaps now we can finally stop worrying about all this, I thought. As would continue to be the case, I was wrong.

Dr. Fickle was anything but subtle. After starting the briefing with the obligatory pleasantries, he cut right to the chase.

"There is still much that we don't know about this new virus. FS-UP, otherwise known as Fissuring Ural Platelets, has confused and befuddled the world's top scientists to this point, but we are confident that we're getting close. In the meantime, here's what we do know. The virus that first was first noticed in England's fatality rate is in the hundreds of thousands. In addition to this, it does seem that most cases are contracted by Caucasians. This isn't to say that other races are unaffected, remember we are still actively learning this as we go. However, early statistics do seem to suggest that Caucasians are more likely to contract the virus than others. Additionally, it appears that, of all things, melanin seems to fight this virus. We don't yet know why, or how, but Caucasians, thus, are more susceptible to contracting this deadly virus."

To say this was a shock was an understatement. I still can't believe it. Did the Director of the National Institute of Allergy and Infectious Diseases really just tell me that I am more at risk of dying because of my skin color? The announcement was made on a Friday, so I decided to lay low for the next couple of days. At least that was the plan. However, as any man could tell you, when a pretty girl wants to go out; you go out.

I may be well off (one of the perks of being a doctor) but Rachel was anything but. An elementary school teacher in the projects, she taught in the same neighborhood that she grew up in. We met one night at a bar while we were out with our respective friends. I'll never forget the first time I saw her, she was wearing black jeans and a denim jacket. She and her friends stood underneath a neon Blue Moon sign. The soft glow of the neon radiated effortlessly off her dark skin so that she looked otherworldly. She had a laugh that both awakened the room and caressed it. I never approached women, I thought it rude to assert myself into situations that I wasn't invited to. However, one can't simply pass up an opportunity for the rest of your life. We made conversation and struck up a fast connection. I was impressed with her knowledge of the medical field, and she thought I was a good listener. We went back to my place that night, I can't remember having ever had a conversation as deep and two-sided as the one we had that night. We continued like that for a little over a year. Somehow neither of us ever ran out of things to say, it was the kind of effortless love that you only ever seem to read about. Around the time of Fickle's announcement, I was considering buying a ring.

We went out that night to one of her favorite spots. Anyone expecting this to be a high-class restaurant doesn't know Rachel. For whatever reason, she'd say, she loved Applebee's but the one across the street from my apartment had the best mozzarella sticks. We sometimes went there three times a week, and even still that was less than she would have liked. We walked in that night and something felt different. We had grown used to the looks. It may have been 2023 in the era of political correctness, but people by and large were still not totally on board with biracial couples. Tonight however felt different. We overcame the judgment each outing, it made us stronger and brought us closer together. The eyes this time, however, didn't stay on us; but instead on me. I could hear whispers but could pick up none of it. Rachel noticed too. When I could bear it no longer, I leaned across the table and whispered,

"Wow, now I know how you feel."

Rachel said nothing. When we returned to my apartment we had one of the bigger fights of our relationship. She said I was being racist, but I couldn't help but poke fun at the comment since I was, in fact, dating a black woman. She didn't see the humor in my truth. Next, she said that I did nothing to help the cause of black people. Now she was really starting to upset me, so I lashed back at her. I reminded her once again that I was head over heels in love with a black woman then I challenged her to look at my Facebook where, in between my posts about sports and meals, were dozens of posts about all life being precious, especially black lives. She didn't miss a beat responding immediately,

"If you really felt that way, you would have come to one of the hundreds of protests I've invited you to," she said.

I was hot, I responded sharply,

"Why do you keep bringing that up? I've told you before, I think those things are dangerous!"

At that, she stood, took a deep breath, and smiled. No matter what, she's always had a way to calm my nerves. She kissed my forehead and hugged me like letting go would be suicide. She apologized for what she said, assured me that she loved me, and then turned to leave, stopping at the door. She looked back at me with tears in her eyes and said,

"It's not your fault. I can't blame you for acting how anyone in your position would act. I'll text you when I get home."

This was to be our last night before the shit of FS-UP finally hit the fan.

With the rest of the world shutting down, our home state of Florida remained steadfast and continued with business as usual. I went to work the following day. As it turned out, even though my state wasn't worrying, my hospital was. During my time out they had completely shifted gears towards combating FS-UP. In a state of emergency, they reorganized the entire hospital which featured two floors dedicated to FS-UP. I approached my supervisor eager to help.

"Which floor do you need me on?" I asked.

"The fourth floor, obviously," she said.

She sounded annoyed, but I was sure she just had a lot on her plate. I got masked up then got going. I couldn't believe what I saw when I got there. It looked like a military hospital, understaffed, and so many patients that their cots lined the lobby. I knew I was in for a long day. I texted Rachel that I loved her and got to it. Eighteen hours later I collapsed back into the locker room. Recognizing I couldn't drive home in this state, I slept in my car. After all, I thought, I needed to be back in eight hours.

What surprised me the most was the following day, we had the same colleagues working on the fourth floor as we had the previous day. Not too outrageous, but five days later when it was still the same crew I couldn't believe it. At the end of my shift on Wednesday, I let my curiosity get the better of me. The more I thought about it the more I realized it probably made sense. When you're in war, you don't split up a platoon. Still, I wondered how the fifth floor was faring. The elevator rested and the doors opened revealing the fifth floor exactly how it was a week ago. I saw my friend Wu up there so I thought I'd go say hi. He looked nervous.

He said things were crazy for them as well, but it didn't look that way to me. Before I left that day I wanted to make sure I talked to my supervisor.

Shandra and I always got along. We weren't the best of friends, but there was a mutual respect between the two of us. I told her what I had seen and she was not happy. She told me I would be fired if I went to the fifth floor again. This wasn't adding up, I'd never heard her raise her voice before but now she was doing it over something so trivial. Still, I had to probe. My recent battle buddies and I couldn't possibly do another week like we had just done. I had to push for more help, so I did. Finally, she revealed, "I will not have your team contaminate the rest of the hospital and our patients!"

Finally, I put it all together. For six days straight I worked with the same people, all white. In those six days, I had to see at least a thousand patients, all white. Come to think of it, Shandra and Wu were the only non-white people I had seen these past six days.

I pondered this as I drove home, but remembered that I had been at the hospital the last several days, I decided to take a slight detour to the grocery store. I had left my mask on in my fatigued drive home and left it on as I walked into the store. Only a few people were wearing masks, not too crazy after all, this is Florida. However, I noticed a printout sign taped at the entrance that read ALL white people MUST wear masks. I couldn't help but double-take. This seemed over the line in several different ways, I mean, aren't I a person? Doesn't my safety matter just as much as others?

The strange ways didn't end there. While looking at almond milk I was approached by an Asian woman who tapped me on the shoulder. I turned and looked to see her scowling at me, she was dressed in white capris and a t-shirt that said Proud Tiger Mom. I thought maybe I was in her way so I stepped aside. I could see that she left her cart and son a good six feet from us. She wasn't wearing a mask and she leaned in close to my face. I would have felt uncomfortable with this anytime, let alone in a pandemic. With a sneer she said,

"Get out of here! You don't belong here! I don't feel safe with you near me or my child, leave now!"

I was shocked. No one had ever talked to me like this before. In a panic, I grabbed a random almond milk, put it next to my avocados, and took off. I had a bigger list when I walked in but I minimized it to get the most important things. When I went to check out the cashier was acting odd as well. I could tell she was a bit nervous even though she seemed quite bubbly with the person in front of me. They had a couple of baggers, but when she grabbed my first tub of sour cream she looked at me and smirked, "You'll have to bag it all yourself." I looked and saw two baggers standing around and talking to each other. Not wanting to cause any more trouble; I nodded, bagged and paid, then quickly left. I felt utterly humiliated. I'm pretty tough, I mean, I am a doctor; I've delivered terminal news to patients and their family members for several years. This broke me and I cried on my way home.

Later that night while eating my world-famous extra cheesy avocado toast with sour cream, Rachel texted me wanting to come over. No matter the day I've had, I always say yes to an opportunity to spend time with my favorite person. She came over and noticed immediately that I was off. She's good with stuff like that. I hesitated, choking down the emotions, but then began retelling the events of my day. The confrontation with Shandra, the grocery store, and how I'd cried on my way home. Rachel intently listened as I recounted the horrors of my day, she's good at that too. When I concluded I could tell she wasn't quite sure what to say yet, so I added, "I mean, I just don't understand. It's like people are treating me like a criminal just because of the color of my skin."

Rachel's face shifted to the same knowing look it always did when she was teaching. She grabbed my hands, looked me in the eyes and said, "and now you understand."

Travis Ray (he/him) is truly nothing special. Works an average job, and is the insignificant other of partner, Del. Armed with them, their cats, and a love of provoking thoughts; he strives daily to be nothing more than an average person.

THE WATER THAT SHAPES US
by Joe Graves

What am I most looking forward to?

I was sitting on the small balcony of my twin brother's home, drinking tea, not sure where to start, and my brother, ever the one who only looked forward in life, gave me this prompt. He had given me a leather-bound paper notebook, and it had cost him a fortune. They were hard to find, but he knew they were the only way I would write. I'd never write my story on any connected device. That would go against everything in my story that I still hold dear.

So what am I most looking forward to?

That's simple. Prayer. I'm looking forward to praying again. Which is why I find it almost laughable that my story begins with me skipping a prayer meeting.

Earlier that day, I had bought a device from a traveling merchant just outside the village limits. I hid it in the pockets of my dress until I could sneak it under my mattress, into a small slit I had cut just big enough for such treasures. It was the only place where my family wouldn't look. I was turning seventeen and soon after, my family would give me in marriage to one of the worst human beings ever to walk the earth. I had no choice.

And yet, I still remember the deep feeling of shame and regret from doing something so deliberately wrong. I wasn't perfect, and would be embarrassed to give you that impression. I messed up all the time, but most of my mistakes were by accident—kneeling at the wrong time during prayers, eating before my father gave the blessing, or speaking too loudly when adults were around. Those were mistakes, worthy of punishment, but honest mistakes. I had never deliberately gone against the code of our village, not like this.

The following night, I pulled the small handheld device out just before we headed to evening prayer; carrying it in my pocket and hoping no one noticed. I kept my distance from my mother and father and two younger brothers, and I'm glad I did. Somehow, I must have bumped the device while in my pocket, and it powered on, buzzing as it did. As I pulled it out to turn it off, I dropped it, and it buzzed on the ground. I looked up, and my family walked on ahead through the path in the woods, ignoring me. I quickly powered it off and shoved it back into my pocket. Then, my stomach, fully convinced that I was worthy of the darkest recesses of hell, decided it no longer wanted to be a part of this. I left the path and threw up at the base of a tree. I watched the yellow mucus and chunks of morning mash drip through the ridges of the bark like water working its way along the cracked and dried dirt after a drought. It was one of my favorite trees along this route, with thick bark and long branches, and leaves as large as my head, that, when outstretched, kept the path cool in the summer heat.

I held back my pebble necklace and long hair, to keep from getting anything on them. I stood up and took a breath, using the folds of my dress to wipe my mouth. My family was down past the next bend and would look for me soon. I looked at my pebble and wiped the mucus that had splattered onto it. Polishing it in my hand, I clicked my fingers into the small crack that had formed when they drilled a hole in the pebble to run the cord for my necklace. Even now, the same pebble hanging from my neck, scratched and smooth from years of polishing, still feels like home. No matter how far I get from home, whether I'm walking on a tree-lined path that reminds me of my childhood or sitting with my brother at a cafe in the city, this pebble is home.

I had to catch up with my family. I stuck my pebble into my shirt and checked to make sure the device was still in my pocket. Its sharp corners, glossy screen, and symmetrical shape were unlike anything else in our cabin of organic shapes and textures.

After prayer started, I excused myself to the outhouse and told my brothers I would practice solitude for the rest of the prayer. I made them promise to tell Mom and Dad, but I doubt they ever did.

With the voices of songs of praise pouring out the open windows of the chapel, I said a prayer—and I meant it—and then headed for the foothills to the west along the golden ridge trail that led to the highest point overlooking the village. I paused halfway up the trail, just past the last cabin in the village, where I powered the device on. It was dark now, and the light from the screen blinded me. Immediately, I checked the battery; my brother told me to always check the battery, for when it's dead, there's no way to charge it in the village. It was at fifty percent. That should be more than enough for a few more days.

I turned it off, placed it back in my pocket, and continued up the hill.

The last time I hiked up here was with my brother—he showed me how the signal worked and explained why it was available on the peak and not down in our valley. He tried to convince me the signal wasn't evil. "It's nothing but a movement of 1s and 0s in a frequency more like a song than the wailing of devils."

I didn't believe him when he said it; you can be certain of that. And, if I remember correctly, I didn't believe him as I stood on that hill a year later, praying that it would connect and praying that God would forgive me for wanting it to connect. I held it up above my head, a trick he taught me, hoping the small bars would light up in the corner.

Nothing.

I set it down in the grass and sat next to it, watching it from a distance, hoping it would do—whatever it was supposed to do. Oh, what little I knew back then!

I turned to the view, and I wish I could remember the view— sadly I feel my memories have all been rewritten with new ones and the mere thought makes me want to cry. But when I try, really try, I can see it, just barely, almost as if it's out of focus: the small fires of the village—hundreds of lights dancing against our homes, and little shadows of people walking in the dark as they head back to their cabins after evening prayer.

Then it buzzed. It had connected, and I jumped up and yelled a little louder than I'd like to admit. Immediately, I opened the app preloaded on the device when I bought it. After a quick scan of my face, it asked me to choose a name. My brother had told me it would do this, and I had spent the last few months wondering what name I would choose if I ever got this far. Whenever I considered it, I was convinced I would choose my given name—how could I choose any other? I don't know if it was the thin air, the night sky, or the empty stomach, but when I was prompted, I selected a new name—the name I had always wanted. Birdie. It sounds foolish now, but that's the name I had always loved. What's not to love about that name? Birds! Free to fly and rest in the limbs of trees. As foolish as it sounds to some, it's been my name ever since. And no one seems to care once they use it a few times. That's the funny thing about names. The more you use them, the less you notice them.

Once I was done registering, I posted the same message my brother had told me to, to the same link he had saved in the notes app: "Looking for a chance to get away." And then I sat and waited for a reply. It would be days before I could sneak away again without raising suspicion, so I needed them to message me back right away.

An hour passed as I scrolled through the primary app, curious if there others who had chose the name Birdie. There were hundreds of Birdies! And then that thing that felt truly original ended up being shared by so many people. I experienced this feeling often in the city. Do you think you're original? Statistically, that just means your data pool is too small.

They never replied to my message that night, not before I had to leave. And of course, I let too much time pass waiting for them.

I had to sprint down the hill, and by the time I got home, my parents sat by the fire near our back door, my little brothers already asleep in our bed. I tucked my shirt into my pants before walking up to our cabin and checked to ensure the device was hidden well in the folds of my loose-fitting dress.

"Did you miss prayer?" my mother asked, without looking up from her stitching.

"No. I prayed outside tonight. Didn't my brothers tell you?" I wasn't very good at hiding things from my mom, and this allowed me to tell the truth, in a way. I had prayed outside, quite a bit, actually.

They didn't ask questions, so I went to my room and slid the device under my mattress, into the little pocket I had made, as carefully as possible, so as not to wake my brothers.

I could hear them talking through the open window.

"She hasn't been the same since—"

What a thing to say. A year had gone by, and they hadn't once talked about their oldest son. It was as if he never existed to begin with. This would be the closest I would ever hear them talk about him, and even then, they refused to say his name.

But my mom was right. I hadn't been the same since he left. But I would say his name. "Jax. Jax. Jax," I whispered. I'd say it all night long. I'd say it to my mother's face—or, at least I always said I would. In the end, I left before I had the chance.

I sat down on the edge of our bed.

In the dim light of the cabin, I could see Jax's pebble hanging behind the bedroom door. He left it when he ran. My mom wanted it destroyed, as was the custom, but my dad wouldn't let her touch it. He had the final say in things like that. So it hung out of sight from any visitors, yet a constant reminder to me of the brother I once had.

Three days later, I snuck the device out from under my mattress, climbed to the peak, and powered it on. There was a message with a set of coordinates: a three-day hike, and the deadline to arrive was only in two days, which meant I had no time to prepare. I had to leave immediately. And late that night, with my family asleep, I packed my things and headed off.

I've never been back since.

***

Rubin was an old man; he looked similar to the men from Water Village, except his beard was trimmed. Much to my surprise, he demonstrated an exceptional level of politeness, especially considering his involvement in trafficking people. He originated from Water Village, a community reputed for its trustworthy inhabitants. He had a family now who lived just outside the city, a wife and two kids, who he was quick to tell me about, and every other traveler who arrived at the coordinates. Within an hour, there was a group of six of us, each handing over to him a small fortune. "Most of this goes towards the expenses, I promise," Rubin would add to the ones more reluctant to cough it up.

The following morning, we woke to the damp smell of a smoldering fire, and I tried to get dry from the dew that fell on my body. I remember being cold and how apologetic Rubin was for not having enough blankets the night before. As was my custom, I walked a bit from camp for my morning prayers, and that's how I missed what had happened. I only found out later, after lunch, that one of the younger women went missing that night. Her sister woke up to her gone, and as one who knew the pain of a missing sibling, I wish I had known earlier so I could comfort her. Most believed she ran off, but her sister insisted someone took her.

This only fed the fears our families had taught us. It was a story told to children, often used to scare us; a story of men taking young women from the villages if they wandered too far. I told myself it was just a story to scare us, and that the girl was fine, but looking back, knowing what I know now, it's possible she was taken. Girls from the villages weren't connected, which means they couldn't be tracked, and that's something those kinds of men found valuable.

The following morning, the older sister also went missing. Rubin insisted she had left on her own in search of her sister, but there was no way to know for sure. We slept in a circle that night, but most of us didn't sleep at all.

The following day, we hiked up so many hills that I wondered if God hadn't placed those hills there to discourage us from leaving. We stopped for lunch just below a large rock overhang, trying to stay cool in the shade. I used the few minutes to wrap cloth around my blistering feet. No one talked, other than the occasional encouragement from Rubin. Later that day, Rubin gave us a few pills to give us energy. I did not like how they made me feel—I had energy, but I also felt nauseous and disoriented. I've refused them ever since, even if they are accepted here in the city. I could tell we were getting close, because Rubin's encouragement happened in shorter and shorter intervals, as if he himself actually believed what he was saying. Then, as one of the young men helped me over the edge of a large boulder, I could see the skyline of the city framed by the setting sun with buildings that reached into the clouds.

I stood there and stared for longer than I remember. It felt as if a day had gone by, but I'm guessing that was just because I was so tired.

That wasn't the first time I'd seen the skyline. I had gone once before, with my dad. It's a customary trip to take before one's confirmation, at the age of twelve. We hiked to a peak south of there, to a lesser view of the city. We were taught that seeing where we came from was necessary before we could move forward with our village. Less than a month later, with the village following me in white robes, I'd walk to the river and draw my pebble from the stream. Not just any pebble, but one that was placed there by my parents when I was born—drilled, tied, and staked in the river that runs south of our village. At our confirmation, we receive our pebble, now smooth from years of running water. The fathers would stand next to me, and we'd repeat these words: "The water shapes the pebbles, just like our families shape us," while placing the necklace around my neck.

I was much closer to the skyline now, this time with my pebble dangling from my neck. The glass buildings reflected the pinks of the sunset, with angles and lines as hard and crisp as the images on the device. Without notice, Rubin walked up and asked for my device. I handed it to him, and he threw it to the ground, stepping on it.

"Can't use that this close to the city—they will see you." He smashed the device with his black boots. "All of you," he continued, addressing the rest of the travelers. "Toss out your handhelds, and smash them—they won't serve you here."

I was about to ask why when he pointed to the far edge of the valley. There was a village with small cabins clothed in trees and one large building in the center, much like our prayer house. It looked like my village. "I didn't know there were any villages this close to the city?"

"That is no village," he said, smashing another phone with his boots. "It's a resort for those in the city to get away and spend a few days away from it all—and it's the only way to sneak you into the city."

"Will we get new handhelds, then?"

"No. The city got rid of handhelds years ago, and to carry one when it's not needed will only raise suspicion. I will explain everything when we get to camp. Let's go."

I had only just become familiar with the handhelds, and I wasn't looking forward to learning anything new.

***

The camp was a short walk down into the valley, so low into the valley that we surrendered the view of the city. There was a small cabin with a few people filling it who seemed to work for Rubin. I stopped and leaned into the room. There were large screens lining the wall, the largest screens I had ever seen—10x as big as any handheld. One screen had a picture of me—and not just any photo: the one I scanned when I created my profile.

Rubin must have noticed me looking, as he closed the door before I could get a closer look.

We sat by the fire and waited in silence other than a few hushed conversations between companions and the sound of wood sizzling in the fire, the remaining moisture working its way out the tops in small bubbles and foam. We don't do campfires in the city, and I miss that too.

I was growing tired and tempted to lie down and take a nap—or go for a walk—I hadn't decided, but knew I couldn't sit there any longer doing nothing when Rubin came out and called people into the cabin. Six others went before my name was called, and each time they came out, they looked different, wearing new clothes and sick—like the fever that killed two of my cousins, with pale faces, holding their stomachs and heads and stumbling towards the fire, where they would collapse. I caught one person from falling into the fire, helping her lay down on her mat. Her eyes were open, but looking at nothing, and she was burning up. I tried to get answers from Rubin, but he wouldn't say anything other than it was going to be fine. "It's a part of the process. Trust the process."

Then it was my turn.

In all that I did to get away from my village, I'm still not sure how I feel about what happened next. I miss my life before this operation. I miss having my thoughts separate from everyone else's. I miss the freedom of the silence. But would I do it again? If that's what it took to get away, yes. So there's your answer, I guess.

After changing into new clothes, I sat down on a medical bed. This operation wasn't like the ones in the fancy hospitals in the city for teens being added to the network. It was in a cabin, with outdated equipment. I believe I saw a mouse scurry along the wall as they were hooking me up. It wasn't the best situation and I'm glad I contracted nothing there. I've heard stories of people not so lucky. They say our reactions were so severe because it's not designed for adults—our brains are just not as pliable—but I think having the right equipment would have helped too.

With my back to the screens, sitting on the medical bed, a woman cut my hair and attached a metal frame to my head. Then, they tied my hands and feet to the chair: "for your own protection" Rubin reassured. I resisted at first, but they were prepared, and two of the other men held me down. I sat like this for what seemed like ages as they attached additional wires to the head apparatus before I felt a small prick into the back of my head.

"Have you ever used ayahuasca?" asked Rubin.

"No." That was only used by the fathers, and only during the solstice.

"Well, if you had, I'd tell you it's gonna feel a little like that."

He stuck the needle into the back of my neck.

It hurt like hell, and I mean that in all the ways I was taught growing up.

At first, I thought, if this is what ayahuasca feels like, why would anyone use it? My head twisted and spun, as if my thoughts were no longer my own, but picked up and placed in a bowl and beaten like the old women who beat eggs until they froth over. It shot pain down into my stomach, and as if to say on record that this was worse than the handheld, my stomach released its contents, and I threw up all over Rubin.

I tried to apologize for the mess, but my brain wasn't able to put two words together.

I remember little else, other than finding a mat next to the fire alongside the others. I watched the flames lick the wood, and the fire never appeared more beautiful than it did in that moment. Soon, the headache went away, and so did the feeling in my stomach. And everything in the world felt good and right and beautiful. I wondered if this is what it felt like when the fathers had their visions.

I learned later that when incorporating adults, they often used drugs to soften the blow and make us more open to new experiences, and the feeling would fade as we became accustomed to the network. I also learned that they had developed a time-release feature for the program, slowly opening up over the next few days. So it wasn't until later that night that I felt it. And it's hard to explain what that first connection was like. It was as if the entire world and all that it contained and everything worth knowing was nothing more than a memory waiting to surface. Or as if I could only dream and find what I'm looking for. I would never have believed you had you told me at that moment that I was granted access to only ten percent of the network. Ten percent was a thousand times more than I had before.

I laid by the fire, between sleep and wake, and dreamed of the city and the people, and they were all there. I could feel them. I knew them—like one remembers the taste of tea or the film it leaves on your teeth when it's steeped too long. They were familiar. I could sense them. I could sense everything.

I thought of my brother and he came to me in my dreams. I

could remember his face and his smile. He lived just outside the city limits, where the trees still grow tall, but where the buildings grow even taller, in a small apartment. He worked in that resort that looked like a village on the other side of the valley. He was married, with a kid—a beautiful little boy. I cried as these memories surfaced.

It was only later that I learned that memory is the doorway to the network, and it's not genuine memories at all but information that lives on the servers. Still, to this day, I confuse the actual memory of finding my brother with the moment when I found him in the database. They say that for those who grew up connected, these blurred memories are not as common, and they are better at differentiating between the two. I'm convinced they just don't care as much. For me, when I feel like I can't separate the network from my true memories, I just think of my family back in the woods, with the cabin and my little brothers sleeping in the bed next to me, and I know those memories are all mine, for the network knows nothing of my family or the cabin or the wooden mantel I would place my pebble on, resting it into one of the large cracks in the hand-carved lumber.

I dreamed all night until Rubin came and woke us up.

"Everyone, we have to hurry. Get up!"

I did nothing before morning prayers, and I hated the fact that I might. Yet, the urgency in his voice and eyes. To be fair, even in the village, we'd skip prayers for emergencies—a pregnancy, death, and other similar events.

I grabbed my mat and dusted off my new clothes, straightening them as I followed Rubin out of the camp. We passed the cabin, and the computers and screens were all missing.

"A few immigration officials are on their way. They will have you arrested if caught here. We must hurry."

It turned out that as much as our village was worried we'd run to the city; the city was concerned too. To keep the social services offered in the city from being overloaded, legal immigration from the outskirts has been made illegal. With these officials showing up, we didn't have the proper time to adjust to the network. Rubin explained as best he could after we had hiked a short distance and gathered around a large tree by a large boulder.

"I would normally give you a few days to get used to it all, but we don't have time. So listen: a short walk from here, a group from the resort spent the week partying. They are waking up and will be just as disoriented as you, which will help. We have gotten you a room at the resort for one night. We have already activated the reentry program in your new chip, and it will start giving you instructions as you go along, but you have to listen for it. It will be like an intuition, or a feeling—a nudge. If you get confused, just try and remember what you're supposed to do, and you will. That's how it works." It was a lot to take in, and I might remember it wrong, but I am sure we had to learn all of this in a matter of moments, with no time for questions. This is not how I'd recommend being introduced to the network. "I will lead you to the party, and you will pretend you were with them for the week. Then, you will ride back with them on their shuttles, spend the night in the resort, and take the shuttle back to the city. And at that point you're in, no one knowing the wiser. It's as simple as that." He pointed ahead to a large rock face behind us. "The area ahead is surrounded by rock walls, and inside, there's no signal, and thus the chips don't work. They come out here to do things they don't want the network tracking. We're going to go into this cove, and your chip will lose connection and you will go through withdrawal, which some of you might find as a relief since you're still getting used to it. Either way, that's the design of this cove. It's why people come here, so that works to our advantage. In their disorientation, they won't remember that you weren't with them. So this is your way to get in. Go in, keep to yourself, don't talk to anyone any more than you have to—the reentry program will guide you from there. Good luck."

He gestured for them to continue and with no other options, everyone stumbled into the cove.

"Thanks, Rubin," I said as I passed him. "And sorry again

about the mess," looking at his shirt, which he had changed since I messed up his other one.

"It happens more than you would think. Good luck, Birdie."

He gave me a hug. He saved my life, and even though I'd never see him again, I'll always remember that hug.

The path led into a bowl made of rocks. The area was void of trees, and the grass was sparse and worn down. My recent memories were quickly replaced with a headache. I tried to think of my brother, but I couldn't remember where he lived—or how to get there. I couldn't remember the city, its buildings, its shops, its people—other than what I actually remembered, which was hard to access over the screaming of my head. It hurt so bad that I nearly tripped over someone lying in the thin grass. That's when I realized the cove was lined with bodies of people sleeping, sitting, and talking, all ignoring us as we stumbled in.

"You got back just in time for the shuttle!" one guy said to us, leaning on his arms while lying down, his eyes glazed over. I smiled and sat down like the rest of our group, spreading out amongst the sleeping bodies. It was only a few minutes later that we heard a whistle, and those sleeping stirred, got up and lined up on the far end of the yard. I followed the others standing in line.

Soon, we were on a dirt path that led to a gravel road past the rock wall where a bus was sitting. As soon as we reached the bus, I reconnected to the signal and the headache slowly retreated. It seemed everyone else had a similar experience of relief.

I had never ridden on a bus before and was feeling nervous when my memories came back—I knew they weren't my memories, but it's hard to describe them any other way. I had never ridden a bus, but I found my seat—15A—and how I knew it was my seat. I couldn't explain other than I just knew like one knows their name. I took my seat and tried to imagine the resort and, like everything else, I could see my room: third floor, fifth door from the stairs. Inside the room was an enormous bed, and along the far wall was a door that led to a balcony nestled into a tree with branches that hugged the building.

No one talked the entire bus ride.

By midday, we reached the resort.

I took the stairs to my room just as I felt I should.

The bed felt as if it was made of clouds with the thickness of jelly from the hooves of cattle. I laid back on it and wondered when I'd be able to go to my brother. It was only a moment later that I learned a shuttle would leave at six in the morning the following day, and the third stop was a short walk to my brother's apartment. It was overwhelming having every answer only a thought away, and all these years later, I still find it overwhelming.

In the morning, I woke hungry and craved something specific: a lightly toasted pastry with berry filling, which was located down in the lobby close to the shuttle. It turns out that these suggestions are always on by default, and I would have to go to a local service center to have those settings turned off. Something my brother would explain to me my first week here, but it felt sincere. I wanted this baked goodness more than I wanted air itself.

But I knew better than to skip prayer two mornings in a row, so going against every inclination of my body, I got up from bed and kneeled, folding my hands into my lap to pray. Except I couldn't. It felt similar to not wanting to and having grown up in a village that prayed three times a day. I knew that feeling all too well. But I wanted to—this time, I wanted to, but I felt distracted and unable to focus my thoughts. I would learn why, many years later, mostly from my daughter who would grew up in the city. The network suppressed such existential experiences, altering our appetite for things like prayer for more beneficial things in society, like berry-filled pastries.

They say you can update the settings, but the application is impossible to complete, insanely expensive, and those who do become almost entirely unemployable. I've never been able to afford such changes, so now I rest on the prayers of those who do.

Unable to pray, and increasingly hungry, I found myself in an elevator, having never been in an elevator before, with no prayers to hold me up. I knew to press the button that had a large L on it and that the L meant lobby, but before the doors could close, someone a little older than me got into the elevator with me. She smiled with the smile my friends would give when they lost a game but didn't want to look like sore losers. I was tempted to wonder who she was—to search my "memories" for her, but it felt wrong doing that with her standing so close.

"Nice outfit," she said as she entered, her smile as insincere as I'd ever seen. I felt my face turn red. They had dressed me in a cabin in the woods, with clothes that would help me pass in the resort, but not much more. Knowing what I know now, I'm confident I looked like a fool. I'm embarrassed just thinking about it.

I could feel she wanted me to respond. I could feel she wanted me to comment on her outfit, too, but what did I know about such things? This is one of the many things my dad hated about the city. Everyone was expected to wear different clothes, but somehow the right clothes, at the right time, in the right way, for the right body—and then be comfortable being judged for it. Before I could say anything, she continued, the elevator doors now closing.

"Did you get that at the shop?"

I looked at the floor. I didn't know what to say. The elevator passed the first floor when she pressed the button, jolting the elevator to a stop. I did not know what was going to happen, but my legs started shaking, and I clenched my fist, prepared to fight if I had to.

"You're not from the city, are you?"

I stared at the ground, fist clenched, heart racing.

"It's ok. I won't judge. I'm glad you're here trying to build a better life for yourself, but let me give you a piece of advice. Strong emotions are hard to hide from the network. So if you don't want someone to know you think they are a bitch, you need to make sure the network knows you want it to be private. It's a rookie mistake."

I stood up straight, confused. "I don't think you're a bitch." I had never said that word before, and I've never used it since. It's such a vulgar word, if you ask me, and I'd never think it about someone like her.

"I hope not, but if you thought it, or something like it, and a part of you wanted me to know it, the network is going to pass it on as a review of our interaction. That's how this thing works—they log every reaction of every kind as a review of your experience unless you tell it otherwise. You can also go to a service center and set the default to private—which your guide should have told you if I'm honest."

I'm not sure my face could have turned more red; the idea that every thought I had about every person from the bus to my room was logged for everyone to see? I wanted to throw up.

"Oh, don't worry: your brief review won't hurt my ranking at all, so no harm done." She turned toward the door and pressed the lobby button. "I'm Abigail. And you're Birdie? That's a cute name."

I let out a breath of air that I must have been holding the entire time.

"And I really do like your outfit," she added. "Sincerely—This is just how I smile."

***

The apartment building rose out of what was left of the forest that surrounded the city: a tower of brick and concrete. My brother lived on the twentieth floor, but as soon as I entered the brick-laid courtyard, I saw him sitting on a bench. He was waiting for me.

It had been a year since seeing him. How do I even describe how that felt? I tried not to cry. I tried to keep it together. I tried to appear strong, but a part of me had gone missing and was now found. I remembered the stories of our God, his love for us, and his search for us, and I had to imagine this is what it felt like to him when we returned home.

I collapsed into his arms, crying in a way I never have before.

"It's ok. It's ok. It's going to be ok. I'm so glad you came!" he reassured me.

"I've missed you, Jax."

He looked at me and smiled. "That's not my name anymore."

"I know. Do you mind if I still use it, for now at least?"

"Sure," he said, "but I see you got 'Birdie' after all," and he laughed at me, just like I knew he would, and it filled me with such joy to hear his laugh.

We sat on a bench close to where we were standing. I said nothing for a good long while as the reality of a new life sunk in. I didn't even realize I was holding my necklace.

"I see you kept it."

That's when I remembered what lay in my pocket. I pulled out his necklace and laid it on the bench next to him. "It's the water that shapes us," I said with a smile, not sure if I meant it as a joke or as sincerely as I ever had. Either way, I meant the next part. I know that much. "We're still family, and we can shape each other."

He smiled at first, but his face got stern as soon as he picked up the pebble. He moved it around in his hands, polishing it before saying anything. "Sometimes the water that shapes us also drowns us." He laid the necklace back on the bench. "If it means something to you, you can keep it, but it's not for me anymore." He slid it back to me.

I kept it, all these years later. It's hanging back in my apartment, out of sight, so as not to bother him when he comes over.

***

I'm not sure which is worse, the voices of our fathers or the voices of every person I walk by in the street. I fear we've traded one for the other, but I made my choice, and I have no regrets. Still, I believe you can't really choose your future until you understand what you left behind. That much of my village still sits with me. That's why we have to go back.

In one month, my daughter will turn twelve years old—old enough to be added to the network, and before she is, she needs to see what we left for herself, just as my father showed me.

Tomorrow, we leave for our journey back to the village.

What I'm most looking forward to? It's prayer. I know my daughter will choose the city; she's been counting down the days till she gets added. Some of her friends already have. But I need this more than her. I miss the silence. I can't wait to quiet myself, with my back against a tree, free from the influence of the network, and maybe, just maybe, hear the voice of God again.

Joe Graves (he/him) is the President of the Ohio Writers' Association and an ordained pastor passionate about storytelling, justice, and community. He began writing in college, producing short films, and has recently focused on completing his first novel while exploring short fiction. Joe's work has been featured in Outcasts: An Anthology, Metamorphosis, The Worlds Within, and 365 Tomorrows.

MUSÉE D'ÉROTICISME
by A.M. Hayden

Religion and sex together may be hard to grasp

So be sure to see all seven floors

If you visit the sex museum after Mass

    A 6' Mesopotamian pottery penis, a painted tantric crevasse

    No need for privacy, confessionals, or closed doors

    Religion and sex together may be hard to grasp

        Some may think it titillating, others will find it crass

        Either way, you will likely want to see more

        If you visit the sex museum after Mass

            While a "Garden of Need" may not warrant a pass

            How about erotic postcards with nuns dressed as whores?

            Religion and sex together may be hard to grasp

                Or what about S&M priests in leather face masks?

                You may be offended, but never bored

                If you visit the sex museum after Mass

                    Nude statues or naked photographs behind glass?

                    One person's art another's blushed porn

                    And all a stone's throw from Montparnasse

                    If you visit the sex museum after Mass

A.M. Hayden (she/her) is the current Poet Laureate for Sinclair College and award-winning Professor of Humanities, Philosophy, and World Religions. Her debut collection, American Saunter, was released by FlowerSong Press November 25th, 2024. Old World Wings, inspired by European travels, is forthcoming by Wild Ink Publishing in Fall 2025. She received the River Heron Editors' Poetry Prize and is a Pushcart Prize Nominee. She lives on a windy little farm with her family, many furry rescue babies, including a blind, three-legged "angel in a dog suit," Vinny Valentine.

THE ISLAND
by Lorisha Adams

You didn't sign up to go to Camp Blitz, just woke up there. Daily breakfast is cold cereal, sometimes fried eggs. By lunchtime, the crew had acquired everything needed to get through the day: a case of beer and a Ziploc baggie of marijuana.

From your time at Camp Blitz, you learned that if you make eye contact with a paranoid person, they'll assume you've been talking to cops. They'll suspiciously squint and repeatedly ask if you're an undercover cop. Then there will be a friend who will cry and tell you about his ex-wife whom he really misses but can't stop drinking alcohol long enough to win her back. Your uncle, who always shows up eventually, will start calling everyone "bastards" and will, for the one-hundredth time, tell the story about the robbery that ruined his dreams of owning a convenience store. Your cousin, with a tiny waist, huge breasts, and flawless skin will, with tears and snot, declare how ugly she feels. Your old friend will hug you and rub your back tenderly, consoling you for unknown reasons. The guy with the muscles will fight, blood and teeth everywhere. He thinks everyone knows that he can't read and can barely write, and everyone does know but they would never mention it. No one tells him that you cannot physically fight illiteracy, you must mentally attack it.

Your philosophical friend makes sense whilst lamenting about American consumerism and institutionalized racism. He might slur here and there but he's smart and could have a successful life if he spoke this way when not high. A friend of a friend is always there and ready for a sexual encounter. You will have to beat his roaming hands away from your breasts and rear. You will have to move and sit next to your brother, who even while intoxicated, is somehow sober enough to protect you.

Circle time at Camp Blitz consisted of everyone sitting around a coffee table sharing a blunt. When it comes around to you, you don't take a puff, you just pass it to the person on your right. They all yell at you to just do it already. You yell back and say that you don't want to start crying about your ex-wife or thinking you're grotesque, or fighting, or touching people inappropriately. At Camp Blitz you learned that drugs and alcohol don't free your inhibitions, they reveal your insecurities and force you to model them in weird ways.

Camp Blitz is located on an island and is cut off from the mainland. Many settle here to escape full consciousness. It helps them float, weightless in the ocean. Those mystical experiences become the sole reason for living. Your Camp Blitz companions needed an outlet, a way to dream about going to the mainland and doing things people do over there.

There are a few ways to get off the island. One, is to be so impressive, play piano like Mozart, paint like Picasso, play ball like Jordan, rap like Jay-Z and the ferry boat will come to take you away. The Chosen One Boat. Another way off the island is to simply get lucky. Your number was pulled in the lottery, do you want to go? Many take the opportunity. Many do not. A third way off the island is brutal. You must practice holding your breath underwater. You must spend days, months, years doing drills, risk assessments, and practice runs. You spend your time building a small boat knowing that your ramshackle creation will not make the distance, thus, in the event of the inevitable breakdown; you will have to swim the distance.

Stories from the mainland somehow travel without a boat. People are rich, virtuous, and comfortable over there. You all desire to go there but you are comfortable among your family and friends. Even as they black out and pee themselves and stumble and fight, they are lovely human beings. They are your protectors.

Your dad disappears into the forest. He comes out sometimes to visit you and the other campers. He wears mud-stained clothing and says, "I love you" through a white-rimmed mouth. He hugs you and asks for resources to take with him back into the forest. You don't know what he does in the forest but whatever it is, it calls him consistently. He seems religiously devoted.

Your mother is an enigma. She used to be the matriarch of the island, nurturing the injured, cooking for the hungry, praying for the troubled. Then one day she disappeared. No gossip from the island or the dark woods. They say she's gone to another place.

Like gossip, books arrive mysteriously on the island. You devour them and finally feel a connection with something. You decide to begin working on your boat. Your campmates call you weird, but you continue to saw and hammer and tinker. You learn to swim and practice holding your breath underwater. Sometimes, it feels like a hopeless endeavor. You give up many times, but something keeps calling you back. After years of preparation, finally, your boat is ready. You hug your beloved and promise to visit.

The journey is long. Neverending, you think. It's lonely. It is dark. The first couple of days your eyes water from the wind and your stomach lurches from the constant motion. Once, the wind conspired and just stopped blowing. Progress toward the mainland halted. You were gripped with despair. You remember the story of a cousin who sailed away and months later her water-filled corpse washed ashore. Gripped with despair you are convinced that this will be your fate too. You wonder why you thought you could make it.

Overcome with despair, you fall into a deep sleep. You slept for three days or three weeks, you can't be sure. After a bout of sickness your appetite returns, and you notice that your food supply will deplete if you don't make it to land soon. You paddle and ration, and paddle more until the god of wind grants you a pardon.

A boat in the distance veers closer. A ramshackle affair like yours. The other voyager waves to you and you wave back. He tells you that his boat has a hole in it and will not withstand much longer. You invite him onto your boat.

You think this is a good idea because if you join your resources maybe you'll have enough to last the journey. As you transfer some of the resources from his boat to yours you notice that he's brought mostly beer and cigarettes, not food.

It's amazing to have someone to pass the time with. When he

forces himself on you, you tell yourself that you're the one who invited him onto your boat. You wanted this. Plus, his rowing is much better than yours. You and he exist only for the sea and each other. You try your hand at fishing. You write fairytales and sing hymns. You dance and wonder and become transfixed with the romantic notion of voyaging with someone you love. That delirious period of confusion and bliss lasts a season or more. Before you know it, you are off course. The boat is sailing aimlessly. You say that it's time to get back on course. It's time to focus on getting to the mainland. Then he reveals that his goal was never to reach the mainland, just to be out at sea, away from the island, away from its mysteries and its cruelty.

You're confused because you could have sworn that when you invited him onto your boat and you bonded and kissed and talked of destinies, that the goal was the mainland. You both had the same goals, the same reasons. You tell him that you cannot remain at sea forever with just raw fish and beer. It won't be enough. He perked up and realized that the beer supply would deplete soon. This sharpened his determination. You both paddle and rest and stay the course.

You make it to the mainland, after months at sea. You walk off the boat wobbly and grateful to be on solid ground. The streets are paved, not with gold like you imagined but are orderly and well maintained. You are amazed at the architectural marvels, pointy roofs, stone walls, and glass ceilings, it's all wonderfully terrifying. You look to him to bond over this new world, but he is uninterested and starts asking passersby where the nearest liquor store is.

You soon learn that the people here are just as inebriated as your family on the island; Maybe even more so. The liquor store is packed with well-dressed glassy-eyed people, who joke about needing a drink to make it through the day. Their hollow smiles mask a deep sadness in their eyes. You long for the island. They were druggies and drunks, but they were yours. You knew them. These people do not know you. They will not protect you. The voyager you once loved wanders away and you find yourself alone.

On the island, you were the smartest, most level-headed. Here on the mainland, you don't even rank. Many are smarter and more level-headed. At school, they make you take tests and assign you a number. You don't understand their tests or their numbers. On the mainland, you've become just another number, just one of five million others. The women with the lightest skin are treated better, more delicately. You long for the times when, on the island, with your dark skin and curly hair, you were treated delicately. Nobody sees you on the mainland. At Camp Blitz, there were times when addicts saw beyond the haze and looked you in the eyes. There were times when your dad came out of the forest and acknowledged you as his. The mainlanders are individualistic. They have been taught how to wrap themselves in a cocoon of falseness. They hide their addictions behind careers and family legacies. They don't sit around a fire and pass around blunt. They smoke in their private mansions.

There was lots of danger on the island. Blasts of gunfire, constant fights, threats and death. But there's even more danger on the mainland. They are skilled manipulators. They smile as they lie. They look peaceful but you can feel the chaos in their hearts. You find little opportunity to thrive.

You work in one of those private mansions on the mainland. Just like Camp Blitz alumni, the owners are always drunk or high off something. People on the mainland were supposed to be sober and intellectual and artful and happy. But you find that they are buzzed, foolish, numb, and miserable. They worship money and recommend that you do so as well. They touch your hair and marvel at your skin tone. They wonder where you come from.

When an expensive item goes missing in the mansion they look to you first. They tell you that your anger is unjustified, gratuitous, demonic even. You begin to hate the mainland. Its beautiful façade mocks you. You feel the way you felt on the island. The people are murderous, inebriated, and miserable. You wonder which place is worse. The one that shows itself openly or the one that hides its treachery.

Weariness hangs heavy on your shoulders. You realize that no matter where you are, the people around will be flawed. You are also flawed and struggling and reaching for something to elevate despair. Anywhere you go the untenableness of life will shine through. You have the urge to build another boat and escape, but you quickly realize there is no escape. You settle into the mainland with all its dark crevices and secret underbellies. You wander among the zombies and tricksters and shadow men in silk suits.

Years have passed and you have melded into the culture of the mainland. They are obsessed with things and some of this rubbed off on you. You find a cave and decorate it with things that give you joy. You find pleasure in collecting things, books, keys, seashells. You delight when you witness small children at play, people hugging, and families walking together. These small displays provide a balm to lingering despair. It reassures you that all is not lost.

Lorisha Adams (she/her) is a reader, writer, and peace advocate. She has pieces published in Literary Mama and Rigorous. She also won the Fairytale Story of Excellence Award in the 42 Word Anthology. She holds a bachelor's degree in human services and lives in Ohio.

SHORTSTOP

by Trent McMahon

Oh, last Friday?

There were so many squirrels on the bike trail that morning, darting around and playing tag with one another. Each time I see a bushy tail jump from one tree to the next, I think about the time one fell on my head. That was when I was seven, so…eight years ago. My aunt had taken me to the park to skip stones across the pond. This was when she could still walk. We had a good laugh about the squirrel falling on my head afterward, about how it wriggled around in my hair a bit before it jumped to the ground and scurried out of sight. About how its tiny paws tickled my scalp. It's a bummer my aunt doesn't laugh anymore.

The river is poking through the trees, small moments of visibility that turn to splashes of color as I pedal harder, pushing the thoughts from my head and concentrating hard on biking faster and faster. I think I'm going to be late for school, but I make it on time after all, with four minutes and thirty seconds to spare before the bell. School is school, and when school is over, it's time for baseball practice.

Should I keep going?

The sun looks like a giant peach I can't touch as I stand on the boiling infield. I stare at it for too long, touching it with my eyes. I see spots, floaters I think they're called. I read that somewhere. They are black dots that come and go, and I have to strain my eyes hard to make sure one isn't a baseball coming straight at my face. As a result, I start trying to dodge the floaters as they careen into view. Just in case. It's just that a lot of them look like baseballs is all.

Coach must notice me acting weird and benches me after the next play. He tells me to sit down and get some water. But he meant it in the reverse order. I take a paper cone from the dispenser, pour some lukewarm water from the orange barrel, and have a seat in the dugout.

I watch the others play ball for the rest of practice. It's no secret that I prefer to watch; the whole team knows, and I guess nobody really cares. I'm too lanky, and some days it feels like I haven't learned how to use my limbs. Some days they don't do anything right but hurt me.

The only reason I am on the team anyway is because Nichi told me to join. *There's always at least one guy on every team like that*, he told me, *who's not very good, but is there for the exercise. You can be ours. JV is chill, you'll fit right in.* He said it so matter-of-factly that I couldn't help but believe him, but now I'm starting to wonder if it was all a trick to keep me around. Which is still flattering, I guess.

Coach is nice enough, about my floaters, but every practice it seems he always has a reason to bench me. Instead of yelling at me or throwing his hat or glove into the dirt like he does with the other boys when they act stupid, he always just tells me to have a seat.

Nichi, who never seems to get yelled at, is the catcher on varsity. He has strong legs and is generally strong all over. In the locker room after practice, it is clear that he has muscles in places the rest of us do not when he takes off his jersey and dons his street clothes. They jut out of his body like pebbles on the beach. The rest of the team is jealous, you can tell. Or maybe curious. After practice that day, a few of the guys on the team, likely joking, asked to touch them, to feel what they were like, but he called them faggots and told them to fuck off.

Those who hadn't heard what they said soon knew from the whispers that swept around the room. Talk about bad timing, to ask a question like that in a room full of teenage boys. But I guess those particular boys haven't lived long enough to really understand bad timing. Their training wheels are still on, to put it a different way.

I can't help but laugh at Nichi's outburst after practice, as he and I push our bikes back along the trail. Nichi asks why I'm laughing, and I tell him that faggot means a bundle of sticks. I'd read it in *The Hobbit* and looked up the historical meaning. It's funny because faggot also means someone who is gay—obviously the way he intended it. *So, it's double funny because you're calling them gay and also sticks, because they don't have muscles*, I tell him.

He laughs. I can tell he thinks it's really funny because his eyes crinkle up. I like it when Nichi laughs. We're new friends this year after having gone up through the grades together without having talked much. A well-timed study hall and a seating chart in French were all it took. Even though we've known each other less than a year, I can feel a deep connection to him, like I know what he's seeing when he closes his eyes. It's really something.

We start biking down the trail, where the squirrels have gone to sleep or are napping at least and pause the conversation. And then I start thinking again.

The "faggots" are JD, Raf, and Saurav, who everyone just calls Splat. At thirteen, they're the youngest on the team, carted over from the junior high every day because they're good and need to practice with the older team. I know better than to call them that word to their faces or to even say the word out loud at all, but it's good to take ownership of words. It helps reclaim their meaning. I read that on a flier a civil rights activist handed me while Mom and I were shopping.

Though it's not for certain I'm gay, but I'm wondering if I might be, so maybe I'm not allowed to reclaim that word yet. Do you ever wonder when your body or mind decides it will be one way or the other? I've been wondering a lot about myself lately. I can feel my body changing and it's weird, like how some mornings I wake up and feel like a completely different person, or how the doctor told me I grew four inches since my last checkup. I didn't give myself permission to change.

Growing up doesn't scare me all that much, and I'm not offended by Nichi's word choice. It wasn't right for him to say it, but Mom likes to remind m, like she did when I told her about what happened later, that teenage boys aren't known for their diplomacy.

How did Nichi using that word make me feel? I guess, if life were a game of baseball, I'd call the use of 'faggot' a foul ball, effort without result. But a foul ball still counts as a strike.

After the bend where Nichi and I part ways with a friendly

wave, I bike at full speed the rest of the way home. There is sweat on my arms and legs from the exertion. Later, much later, after dinner and before my bath, I lick my arm and taste the salt that has dried on my skin. We really are extraordinary machines. Mom listens to that song sometimes when she's lounging around; it's by Fiona Apple.

Have you heard it?

Later, I get a text from Fritz on our team's group chat, inviting me over for a sleepover at 21:00. In all honesty, Nichi is just about the only reason I would want to go to something like that. Not to diss the rest of the team too hard, but they're not like Nichi, who is quiet but secretly funny, stern but lighthearted, sometimes dark even, gloomy, and known for his little explosions, like the one in the locker room, but is still kind-hearted and intelligent. The others are constantly loudmouthed and crass and get horny from a badly timed sneeze or by looking at the pyramid of oranges at the supermarket. You get the picture.

I ask Mom if it's okay to go and she's okay with it because she and Fritz's mom sometimes hang out on our patio and drink. We're sure they're texting behind our backs. It's weird when moms become wine friends. I tell her it's not set in stone yet, that I'd let her know for sure in a bit. I didn't tell her why, but it's because Nichi still hasn't confirmed he'd be there. She and Dad are in the kitchen, making dinner together, which is sweet. Not that they'd ever hear that from me, but I really am glad they're happy together.

I scroll through the conversation to see who's all coming—looks like Splat and JD, as well as a few other boys from the team: Staniel, Quandong, Theo. They're all right but no Nichi yet. He's always slow to text back anyway, if at all. I bide my time and take a bath. As usual, while the tub fills with water, I click on the portable, waterproof radio, switching the dial to a station I like.

After getting into the bath, the radio starts playing mostly ads, which is annoying. When I dip my head below the water, the ads turn into Underwater Music. That's what I call them anyway, and it makes them better. Sound works differently underwater because the water affects the way we hear. I read in a book once that sound waves actually move five times faster underwater. Try cracking your knuckles underwater sometime. It's wild.

Under the bubbles, I build an imaginary city in my head where roads and cars are illegal. The city is small but dense, with vast underground malls and eateries and tall, tall apartment buildings shooting up into the clouds. Subways take you anywhere you want to go. Everyone bikes around too. I am an adult and living in the tallest building in the city, on the highest floor. I'm roommates with Nichi. Sometimes we take the stairs for fun if we meet in the lobby after work, a race up 130 flights. By the time we reach our apartment door, we're as salty as the sea.

The Underwater Music continues playing while my stored oxygen depletes. I try to imagine that Nichi and I are more than roommates in this fantasy world—that we're dating, married even— but it's too weird. Or am I just telling myself that? Under the water I am dying, which is absolutely what happens when you hold your breath for an extended period — a little death, an inch-race towards death up until it's not. Sometimes it's scary to think how many seconds or how many inches a person might be from the end.

My head emerges when I hear a vibration in the Underwater Music: my cell phone. It's Nichi, the friend version, the present version, the group chat version. All the text says is *Sure*. I wait a few minutes before adding my response. I check the clock on the radio—it's only 20:00. I do this thing I call "Play God," which is when I unplug the bathtub drain, let it drain for a while, and then cover the hole with my foot. It's fun if you think about it in different ways.

I dry off, change into something casual (our team's shirt and a comfortable pair of shorts) and, am ready to go. No more salt skin. I snag some banana chips and cans of sparkling water from the pantry and put them in my backpack before telling Mom and Dad that I am heading over to Fritz's place. I kiss them each goodbye and we go through the routine of "What and What Not to Do." As if I need reminding. Mom tells me to say hi to Fritz's mom, which is dumb because they have probably already texted each other or shared some dumb inspirational article or wine meme earlier that day, but I zip my lips up tight and nod as I rush toward the door. Outside, the sun has dipped beneath the trees and has stained the sky red, the color of pressed grapes, the empty lot across the street, the color of love and Spanish mysteries. I read those descriptions in Dad's copy of *On the Road.*

　　Beautiful, don't you think?

　　Fritz lives up the hill from us, the next neighborhood over, in one of the houses Mom dreams about. By the time I ring the doorbell, it sounds like everyone has already shown up; I am a little bit late but that's trendy, I remind myself. There's a distant rumble of feet slapping against the wood floor, stampeding toward the door. I am ushered in by seven or eight guys, thrown, into multiple conversations at once. It's overwhelming, but in my head, I imagine the Underwater Music and how it sounds so serene and not rushed and not real, and I manage all the sensory information without too much trouble. By the time we make it to the kitchen, Fritz's mom has an avocado toast waiting for me. She's pretty cool even if she is friends with Mom, I guess.

　　In all the commotion I didn't even notice Nichi hanging out in the back, sulking, like the only reason he joined the stampede to greet me because it'd be weird to stay in the basement with Fritz's dad, who basically just games down there from the moment he gets home from work until whenever he decides to go to bed. I've never seen Fritz's mom even talk to him, if you can believe it. He's not too bad. Some of the guys really like him, anyway, but if I hang around him for too long, I start to get sad for some reason.

　　Before I can even get a bite of my avocado toast in, Quandong and Splat inform the group that their ping-pong match was paused for this, so…

　　So it's back to the basement, my toast in one hand and a can of sparkling in the other. It's one of those basements that's really just another story of the house built underground. There's carpet, even a kitchenette down there. At my house, the basement has stone flooring and a drainpipe for water to go down when there's a leak after a big rainstorm.

But I'm not trying to complain about being poor or anything to you. It's just facts, promise.

I linger in the back of the circle while the others gather around the dueling pong players. There's no denying their skill, which far exceeds mine; like, it's not even funny. They move in almost blurs, catapulting the white ball back and forth until it's a comet-like streak flowing between them, like they're Super Saiyan. I switch my gaze to watch the faces of the boys and suddenly feel all alone because their excitement is not my excitement.

This happens a lot these days, especially after practice when the guys start talking about girls they want to "fuck," (their words, not mine) or who has big boobs in their class. This kind of talk is confusing me even more, about whether I might be into guys because I really don't care about any of that. Mom likes to tell me that, whatever the outcome, she and Dad will support me, but there's still a part of me that's unsure if that's the truth. The whole truth anyway. It's because she'll also say things like, *Maybe you just don't like those conversations because you know better than to demean women and that's all.* Or, *This all might just be a phase we can laugh about when you're older.* She might be right, but (1) I think she forgets I'm still a teenage boy sometimes, and (2) even if it is a phase, it isn't all that funny. Still, I love Mom, so of course I can forgive her for being unintentionally prejudiced. I saw on TikTok that these sorts of things are called *microaggressions* and that they're really hard to avoid.

As the ping pong game continues, I sing a lyric under my breath to push away the negative thoughts. *Dark blue, dark blue / Do you ever feel alone in a crowded room?* Jack's Mannequin. Another one of mom's old CDs is making its way into my brain.

I crack open my backpack and offer a bored Nichi some of my banana chips while I'm attacking the avocado toast. He takes them with a small nod in my direction. I ask him how things are going. He says, *Fine. *crunch, crunch, crunch**

I say, *Me too. *silent chewing* But I'm wondering why I showed up.* This isn't really my thing. It's okay to say it out loud to Nichi because nobody is paying me any attention.

He makes the long, low noise under his breath that I've heard him make a million times. The noise clearly says, *Ah, I see...* without uttering a syllable. I asked once, early on, maybe after the second or third time seeing him outside of school, why he makes that noise, and he told me it's commonly used in Japan, where his parents are from, as a way to acknowledge understanding. I nodded, even though it would be the perfect time to make the noise we were discussing, but I didn't want to come off as insensitive. So I nodded.

Makes sense, I told him. *Where in Japan?* He said, *Yokohama,* but I wasn't entirely sure where that was, so I just nodded again and said, *It must be nice there.*

Before his memory can answer me (I looked it up later, though; it is nice there), we are interrupted by a scream of triumph from Splat, who won the ping-pong match. Everyone is cheering for him, even Quandong, who apparently almost won. I guess it's all in good fun. Not pointless if you think about it that way, as fulfilling some kind of role in the dynamic of the group. Those kinds of things are probably important at the end of the day.

After the cheers and whatnot, there's this collective feeling of *What's next?* in the air, and nobody is sure what to do. Someone suggests we go outside, and when someone then suggests hide and seek it suddenly sounds like the perfect plan. I say nothing, not wanting to betray my position of careless outsider with Nichi, a member of the rat pack, budging only when Nichi indicated it was acceptable to do so, the dialogue of his body language and mine trying to sync.

And so, we're off once more. The stampede moves its way back up the stairs and out into the night. The breeze hits my face, and in the fabricated lightness of the city beyond, I see the two usual stars poking through the pollution, the strong ones. Theo is the first seeker, his voice crying out through the night toward 100, and the rest of us divide off and float into the darkness like sea divers.

This way says the darkness. Nichi. His voice is slow like always, but I can tell even he is excited by the game; it's hard not to be. We take off together down the Fritzes' sloping lawn and onto the pale concrete of the road that braids itself with the darkness. Side by side, we cross into the wilds beyond.

This is what I heard Dad call the "real curb appeal" once, how all the homes up here, with the neat, trimmed lawns, all dissolve into woodlands, prairie flowers, and bugs, bugs, bugs. The rich are not required to share a view with anything but the world itself. Nichi is running ahead of me now, standing mightily against the sky, where there hangs no moon, no ghost peach for my eyes to taste. I realize in this moment that I am stuck to him like metal to a magnet, like a flower to its stalk, its roots. It feels right, but it probably isn't right to think so. My legs slice their way through the tall grass as he pulls me along into the unknown. Bugs scatter as we pass, small and frightened, inconsequential to our adventure. I want to pause the world and calm the thoughts that start welling up deep inside me. But there isn't time for that now, as I realize that Nichi could take me anywhere he wanted to, and I would follow without question. And that I wouldn't want it any other way.

Can we take a break? I need some time before the next part.

Nichi leads us to a culvert that runs under the road, my trainers soaking through in an instant, cold and unreal, like water sourced from Lethe, one of the other rivers of the underworld. It flows backwards and forwards in my mind, swelling up to the edges of my thoughts, so that the world I'm slipping into with Nichi—this strange, dark, oval existence—becomes waterlogged, blurred. Being alone with Nichi like this, in a vacuum, feels intimidating, peeled-scab raw. We take our phones out, and the glow allows me to feel more situated in reality for a few seconds before dissolving once more into the fluid world of the culvert.

Someone spray painted a penis in the concrete, neon-green, and almost phosphorescent in the phone light. Amazing timing. If we weren't trying to be covert, we'd probably laugh. Laughing with Nichi. I'm reminded of the bike ride earlier, his genuine laughter at my joke. His crinkly eyes. The scene replays behind my own eyelids like a family video. I like it when Nichi laughs.

The shivers start in after a few minutes of waiting. A wind blows from somewhere deep within the culvert, flittering across my eyelashes like a magic spell, catching the ridges of the piping, creating a musical tone that blows through me. It sounds like something a nymph might play to lure unsuspecting victims into their hollow. The icy water sends sharp pains up my legs, and the floaters from baseball practice return to my eyes, darker than the night, like burnt-out stars hovering in inky space. I'm shivering from the cold and also from the nerves about what might happen. About what this strange situation might do to me.

We dare not speak for fear of disclosing our location. Every so often there is a stamp-stamp-stamp of feet on the road above like the marching of troops, but it dies away quickly, muted by the water, the metal, and the beating of my heart. Our legs ripple closer together, until our new hairs are touching, standing on end with our goose-pimpled skin.

It is going to be alright, one hair whispers to another.

Faggot, it whispers back.

I almost laugh for real, imagining our talking leg hair. I look at Nichi's barely illuminated face but can see nothing, no expression looking back at me, the mouth a thin line neither lifted either up or down by the muscles in his face. I'm probably going to regret this, but I can't stop myself. I move, though I am uncertain if it was actually my own doing or from the magical frequencies flying around.

I use my hands to wrap myself into his body, bringing us together. In these moments there is no thinking, just doing. I'm practically trembling, disrupting the water like I am the tide against the coast that is Nichi, who is unmoving, unaffected. Does this mean he is okay with what's happening? I can't see his face in the dark, but he doesn't flinch or yell at me like he did when the other boys invaded his personal space. So, I stay where I am, clinging to him, smelling the remains of soap on his body, the detergent on his clothes. Ocean breeze, a slight, salted edge.

Do I get special treatment from him for a reason? I think. Or it is like with Coach, who mysteriously withholds his anger, frustration, and agitation at my poor performance? Is there some reason I don't understand what causing this, whether about myself or the others? I am dying to ask him but now is not the time. Later.

Or now, with you, I guess.

He is warm and I can feel his steady-beating heart bumping against mine. Extraordinary machine. I don't dare do anything but remain as I am now for as long as possible. I can't even imagine the thought of kissing him. It's far, far too much.

We are finally found and break apart, the magic spell broken by Theo, the bastard. We exit the culvert individually and scramble up the hill in a mad dash for home base. Nichi easily outruns me, and I am tagged out almost instantly. Martyrdom is never easy.

We play a few more rounds in the dark. I no longer hide with Nichi. It seems right to create space, though he seems unaffected by my embrace, or at least does not mention it to me afterward, almost as if I dreamt the whole thing up. We play until Splat hides himself away so well that we give up and scream to the darkness that we're going inside. Ten minutes later he returns to the house with several grass stains on his jeans, hair matted with dirt, and a cut above his left eye. He isn't about to tell us where he disappeared to, and we respect that, the honor of it all.

We finally get Fritz's dad off the console around midnight, and we take turns shooting each other and then shooting other people online. Then we switch over to soccer. And then baseball—each of us with a controller, controlling our real-life positions on the screen. It's so much easier to concentrate here than on the field.

While we play the game, I can feel the team becoming more comfortable with me. It helps that I've played this game before and helped lead our team to several impressive saves. They include me in jokes, something they usually don't do at practice. If only I could play this well in real life—they might respect me more. But as I feel them start liking me better, I also can't escape my thoughts about what happened in the culvert.

It's like an out-of-body experience, being in two different planes of existence at once. I'm with Nichi there, but he is here as well, as we work together to play infield. As I wrap my arms around him there, I see the others here, each controlling themselves on the screen. There is a constant understanding between our actions and our thoughts. I am my own team, several personalities all at once, all working together to succeed in life.

I like Nichi, but is that enough to consider the possibility that my liking him might be more than friendship just because I might be gay? It's also important to consider his feelings. I can be attracted to him without reciprocation, probably? Is that healthy? Isn't it better to find in Nichi a sexless love, like a brother? It's a resounding YES in my mind, especially since I haven't talked to him much since we were caught, but I am not sure if it's possible. Nothing I have read or watched has helped me figure it out, which is a first. Mom and Dad definitely won't be any help with this either.

Will you?

I read on a baseball forum that shortstops are the most defensive members of the team, asked to defend the infield, bounce between second and third as needed, fielding balls that come in reverse toward home plate, where the catcher waits. I may not seem defensive, but I have trouble really opening up to anyone my age without taking the time to consider the risks. To me, that's the definition of defensiveness.

Maybe that's what my problem is; it's something I want to work on anyway. Sometimes your flaws are really just perks when you redefine them and own them.

A clock chimes somewhere in the sleeping house above—02:30. We play and play until we fall asleep one by one, on couches, in piles of blankets on the floor, on the treadmill. Nobody seems concerned that I'm going to be sleeping in the same room as them, which is reassuring in a way. Is my life going to be filled with these little uncertainties? Eventually, the catcher and the shortstop are the only two awake, their characters unsure how they are going to make the game work together, with just the two of them. Baseball would be pretty boring without the other positions, I guess.

I get up from the couch where he and I are sitting, and move to the other side of the room, to an empty corner. Something tells me it's a good idea to put distance between myself and Nichi tonight. Not that there are weird feelings between us or anything. At least I hope not. I guess I don't know. Why hadn't I thought to just ask? Why am I not doing it now?

I try saying goodnight to Nichi as normally as I can but my voice catches in my throat. He laughs from over on the couch, and while I'm not sure why, it makes me feel better about things. That laugh again—I can tell it's going to be all right whenever I hear that sound. He probably can read me like a book anyway.

The carpet is surprisingly soft and comfortable, and I close my eyes. Nichi turns the TV off. There are the shuffling noises against the carpet of a person walking carefully around a group of sleeping teenagers. That's a very specific sound you'd know right away, isn't it? Followed by stillness that seems to last longer than necessary, as if the darkness is trying to tell me something important. Then a warmth coming from somewhere nearby.

I open my eyes and see a familiar outline settling in next to me on the floor.

Trent McMahon (he/him) works in higher education and received his degree in English & Creative Writing from the University of Iowa. His work has appeared in Earthwords. More of his work can be found at https://trentmcmahon.com. He lives in Columbus, Ohio.

PORNOCOPIA
by Jay Osborne

I was twelve years old and on my way to Sunday School when I first discovered sex. I made the discovery when I stopped to invite my heathen friend Mike to church as the teen evangelist club had encouraged me to do. Mike was not at home, so I decided to look in the tool shed out back. Mike wasn't there either, but I was stunned to discover that the shed was a cornucopia of pornography... Is pornocopia a word?

Having descended from a long line of asexual ministers, sex was as unknown to me as a Swahili. My parents had always slept in separate bedrooms. I'd always supposed my brother and I were the products of a petri dish experiment gone awry.

Nothing in Leviticus had prepared me for a workbench covered with hundreds of copies of Playboy, Penthouse, Hustler, and other more specialized and mysterious magazines. My own recent birthday gift of a set of Encyclopedia Britannica suddenly seemed worthless in comparison. I'd always felt superior to Mike who had failed fifth grade twice yet now I knew that he was years beyond me.

I spent 15 minutes perusing the material before noticing that I was late for church. Halfway across the yard, I realized that I was in such a daze that I had left my Bible in the shed.

When I went back to retrieve it, I grabbed a copy of Naked Love off the top of the pile, crammed it down the front of my pants, and pulled my shirt down over it.

At church, the enormity of my sin pressed against me. God in His infinite wrath had already elected to punish me by giving me x-ray vision. The clothes simply vanished off everyone I looked at. Even Dad up in the pulpit was not immune. God's curse was much more powerful than the worthless x-ray spectacles that I had purchased from an ad in the back of a comic book a few years before. This new power was completely uncontrollable and now I understood Superman's devotion to good deeds as penitence for all the wicked things that he had seen.

Dad's sermon on the destruction of Sodom and Gomorrah only triggered a spontaneous song in my head that began with the lyrics, "Sodom and Gomorrahia, They fill me with euphoria…" I earnestly prayed that my problem would suddenly vanish but when I got home and looked in my pants, it was still there, a sure sign that God had abandoned me.

When I got some time alone after lunch, I realized that my choice had not been optimal. The magazine was all black and white and filled with unairbrushed naked couples frolicking on a farm. Most distressing of all, was that there was a naked man on every page. This was bad. If I had learned anything at all in gym class, it was that there were certain things that you did not ever want to look at. An appendage on the page was as unwelcome as a gizzard in your chicken sandwich. I decided that the best way to begin my spiritual redemption would be by cutting out all the male parts. Maybe later when I was stronger, I would cut out the female parts until all that would be left would be the grainy black and white photos of the farm and then I could throw it away, unless by that time I had become unnaturally attracted to the pigs. I shuddered at the thought.

I moved out to the garage with the magazine and a pair of scissors and started cutting. After cutting across the page to the proper location, I found that three quick snips in the shape of a triangle were sufficient to remove the offending parts. One problem was that sometimes this ruined the image of the woman on the back. Eventually, I stumbled onto another novel use for duct tape and began covering the troubling parts. The same quick three snips for triangles worked well until the automatic garage door began opening and I had to run into the house with the magazine before Dad flattened me. I hid the magazine under the bed and pretended to sleep but was unable to as my copy of Naked Love battled against Paul's First Letter to the Corinthians for dominance in my mind. I knew I was going to Hell if I didn't get rid of it, but I couldn't bring myself to abandon my treasure. I envied my younger brother in the other bedroom whose sleep was untroubled by thoughts of Naked Love. Before midnight, my mother and father opened the door, switched on the light, and walked over to my bed.

"You forgot these in the garage," Dad said as he opened his hands and let a handful of confettied male parts rain down upon my bed.

I wanted to say something to explain myself to them, that I wasn't collecting the cutouts, but doing the Lord's work by snipping them out, but all that I could think to do was to hand over my prized copy of Naked Love so they could see for themselves. They flipped through it for a minute without saying a word.

"See I covered them," I said meekly.

"With silver panties," Dad said with disgust as he tossed the magazine onto my bed. Mom leaned down next to me and through drunken tears said, "We will never speak of this again," which of course meant, "You'll never hear the end of this you sick sick little bastard," and then left the room to cry or drink or both most likely. Without another word, my father grabbed the magazine that he had just given back to me and left the room.

As I lay in the dark room, illuminated only by the fire of my father's book burning in the backyard, I contemplated all that I learned about sex. Sex was bad, evil, trouble, complicated beyond belief, and certainly not fit for human consumption.

It was probably even worse if you ever had it with another person.

Jay Osborne (he/him) received a Bachelor of Arts in English from The Ohio State University. He has written lyrics for the Columbus band Heartbreak Orchestra and for Karma Beach. He is currently a tabby rancher in Southeastern Ohio.

THUNDER AND ICE
by R. Luce

Will Beesom woke up long after morning had been chewed, swallowed, and fully digested. But for all he knew, it could have been almost any time of the day. He only knew that there was enough light coming through the dirty window to reject the concept of nighttime. He had no watch to look at, no cell phone, and there were no clocks on the walls. Time and place were concepts that other people built their lives around; he did not. He had been awakened by February's cold accumulated on his skin, sinking into his bones, and agitating his brain to do something about the shaking of his body. Though he had tried to swat it away like a bothersome fly that chooses a spot of bare skin to crawl upon, the effort hadn't worked. The cold was a masterful dodger and would not be flicked away, could not be flattened by a hand crash, and would not leave unless all skin could be pulled beneath blankets or heavy clothing that Will didn't have.

His brain whirled in the aftermath of the drugs and alcohol. As he tried to remember how he had ended up in this place, the best he could conjure were shadows of flickering gray images like the snow and noise of an old TV absent an antenna. His head hurt; his stomach threatened to make him wretch. His body was shaking. He raised his hands to catch his face as it fell forward. After a minute or two, he started taking in the space where he found himself. He was sitting on a stained sofa—some shade of brown—that reeked of embedded sweat and cigarette smoke. Everything he could see looked like it hadn't been cleaned for years, and had not felt warmth for even longer. There were other people in the room: two couples lying on the floor—each of the pairs pressed against one another for warmth—and a man sitting in a chair in a corner smoking a cigarette and tapping ashes onto the floor as he stared at Will.

"Spare a cigarette?" Will asked the man who sat low in the seat of a ragged chair that had tired of holding too many people for far too long a time. The man said nothing, and held out the pack. Will stepped unsteadily over the bodies between them and took a stick from the half-empty pack. The man reached into his pants pocket for a lighter, and plunged the flint wheel to spark a flame.

"Where the hell are we?"

The man stared back at him, took a drag on his cigarette then responded, "You just said it, man: Hell."

"Where's the goddamn heat? It's freezing in here."

The man looked at Will, and spoke in a flat voice, "Ain't nobody paying for heat here."

"Where the hell am I? For real."

"John's place." Seeing the confusion on Will Beesom's face, he added, "Canaanville, Man. Where did you think you were?"

Will thought about asking who the hell John was and how he ended up someplace called Canaanville, but realized he didn't care. "How far are we from Columbus?" he asked.

"Maybe sixty, seventy miles." the man said. The man turned his head and stared out through the smoke-dulled window.

"Was there anybody with me when I got here?"

"No idea, Man."

Will finished his cigarette, crushed the hot ash against the sole of his shoe, and tucked the butt into his pocket as he stood up and began looking carefully at each of the bodies lying on the floor, their faces pressed against the worn carpet or into the bodies of the people beside them. Bobby wasn't among them.

"Bobby!" he yelled. "Bobby, where are you?"

"What the fuck?" a man's voice from down the narrow cattle shoot of the trailer's hall shouted threateningly. "Quiet down!"

"Jesus, Man!" the guy sitting in the corner chair said.

Unfazed, Will went down the pathway toward the three doors beyond the destruction of a bathroom. When he opened the first of the three, a man lying on the floor beside two others told him to get out. Will said he was looking for Bobby.

"Ain't no fucking Bobby in here. Get out!"

The next door opened to a tiny room that would have been

overcrowded with a single bed and a small dresser had they been there. Bobby was lying on the floor in the fetal position shaking violently and making puppy-like sounds of suffering. When Will spoke, Bobby raised his head, his eyes the eyes of a rabid dog. Slobber rolled down his chin. His fists were clenched.

Will spoke to him again, "It's me, Man: Will! It's me, Bobby."

"They're gonna kill us."

"Ain't nobody gonna hurt you. I won't let 'em." Will kneeled down, lifted Bobby's upper body, and wrapped his arms around him. He held him close for a long while, lay his hand on Bobby's face, and made small circular motions with his fingers against the soft whiskers and the whiskerless skin behind the ears. When he could feel the heat being passed back and forth between them, Will whispered, "Let's go home," kissed the side of Bobby's face and lifted the skinny bag of bones Bobby had become to a standing position.

"I'm scared, Will."

"I've got you, Bobby. I'll take care of you." He took the zipper ends of Bobby's thin black nylon coat, connected them, and slid the tongue up to the top of the zipper teeth, holding him by one arm as they walked. As they got to the entrance door, he looked at the man in the low-slung chair and asked, "Hey, Buddy, which way to Columbus?" The man, no longer looking at him, mostly staring into space, turned toward the window and lifted his left hand and pointer finger, aiming right. Will pulled Bobby through the door and closed it behind them.

With each vehicle sound coming up behind them, Will turned and gave the universal hitchhiker's thumb. After a couple miles of stumble walking and being shunned by drivers in dozens of cars passing them by, an old, red Ford pickup truck with rusted fenders, and numerous dents and scrapes, pulled off the road and waited for them to come up to the side of the truck. Knowing that putting Bobby beside a stranger was likely to freak him out, Will opened the door, thanked the old woman at the wheel, took hold of the front of Bobby's jacket, and climbed in, pulling Bobby up into the cab behind him. Will told Bobby to shut the door. Robot-like, Bobby tried to obey, but almost fell out of the door. Will caught him, pulled him into place, and then lay across Bobby's legs to reach the door and pull it hard against the frame.

Feeling like he owed some kind of explanation, Will—through his chattering teeth told the woman he was sorry for the fuss. Bobby just wasn't feeling well. He thanked her again for the ride.

"You boys looked awfully cold out there. Where you headin' to?" The woman's voice sounded unphased—relaxed, gentle on Will's ear.

"Columbus," Will replied as he tried to control the shaking of his body.

"Well, that's just where I'm headin' to. You from around here?"

"No. Columbus," Will said.

"What's got you boys way out here on such a cold day?"

"It's a long story," Will said as Bobby pulled his knees up high, planting his feet on the seat, and wrapping his arms around his knees as he shivered against the door and the window glass. "Just as soon not bore you with it."

"I'm Elma Worthing," the woman said.

"I'm Will; my buddy here is Bobby … like I said, he's not feeling too good today," he said.

Will and Bobby rarely got rides from women, probably for fear of picking up drug addicts, rapists, murderers, or all three for the price of one, Will suspected. This one didn't seem the least bit concerned about any of those things. She seemed to want to talk like he was a real person, as she knew him like he wasn't just a hophead hanging out with a tweaker. He told himself she sounded kind of like a grandmother he sometimes imagined—not his own, but one of those good grandmothers you see on TV around the holidays. He tried to look at her as much as one could while sitting side-by-side in the confines of a too-narrow seat in a rattling metal box bouncing along the pavement at sixty miles an hour. She was bundled up in a coat unbuttoned at the top, scarf, hat, and boots; it was difficult to make much judgment about her other than she had a kindly face of sagging skin, wisps of gray hair hanging out from under her toboggan, a hint of gloss on her lips. Her wrists, or at least what little of them he could see above her gloves, were thin and wrinkled. Her voice was old-woman thin—a voice that presides not because of strength but because of self-respect and respect of others. She engendered a vision of an extended network of friends and a Hallmark-card-like family that always comes home for the holidays: hearth fire, candles, the smell of fresh-baked made-from-scratch pies.

The warmth coming from the truck's heating system felt good on Will's feet and legs and slowly made its way up his body, allowing him to unzip his coat. He asked Bobby how he was doing and if he was getting warmed up. Bobby shook his head up and down, breaking the side-to-side motion that had been going on for the past several minutes. "Why don't you unzip your jacket, Bobby, so you don't get too hot."

With trembling hands, Bobby obeyed, and felt for the zipper. Seeing him struggling, Will took over, found the zipper tongue, and pulled it down, releasing both flaps of the jacket. Bobby was fidgeting more extensively than he had been even moments before, sometimes it seemed as if he wanted to bounce in his seat, and he was mumbling to himself. Will put his hand on the inside of Bobby's left thigh and whispered to him, "It's okay, Man. It's okay."

Will felt himself twitching now and then too. He worried about the woman, and feared her stopping and putting them out. He worried about how she might be feeling with him wedged up against her so tightly that he could feel the contents of her coat pocket against his hip, wondering if she felt him shaking as his body fought the drugs and a desire for more. For a long time, she made no comments that suggested she was aware of anything other than getting down the road and helping Bobby and him get out of the cold. She made small talk about hitchhiking, the weather, and what the world was coming to. Will tried to reply politely when she asked a question, tried to remember to express some kind of interest in whatever she talked about . . . to, at least, say "uh huh" and "no kiddin'" at appropriate times, but when she stopped talking and gave him room to contribute, he could think of little to say; he wished she would just deliver Bobby and him home without words, but words would be the price he paid for the ride.

After fifteen or twenty minutes of travel and Will's attempts to make small talk, she shifted the topic gently, "Looks like you guys have had a bit of a rough time, if you don't mind me saying so," the woman said.

Fear raced up Will's backbone, "Yeah. Guess so," Will said warily. "Shows, huh? Sorry if we don't smell too good. Didn't get a shower this morning."

"The old smeller doesn't work that well anymore," the woman said. After a pause, she leaned forward trying to look around Will to Bobby, and asked, "How you doing over there, Mr. Bobby?"

Will looked at her profile as she turned to focus on the road, and watched her give an occasional glance toward Bobby to see if he was going to answer. Talking to himself more than to her, he said, "They planned it. Watched me sleep." He gripped Will's arm.

"I'm right here, Bobby. Come on, man. Relax. She's OK."

"Sounds like he's not doing too well," she said to Will, as though Bobby was out of hearing.

"He'll be okay."

"Meth?" she asked in a matter-of-factly way. Will turned to her, wondering how in the hell someone like her could have a clue what meth is, let alone how it fucks with a user's head.

"That stuff's nasty shit, Will," she said, surprising him again.

"No shit!" Will responded, chuckling at her use of the word shit. "How's a nice lady like you know about stuff like that?"

"What? Because I'm old, I don't know anything, don't read, don't learn anything beyond my own generation? I've been around the block once or twice … know about it because I was an ER nurse for a long time. Just retired two years ago. Seen a lot of that stuff come through the doors." She poked him with her elbow, and smiled through the statement, "You boys look like you would be pretty good-looking young men if you got off the drugs."

"So, you're saying we're not good-looking?" He joked with

her, though he felt the sting of remembering Bobby and himself growing up best friends, thinking themselves "hot" and believing that women would fall at their feet and other men would envy them … a long time ago and a world away from this one.

"I'm saying that stuff isn't doing you any favors. That's all." She paused for a moment, and then, "Sorry. Didn't mean to preach at you."

Will said, "No problem. I appreciate the ride."

"No problem," she repeated back to him as she rolled her eyes to the right like a parent to a teenager. Then she went silent, stared ahead at the highway except for the occasional glance in the rearview mirror, and turned on the radio. Country music. Will kept his mouth shut about how much he hated it. He tried to shut it out, wished he could think of something to say to get the old woman talking again so she would turn it off, but he could think of nothing that might interest her. After a few miles of twanging guitars and mournful voices, he felt himself drifting toward sleep. He fought to hold his eyelids open as they rode for miles without talking, just listening to songs about crying at a bar over a lost love, driving 18-wheelers, cheating hearts, and old dogs. At one point, he felt Bobby's body turning toward him, the laying of his head against Will's shoulder. He put his arm around Bobby and pulled him to his chest, held him as the lover he had been when they needed money, and discovered the porn brokers would pay. It was nothing—just a job, no big deal—at least that's what they told themselves for a while. Then came the day when they lay together for themselves, not for money, but because they wanted to, and Will said he loved Bobby, always had, and Bobby said, "Me too." When he awoke to some man's gravelly voice singing about having honky tonk blues while a steel guitar screeched in the background, he wiped his eyes on his coat sleeve, and said to the woman, "Sorry. I nodded off there."

"You weren't out long. Don't worry about it. If you'd been bothering my driving, I'd have hit you with my elbow." She turned his direction briefly and smiled, winking her eye mischievously.

About five miles outside Columbus, Elma turned off the radio and spoke again. The abrupt stop in the monotony of the music and her words broke the hum of the motor and the clattering of the untethered tin of the beaten truck body, broke his fall off the razor-thin wire where reality and fantasy converged. "Can I say just one more thing to you about the drug thing, Will, before we get you into town?" When he told her she could, she said, "If I asked you this question: 'Do you like your life and your future,' what would you say? You don't have to answer. Just think about it. And if you don't like the life you're living, I just want you to know that you don't have to keep living it this way. I don't know you. Don't know what's gone on in your life. It's none of my business. But if you want help, there are people who would help you and Bobby make some changes."

"Thanks, Elma. I'll think about it." He said it knowing he had thought about it many times, told himself he hated what he was doing with his life, and there were times he thought maybe he could do it—quit, that is—maybe tomorrow, or soon, maybe. He thought about waking up in a clean room under clean sheets and getting ready to go to work doing something that mattered, having money that he earned and had not stolen or sold his body to get… but then there was Bobby to think about.

As Elma pulled up to the curb on the corner of Fourth and Spring as Will asked, she said, "OK, Boys! This is the end of the line." Will reached across Bobby to open the door and pushed him to move. "No, not here." Bobby started yelling. "They're over there," pointing in the direction of the adjacent corner where people stood waiting for the light so they could cross.

"It's OK, Bobby. I know those people," he lied. "They're the good guys. I've got your back, man. Come on. Let's let Elma get on her way." Then they were standing outside the truck looking back through the open door, "You're a good person, Elma! Thank you for the ride and the conversation," Will said, and he meant it. When Elma wished them well, he closed the rusty, screeching door and waved goodbye. For a moment, he watched the beaten old

Ford shimmy down the street until it was swallowed in the traffic and blocked from view by a bus. He told Bobby he had liked the woman, then turned and started walking.

They made their way down Fourth Street for a short distance, turned right onto McKee Alley, and went another four blocks beyond Grant Avenue. All the while Bobby was carrying on about the theys and thems and the cameras until he hit upon the question: "We gonna see the man, Will?"

Will put his hand in his left pocket, pulled out a wallet, took seventy dollars in cash and a credit card and stuffed the loot into his pocket. "Got us covered, Bobby." He looked at Elma's picture on the license, stared at it, and rubbed his fingers over it. "I liked her," he reminded himself as he folded the leather casing, carried it like a spent cigarette butt to the trash bin near Faith Mission, leaving the library card, AAA and ACLU membership cards and license belonging to Elma Worthing caressed in the folds of old leather. He hesitated briefly, looked up at the sky, then dropped the wallet atop the heap of life debris dropped from the hands of many strangers.

Ron Luce (he/him) writes novels, plays, short stories, essays and poetry. His most recent publication is the novel, Star Late Rising (2024). He has a BA from SUNY Brockport, and an MA and PhD from Ohio University and taught in higher education for many years.

THE ARAN SWEATER
by Gabriella Ercolani

Late October's brisk wind ushered in sweater weather. Somehow our yard, in fact, everybody's front yard, slept beneath a blanket of orange, yellow, and red leaves.

The brightly colored duplexes starting from the dead end went from yellow to blue to green on our side of the road. Everybody's house looked the same on the outside. Everybody's house looked happy.

"Knitting weaves a magic spell, Fiamma. When you knit you put your emotional intent into each stitch."

"Is that why I love wearing sweaters you knit for me, Mommy?"

"Si, cara mia. Because when I knit for you, I tell you how much I love you. But you can knit any emotion at all into the magic of each stitch."

Quiet held us both in the palm of its hand while my father slept. My mother worked the yarn very slowly so that I could watch and learn. The white of the scar on her thumb moved and flexed as she cast on stitches. It would always be there, I realized.

We cast on enough stitches for me to make my own scarf. Sixty stitches. I counted them all by myself. But my fingers were starting to cramp, and the yarn tickled.

"My hands feel funny."

"You'll grow accustomed to it. It takes time, sweetie."

Mom made my ball of yarn from all the different colored remnants she saved from previous projects. There was the hand-me-down couch she had reupholstered. Part of the couch matched bits of the curtains in my bedroom, another part matched some of the living room curtains, while the cushions and armrests matched almost all the kitchen drapes.

The morning sun filtered through the patchwork of the living room curtains. Pieces and parts all sewn together, all different colors. Mom cried when she hung them up. She missed a better standard of living. But one of the best qualities I inherited from my mother was her ability to endure difficulties by finding something positive in every situation.

"You know, with the sunlight, these almost look like the stained glass windows in church. All those broken pieces put together to make something beautiful. What do you think, sweetie?"

I smiled at her. Her ability to look at life from a slightly different perspective caught my attention even then.

We heard a cough from upstairs, and Mom stopped knitting, looking up with a frown. I already knew I would be expected to keep the events of the previous night a secret. We had put back all the books and records on their shelves. And Grandpa Willie's old black leather recliner sat back in the corner by the stairs, with Grandma Peg's antique book lamp by its side. My mother had woken up early to clean up. We'd done everything but vacuum so as not to make noise. I could still smell the Lestoil coming from the kitchen, where she had cleaned all the trash and food from the counters and floor. Our whole apartment looked as if nothing had happened, but I still remember the sense of desperation in my stomach.

My mother doesn't remember a time when she couldn't knit. She had been taught by her mother and my Zia, Mom's sister, back in Italy while still a child, barely old enough to hold the needles. Her mother broke her natural left-handedness, slapping her hands every time she got the stitches backward. She learned to be right-handed. Even then she knew to keep quiet.

I never met my Italian family because they never came here. But I knew that my Nonna and Zia could knit and crochet lace. They made lace curtains and tablecloths, my cousin's communion veil. They used to sell their creations before the war. I kept the few pieces of lace my mother brought here when she "ran away to America" as she puts it. I remember the two small circles Mom and I wore on our heads every Sunday at church, a table runner, and two doilies that Mom put underneath each lamp on the end tables on either side of our couch. Right before she came to America, Mom and Zia had cut rags into long thin strands they then tied together, and they knit those strands into shopping baskets. We took ours to the farmer's market every Wednesday and carried home our fresh vegetables in it.

We heard a cough again. Our lab mix, Sadie, woke up and lifted her brindle head toward the stairs, but she didn't wag her tail. I looked at my mother.

"Shh. It's ok."

My father had come home wearing the first Irish cable knit sweater Mom made for him. The charcoal-colored wool and his ruddy skin met at the neck. He wore jeans and tan, moccasin-style shoes. He had gotten a raise at work, so we'd left the projects, a collection of brightly painted row houses, for a condominium community made up of brightly painted duplexes. That was the previous year, when I was four and a half.

My mother said the pattern of the sweater was tradition. Every family in Ireland had their own design. When a fisherman drowned, identifying the body began with the pattern of their sweater, because the sea would make the man so bloated you couldn't recognize him. Each man's sweater acted like a driver's license left in a pocket or a fingerprint. I can remember my father telling me stories about how his Grandpa Willie and my Grandpa Jackie used to fish off the coast of Galway before coming to America. They wore the same kind of sweaters in the old gray photos we had of them. I spoke to Grandpa Willie's ghost sometimes, because my mother taught me that our ancestors never leave us, not even in death. I wondered what it was like to fish in the ocean. I wondered why my mother would want Dad to always be identifiable since I'd never seen him fish.

Mom looked at the yarn in my hands. It was time for the next step. She tried to speak, but her voice caught in her throat. I watched as she swallowed hard and took a deep breath. Then she looked down at my hands.

"Ok, now change hands. Bring the needle up into the first stitch. Now wrap the yarn between the tips of the needles. That's it. Pull the left needle. Not that one, the other one. Up and over. Good.

Just keep doing that."

"Like this?"

"Yes. Try not to hold on too tight." My mother glanced away from me, at the statue of the Black Madonna and child that sat on a little shelf above the black leather recliner. It had been given to us by my Zia when my parents got married. I took it down once and opened it up. If you turned it over and opened the hole in the bottom, you'd find prayer candles and a rosary inside it. I remember Mom explaining to me how to set it up like a little altar and ask the Blessed Mother for help if I ever needed to.

"Where does this piece go?" I asked her.

"Wrap the yarn around your pinkie, not too tight and not too loose. Now pick it up."

I could hear my Dad in the bathroom at the top of the stairs. We heard him pee and then flush. Then he started coming down the stairs. Sadie got up and went into the kitchen. He stood on the last step, watching us. His eyes studied us sadly like he wanted to say something, but instead, he looked down like he had a cloud in his mouth. He let out a big sigh and blew the cloud out.

"You're going to teach her to be just like you," he said, with his hand on his hip.

"It's an important life skill," Mommy told him. She kept on knitting.

"House looks nice."

"There's coffee in the kitchen."

Once I got my needles going, Mom started knitting at her regular speed. Her fingers worked the yarn so fast I just looked on in wonder.

We knit in silence for a while. Dad went out on the back porch with his coffee and smoked a cigarette. Sadie came back to sit by our feet. I heard my father out back talking to one of the neighbors. I wished he'd get into one of those long-winded conversations where he lost track of time. But he came back in and I heard him pick up the phone. I loved the sound of the rotary dial, the way it whirred back around after each number, slowly making that connection to somewhere else. He told the person on the phone that he was sick and wouldn't be there for his shift. He had to tell them twice and promised he was telling the truth. He came back inside and went back up to the bathroom to throw up. We didn't see him again until almost dinner time.

Mom had a midterm that day at school. Usually, she'd wait to study until after I went to bed, but that week she'd been letting me play with Jessie next door, so she could study after school all day and night until Dad came home from work. She would read to herself out loud because she was still learning English. She read her books until she looked tired. She always looked tired, but that week she looked like she'd been running towards something, instead of running away. I used to see inside people through their eyes, and that week, my mother's eyes looked hungry. Maybe that's what Dad saw in her eyes. Maybe that's what had made him so mad when he'd come home the night before.

"You're doing this all in a language you can barely speak. How are you doing that?" Dad asked her that a lot and she never had an answer, at least not one that satisfied him.

Jessie and I hid our friendship from Dad because of what happened the day we moved in. Mom got the scar on her thumb that day. She didn't have very good balance because part of her right big toe was missing. They had to cut it off after she got frostbite back in Italy during the war. She and Dad were moving the couch in through our new front door and she lost her balance and dropped her end. When she fell, she landed on a glass of beer on the steps. She put her hand down to keep from falling any further and that's when her thumb split open.

"Just hold up your end, Minerva!" Dad yelled.

"Marty, I can't, it's too heavy," she said, not feeling the wet of the blood yet.

"Just hold on for one more minute." He couldn't see Mom's thumb from where he stood.

But she couldn't hold on. She dropped the couch halfway up the front steps, making my father stumble backward. He glared at her. Mom started to cry and ran inside. I'd offered to help, but my father just hit me and yelled at me to go inside. Jessie and her parents saw the whole thing.

"Hey, let me help you with that," Jessie's dad said as he ran over to our steps.

"Thanks, man." I heard my father say in a controlled tone.

They got the couch in the house and then Jesse's dad made the sort of statement that normally made my father mad.

"You know if you ever need to talk to someone. If you want to do something, you know to relieve your stress, not take it out on your family."

When Dad finally spoke, he offered Jessie's dad a beer. The two of them sat out on the front porch. It seemed like Dad would have Jessie's father to help him unload the rest of our belongings after they had a few drinks. They sat together on the porch for a long while. I sat in front of them on the soft summer grass and listened as Dad talked about growing up in Brooklyn with my Great Grandpa Willie, Grandpa Jackie, and Grandma Peg. He enjoyed telling the story of his Grandpa Willie's bar, where he started working before his sixth birthday. I'd heard Dad tell the story a thousand times about how on the first day of his first summer vacation, he had to pick up a case of beer and push it up the stairs from the basement one step at a time. By August he could carry it all the way up the stairs and unload a case of beer into the coolers all by himself.

"I had arms of steel like Marlon Brando in *A Streetcar Named Desire*, plus when you get a couple of hot licks with the belt for dropping a case, you learn to get strong real quick."

"Sounds like a hard way to grow up," Jessie's dad said, peeling at the corners of the label on his bottle of beer.

"It's all I know," said Dad, "I don't know no different."

Jessie's dad listened to Dad's story politely, smiling from time to time, nodding his head. He had the nicest hands I'd ever seen on a grown man. His soft pink fingers and clean nails looked almost feminine. Had they not been so broad, had his fingers not been so wide and long, they might have looked delicate. My father had man's hands. They were dark, almost black in places from machine oil. The smell of oil would always cause me to recall him. He picked at his fingers too so that the corners of his nails were always bloody. I could tell my father worked hard for his money. I wondered about Jessie's father if he did anything at all with hands like those.

Jessie's dad interned at the hospital just two blocks from us. He wanted to specialize in trauma surgery.

"Do you cut people open?" I asked.

"Sometimes," he said. I wondered why his hands didn't have blood on them until I remembered that blood washed off easily when you got hurt.

I liked Jessie right away. We were in kindergarten together. Jessie's mom and my mother knit and went to church together. They would light candles and burn sage throughout the house. They taught me how to pour thin, almost indistinguishable lines of salt on the windowsills. My father never did warm up to Jessie's parents. He kept saying he didn't trust "those kinds of people." They factored into a lot of his rages, including the one from the night before, when he said I couldn't go to school and Mom couldn't take her midterm.

When their fight woke me up that night, I thought the problem lay with me. I knew he'd never wanted to have kids. He told me that every time he got mad. But instead, I heard him disparaging my mother's attending college. "I make a good salary. I bring home 324 dollars a week! What the hell are you going to do with a college degree anyhow? You're going to leave me, aren't you? That's why you're doing this!"

"It's not about that, Marty. Please, you'll wake up Fiamma." They had no idea I was already awake and listening in the hallway upstairs.

"Am I not good enough for you? You spend all your time with those books. You never spend any time with me! We used to have fun, remember? You're no fun anymore! You're always so goddamned serious now!"

"I just need something that's my own! Please!"

Then I heard things crashing, and I crept back to my room and hid underneath my bed with the dog. Mom found that antique bed frame on the side of the road, disassembled, in someone's trash. She pulled over and got all the pieces in the bed of our truck. She drove home slowly that day and put the bed frame back together that night. I would no longer have to sleep on a mattress on the floor. The height of the bedframe meant that Sadie and I could sit up underneath it without our heads touching.

"I know you're scared Sadie, but if you just go down there and bite him, he would stop. Go down there and bite him, Sadie! Go on!" I whispered, but she wouldn't go. Dad had thrown her out a window once. I don't remember that, but Mom told me about it later. Sadie always feared him after that.

About a week later, on a rainy day, I came across the bucket when I went downstairs to play in the basement. The bloated maxi pads, bloody cotton balls, and facecloths were all soaking in the water which reeked of urine and vinegar. Beside the bucket, sat a trash bag full of maxi pads and bandages that had been wrung out. While I wondered what purpose saving up her blood achieved, I immediately understood that this concoction had something to do with why Mom had peed into a mason jar just a night earlier. That night, Jessie's mother came over and Mom brought the bucket upstairs.

"Marty got asked to put in overtime tonight, so he'll be there for all of third shift."

"Perfect," said Jessie's mom. "The wool should be dyed and dry by tomorrow."

Jessie's mom came from Basilicata, about five hours south of my mother's hometown in Italy. She had dark hair and dark eyes just like my mother. She wore a medallion of the Black Madonna around her neck. Mom said she noticed it right away, the day they met. It always made her smile because it reminded her of a time when she had gotten sick as a little girl in Italy.

"I hadn't walked in a month," she told Jessie's mom, "and an old magari woman came to our house and said a prayer over me, about a fawn and going west with the fawn. La Madonna Negra would bless me and make it happen."

Jessie's mom had smiled, nodding her head. "La Madonna Negra watches over all women. Your family has the gift?"

"My grandmother did, but she died before I was born," Mom said.

"That's why the woman came to you, because you belong to her people. Fiamma has the gift too, but without a teacher, I don't know. The old Gods might make the road hard for her unless she finds the fawn."

Mom had taken our statue of the Madonna and Child down and set it up as a mini altar, lighting the little candles that were inside it and setting them on either side of the Dark Mother. They had poured the bloody water through a colander and boiled it. Jessie's mom pushed the skeins of yarn down into the bucket. Then they said the rosary in Italian. The darkness in the house closed around the light of the candles and made me feel as if the Dark Mother held us in the palms of her hands. The yellow curtains which drenched the kitchen table in filtered light during the day, looked like rippled walls, reinforcing the room and enclosing the magic even further. Jessie's mom and my mother lit a black candle. I watched as Mom pricked her finger and wrote on a mirror with the blood from her finger. She laid the mirror in front of the Black Madonna. I had been hiding just outside the living room door, by the couch, watching them. I must have made a noise because Mom turned around and saw me. I thought she would scold me, so I started for the stairs, but instead, she called for me to come to her.

"Do you remember when I said you were a magical child?" I nodded and looked on in confusion, as she swept a curl from my face. "Someday I will explain all of this, but for now, I want you to go back to bed and think of all the things that make you happy. And Fiamma, please keep this a secret. Ok?"

"Ok, Mommy," I said, touching my hand to hers as she cupped my cheeks in her palms.

Jessie's mother smiled at me and wished me sweet dreams, "She's the spitting image of her dad, Minerva." Mom pulled her hands from my face then and sent me to bed.

The following weekend, after Dad made us his famous scrambled egg and pancake breakfast, we all sat down in the living room to watch the Saturday morning cartoons.

"You making yourself a tan sweater, doll?" my father asked as he played with the rabbit ears on the television set and sat back down in the recliner.

"No, it's for you," Mom said, not looking up.

Dad just smiled and stared at the TV. I held up my scarf and frowned. It looked like a worm that had come out during a rainstorm, scrunching up and then making itself long again trying to get somewhere.

"It's all uneven, Mommy. It's not nice like yours!"

"You just need practice. You'll get it in time."

I lay in the bathtub that night in the pink of our bathroom, holding my nose and seeing how long I could stay with my head under the water. I relished the quiet under there. The whole house felt still and calm. My father was always charming and calm for a few weeks after one of his blow-ups. The night after his hangover, he took us out to dinner and even let me get lobster. In the past, we'd gone to Paulie's pizzeria, where they let me go back into the kitchen to watch them throw the pizza dough in the air. But that night, Mom made ravioli and cabbage, which I loved for its buttery flavor.

Mom never said anything about missing her test. She never said anything about not going to school anymore. I enjoyed having her home with me all the time. She ended up taking me to the library more often. She enrolled me in two children's reading groups, one co-ed, and one just for girls. We never missed that one. I read about Amelia Earhart and Cleopatra and Florence Nightingale. I told Mom I wanted to learn how to fly when I grew up and she said she didn't see any reason why I couldn't do that.

By the time Mom finished the Aran sweater, a blanket of snow had covered the world outside our windows. I pined for Christmas, counting down the days on my advent calendar. I hated my scarf, but Mom had been right about the sweater. The sandy color did suit Daddy's Irish. His cheeks and nose looked extra rosy against the purplish brown of his neck while he shoveled the driveway. I watched out the window as Jessie's father pushed her down the hill on her sled.

Because we lived in a cul-de-sac, no cars came through our street, and the city plowed our road last. That made our street the perfect sledding hill. Jessie's Dad pulled her back up the hill in front of our house after every time she sled down. I watched her as she squealed and threw her arms over her head, her dad running behind her, cheering her on. Jessie's dad never spoke to my father again after the day we moved in. When I asked Mom why, she told me some people just don't know if they should get involved. I didn't know what that meant, but Mom said, "It's just not done."

After the ravioli was done, Mom called me into the kitchen and told me to go upstairs and wash my hands for dinner. I asked her why I couldn't just wash my hands in the kitchen, but she said no and to go upstairs. I saw the bottle of Jameson on the kitchen table, so I obeyed.

That night started off as a good night. The charming father I adored always came out after one or two whiskey sours. He let me experiment with the salad for dinner, and I put raisins and strawberries and blueberries in it. He said that's how rich people made their salads. After dinner, he let me open the sofa bed so that we could make a fort underneath it. We used every sheet in the house and Mom couldn't come in unless she guessed the password which he always changed. Then he tickled me. He tickled me so hard that I couldn't catch my breath. I kept begging him to stop but he wouldn't. He tickled me until I threw up all over the living room carpet. That's when he got mad.

Dad had a system to the way he hit me. First, I had to go upstairs, and my pants and panties had to be off. Next, I had to lean over the toilet bowl, holding on to it.

"The longer you scream, the longer this is going to take," he told me. He would strike me hard, with all the force of a grown man's strength. He spoke to me in a soothing calm manner, between each strike of his hand, as if my pain and terror were the healing tincture he needed to subdue his mood.

Afterward, Mom gave me a bath. She put cold cream on my bottom when I got out and told me not to drain the bathwater. Then I went to bed and waited for the fight, but it never came. Instead, I heard my mother laughing. When I crept down the first three steps of the staircase I could see them on the living room floor, kissing and speaking softly to one another. Dad got up and poured himself another drink.

"That sweater looks so good on you, honey." I heard Mom say.

"It does, doesn't it?"

"Why don't you go upstairs and take a shower? I'll finish cleaning up down here. Then we can go to bed early tonight."

I saw my father stare down at my mother, before tilting his head back and finishing off his drink. I went back to my room quietly, but I had plenty of time. He started talking about something else and another hour passed before he made it upstairs. I heard him stumble on the stairs and knock into the photos on the wall. Sadie pushed her head up under my hand as it hung over the edge of the bed. I heard Dad turn on the water for his shower. But Mom never came back up the stairs. I must have fallen asleep before she did.

The next morning, I woke up to the sound of walkie-talkies coming from the front yard. The flashing lights of police cruisers shone through my bedroom window. I pushed my desk chair over to the window, stood up on it, and looked outside. Two police cars sat on our front lawn, surrounded by neighbors. The policemen walked up our stairs just as Sadie and I entered the upstairs hallway. Mom led them into the bathroom.

"He must have just turned on the water and slipped."

"Why is the tub full, Ma'am?"

"Oh, my little girl had just taken a bath. She forgets to drain the tub all the time."

"Was he drinking?"

"Yes sir. He was very intoxicated."

He was still fully dressed, having tripped on an untied shoelace and fallen into the tub headfirst. He wore jeans and the Aran sweater Mom had made him in his family's cable pattern. It was almost supper time before they took his body away.

I cried because I didn't understand what happened. But my mother scooped me up in her arms, the way she did at night when she would come into my room and hold me for her own comfort.

"It's ok, sweetie. Mommy's got you. Mommy's here."

Gabriella Ercolani (she/her) has been writing since the age of ten, after hearing "A Day in the Life" by the Beatles for the first time. She won the Marshal B. Woods Literary Award for her play Ave Maria. In 2019 she received her MFA in creative writing from Lesley University. She lives on a small farm in northeast Ohio with her husband Michael and their pigs, chickens, ducks, and five dogs.

LOVE BLOSSOMS
by Michael Sepesy

In the heat of the Amazon wild, we erected our portable lab, Dr. Galatea and I. A local indigenous tribe's rumors of a "love blossom" had attracted investors, who recognized the market potential for a genuine aphrodisiac.

"I'm not sure why anyone would pay for that," Dr. Galatea said as we pulled the canvas covering over our tent's aluminum frame. "I've never been interested."

"Some people have nothing else in their lives."

We were perfect working partners—both plain and dull in our individual ways, our focus on the work.

"What does the plant get out of it," I asked while we organized our workspace, "getting other organisms to mate?"

"Reproduction? Self-defense?"

We kept our team small. Our guides by now had left and would return in a couple of months with more supplies.

The journey was brutal—flesh-eating grasses, acid-spitting murder hornets. We watched a cat-sized spider eat another cat-sized spider.

"I'd prefer to take my chances with the plant that makes people fall in love," I said.

Weeks later, a trail of bones led to a clearing--vines spiked with thorns, woven within a thicket of ailing walking palms, lashed the trees' spindly stilts in a taut web. Carpeting the ground, the brittle mammal remains—decaying monkeys, intertwined, limbs latched together—crunched underfoot.

Scarlet flowers, just as described, speckled the vines' woody stalks. When our hedge shears snapped through the dense tendrils, a puff of mist clouded the air.

Galatea coughed, and staggered back.

"Are you all right?" I stumbled to her, my vision blurred with tears. Her fingers grasped my sleeve, tugging me away, and we scrambled from the sweet-scented swirls of dust around us.

***

Safe in the lab again, we secured our samples. Each of us examined the other: eyes red, pupils dilated, cheeks flushed.

"We'll have to monitor ourselves for more symptoms," she said, a lilt of music in her voice.

The moments slowed to a thick syrup and stopped. And then it began.

She stood close, the musk of her sweat heavy in the small space between us. My hands like someone else's hands reached through the timeless space to peel away her damp clothes as she did mine, and we were on each other like jungle cats, quickly rocking and rutting in a huddle of limbs, each inhaling and exhaling the other, and even after it builds and builds to its finish, we keep at it, a single beast with a single purpose—this is what we are now, this grunting and clutching and slap slap slap of body parts and wet mouths going dry on the salt of each other's skin, this single instant without hours or days, the friction of the flesh rubbing raw, wearing ourselves away, the thirsty, thrusting burrowing, desire spilling over into suffering—how long? how long have we been here?— the splintering, searing ache in the joints and hot needles of pain in my spine, hip bones clicking, the gouging pain in the ball and socket joints, and we keep on, fat shrinking, muscles wasting, until there's only the hard grind of bone on bone, eye sockets sinking, and cheeks growing hollow, the astringent stench of acetone—the smell of nail polish remover—wheezing out of us as our starving bodies devour themselves from inside, the skin splitting, shredding, tearing away, the licking, the biting, the chewing into each other, but nothing can cease the relentless want, the need, the mindless clawing for the other, until they appear at the door, our guides with supplies, withdrawing with horror, as we beg for them with what breath we have to stop, to stay, to

"KILL US!"

"KILL US!"

Michael Sepesy (he/him) is a Cleveland writer and playwright whose work includes published pieces appearing in Angle Magazine, Cleveland in Prose and Poetry, and The Best Women's Stage Monologues series as well as plays produced and/or developed by Cleveland Public Theater, The New York International Fringe Festival, and other venues across the country. He has been a recipient of the Ohio Individual Artist Fellowship among other awards, including for his short film work which has been featured at the Ohio Independent Film Festival, and he holds an MFA through the Northeast Ohio MFA (NEOMFA) Program and a bachelor's degree in English and graphic design from Cleveland State University, where he currently teaches.

THE INTERCESSOR
by Corrina Malek

Rosa is suffering. They're all suffering, but especially Rosa. She's in the final stages of Alzheimer's which could continue for a few agonizing weeks or maybe even a year. The doctor and nurses here have no idea how long she'll last, and I can't blame them, really. It's a horrible disease and every patient is different. It's hard to tell what will happen. Only God can predict the timing of the final outcome.

This is where I step in.

Rosa is now bedbound and really should be moved to our other facility. We try and get her up occasionally, but if it takes more than two of us, technically she needs to be at our Westfield location. It's hard on the residents and sometimes harder on the families to move them, so we try and do our best to accommodate.

Rosa is not yet in hospice care but really needs to be. Her family refuses to put her on it, for reasons that are never shared with someone like me. Her daughter-in-law, Cecilia, is the only one who visits anymore, and I have a feeling she drew the short stick. I've tried many times to talk with her, but I don't want to overstep. It's a complicated dance.

"She's quiet now, but just about every hour she does moan a bit," I told Cecilia recently, who was standing at the foot of Rosa's bed, her arms crossed, studying her ailing mother-in-law. Cecilia has a permanent frown, similar to what I've heard called "resting bitch face." Rosa was tucked in beneath a thin light blue blanket and looked unbelievably small in her twin bed. We're required to weigh her every week, and the poor thing was down to 99 pounds this past Sunday. I couldn't recall her admittance weight, but it was definitely over 120 pounds. Her frail body swims in her once snug sweaters. It was weeks ago that I dressed her in a sweater; now she just wears pajamas.

I waited for Cecilia to ask me what could be done for Rosa, how could we help, was there anything we could do? Instead, she uncrossed her arms and moved her bejeweled hand to her hip, letting out a sigh.

"Is she eating?" she asked and raised her eyes to mine.

"Very little," I said, smoothing Rosa's hair away from her face. Tammy, one of the nurses here, gave Rosa some pain meds and it looked like they were finally kicking in. Her face was placid and still.

"OK, well, I'll be back," Cecilia said, picking up her purse from the recliner. She pulled the straps high up on her shoulder and patted the bump at the end of the bed where Rosa's feet were.

"See you next week, Brenda. Call me if there are changes." She sighed again. "I don't suppose there's much we can do for her at this point."

"She's in God's hands now. Take care, Cecilia. We'll call you for sure."

Cecilia glanced back at her mother-in-law, nodded at me, and left her room. There was more we could do, and it frustrated me to no end that Rosa's family denied hospice care–care that could administer morphine on a regular basis without going through the hoops we had to go through here to give meds. Care that would include a hospital bed to make changes easier. Care that would include extra nurses and aides and overall attention. And care that was free! I didn't understand the family's choices, but I didn't have to. Ultimately, Rosa would be cared for.

It was hard to believe May marked my 27th year at Mystic Hills and being an STNA–a State Tested Nursing Aide. I never had the money or grades to be an RN or LPN. And frankly, being a Nursing Aide suited me just fine. I didn't have the pressure of administering meds, but still got one-on-one time with all the residents. Sure, there were times when I was pouring cups of ginger ale and bussing dinner tables that I would think, this? This is what I do now? But it was all a part of holistic care. The residents here mean the world to me. They arrive here at their worst: Minds and bodies failing and families who sometimes care and sometimes do not care enough. I am here and I care. I will see them through their worst.

Mystic Hills wasn't a religious organization, but that was okay, I brought God and my prayers to all the patients there. I was close to Pastor Grexel and we always discussed who needed to be included on the church bulletin's prayer list. I couldn't, of course, divulge any personal information about our residents, but I was free to include them in the bulletin and enlist my fellow prayer warriors. I had been a member of St. Michael's Lutheran Church for well over 40 years. I was baptized there, confirmed there, and if I had ever been blessed enough to find my soulmate, I would have been married there as well. But marriage is not for all, and I know God wanted me to offer His peace and healing within the walls of Mystic Hills. It's my calling in life.

My father passed away far too early in life. I was barely into my teens when he was killed instantly in a head-on car crash on a rural highway. The bag of corn he had on the seat next to him remained untouched, but he did not survive. For years I couldn't look at a corn cob without thinking about that detail, one that I wished my mother had never shared.

My mother, on the other hand, died slowly. It took two long years for her pancreatic cancer to win. It wasn't much of a battle, really. My mother never had the will to live after losing my father. I took care of her, though, kept cold washcloths on her forehead, gave her lavender-scented sponge baths, and played her favorite music softly in the background. My little brothers lived across the country then, but they wouldn't have been much help anyway. It was me, always me.

After my dad had passed, my mother never really reclaimed her role as a parent. She performed the essentials, of course, but the weight of true caretaking fell on my young shoulders. While our family had always been religious, it was especially in those years that I leaned on the church. And unlike family friends, whose sentiments and casseroles ceased after a few months, the church was always there. What a wonderful congregation! Those women, in particular, became surrogate mothers, aunts, and grandmothers. And after all those years passed, it was Pastor Grexel who felt more like a true father to me, my own father's memory fading with each passing year.

I remember when sweet Martha Weinstein was admitted. She was so tiny! Four feet ten inches tall and such energy. What a fireball! With her little round face and button-dark eyes, she looked just like a doll. At 80, her hair still hadn't grayed and fell in loose dark curls that she kept short, in a Little Orphan Annie style. Her family brought her to Mystic Hills when she started leaving her garden apartment at night. Fortunately, most nights when she was roaming around their small community, some helpful neighbors found her and took her home.

The one night when she was gone for hours put Martha's family over the edge. They drove all over town looking for her and contacted the police as well as their local hospital. She was found in the park near the pavilion, trying to bag up what was in the garbage can and saying, "It's trash day, isn't it?" Martha was also turning on her gas stove and leaving her refrigerator door open. Her daughter caught her trying to fish a piece of bread out of the toaster with a knife and her granddaughter just barely managed to stop her from putting her hand down the garbage disposal while it was on. The list of offenses went on, and her family struggled to care for her. I assured them she would be safe with us, and she was.

But dementia runs its course and in due time, Martha could only babble a few indecipherable words. She was wheelchair-bound; her head permanently slumped over.

I remember June 16th, 1998 vividly. It was a Tuesday, and I was working a double shift. Shortly after "movie night" I walked over to Martha's wheelchair which was parked at the end of the long beige couch, facing the TV. I pulled out a tissue from my pocket and gently captured the long strand of drool that was dangling from the corner of Martha's mouth.

"There," I said. "That's better. Let's get you to bed, Martha."

I wheeled her down the long hallway. Martha's room was the last door on the right, just before the emergency exit door.

I pulled her yellow quilted sweatshirt over her head and decided to let her stay in her undershirt. I stopped putting a bra on her weeks ago. Her daughter Eunice had commented on it, but when I explained that it was likely more comfortable for her to wear an undershirt and not have bra straps digging into her back, she agreed.

The gray sweatpants came off easily enough. Thank God for elastic waists and wide-bottomed pants. I selected a pink floral nightgown from her small chest of drawers and pulled it over her head. She made no sounds, no gestures, her brown round eyes barely blinking.

Changing her Depends was a bit more work and I could have asked Candy to help, one of the other aides on duty that night, but I needed to take care of Martha myself.

Martha had lost so much weight in these past few weeks that hoisting her onto her bed was easy. She no longer would go to the bathroom on her own, so no need to put her through the misery of sitting on the toilet. Once in her bed, I tucked her in with her plush lavender paisley comforter. I looked at her sweet, blank face for a moment and suddenly realized I hadn't brushed her teeth. I debated internally for a moment and decided it wasn't worth disturbing her.

It was then, when I was thinking about her teeth that her eyes moved and met mine. It was an instant, but it happened. She looked at me. Really looked at me. She was trying to tell me something, communicate somehow. I knew it.

I also knew that Martha was suffering. Her best days were clearly behind her. So many residents, despite their illness, could still experience joy. They sang, laughed and some even danced. They participated in the ball toss games and a few tried to work puzzles. Many were no longer verbal but were still voracious eaters. Some were left with just the ability to smile when a loved one would visit or when shown a photograph.

But not Martha. She no longer laughed, no longer smiled, no longer existed, really. Her family visits were fewer and shorter.

In that moment, when Martha looked at me, I knew what needed to happen. I knew what I needed to do. What God wanted me to do.

I grasped her hands that I had folded across her chest and moved closer to her face.

"Don't worry, Martha," I told her. "I understand and I'm going to help you. You don't have to go through this anymore. You are going to be with God now."

And before I could give it another thought, I closed the door to her room and locked it. I then took the pillow from the easy chair beside her bed and placed it over her face. I barely had to apply any pressure. I held it there for several minutes, only feeling her body slightly convulse under the pillow. She didn't move her arms or hands at all. She surrendered.

For a moment, I thought nothing had happened. I removed the pillow, unsure of what I'd find. Her eyes were closed and her mouth was open. She looked exactly like she did when sleeping—so much so that I put my ear to her chest to see if I could hear a heartbeat. Nothing. I looked at her one last time and instead of feeling any sense of guilt or horror, I felt amazingly light. I had freed her. No pain, no struggle, no having to endure. She was with the Lord.

No one was surprised the next day to learn of Martha's passing. The late evening shift had looked in on her but must have assumed she was sleeping. It was the morning team who found her and shared the news when I arrived at work later that next day.

The tears I cried for Martha were real, and my grief was genuine. Her family, while sad, were visibly relieved. Their lined faces and puffy undereyes seemed almost transformed when they came in to clean out Martha's room. Her daughter and granddaughter both hugged me that day, as they carried out the last of Martha's belongings.

"You were so good with her," Martha's daughter said, her eyes glimmering. Her face seemed smoother now and despite her grimace as she regarded the now-empty room, there was a resoluteness about her, a new sense of purpose maybe. Her once tired eyes were reviving. The three of us stood on the threshold of Martha's room: me, her daughter, and granddaughter. Relief washed over all of us. Of course, no one benefitted more than Martha. I had freed her from the chains of this horrible disease. She was the first one I brought to peace.

I've kept their names in my Bible. For each soul I've released, I've placed a colored bookmark with each name next to a particularly meaningful verse. I'm up to 13 now and have all the colors of the rainbow sprouting from the top of my Bible.

Outside of the church, I didn't have many friends. I was friendly, of course, with all the staff at Mystic Hills, but I never felt the connection I sought—the comradery of caretaking with a higher purpose. So many of the aides were there for the paycheck, which frankly, wasn't much. I know I wasn't right to pass judgment, but it was hard not to be angry as I would see aides just sitting at the kitchen bar chairs, playing games on their phones. Games! These residents needed us and they were playing games? After doing this job for so many years I'm fully aware one can't be "on" 24/7, but these residents need us. We owe it to them to give them care, love, and attention, especially when no one else will.

I shared my frustrations with Pastor Grexel, who was always so kind, so patient. He listened intently, leaning toward me, his forearms resting on his thighs and his hands clasped together.

"Brenda, you are doing marvelous work. You are serving the Lord in ways that most cannot. I trust many of these aides who work with you are fairly young? Inexperienced?"

I nodded. "Candy is a bit older, and she cares quite a bit, but the rest of them...yes they are mostly younger."

"You must trust in the path, trust that you are setting an example for these young women. We're not here to judge or alter God's plan. The work you do is extraordinary, and the others will follow suit, in due time. And..." he paused, holding his hands up in a shrug, "if they don't, you must trust they are on a different journey, but you can continue your sacred endeavors."

He leaned closer and grasped my hands. "Brenda, God trusts in you, focus on your faith and God's will. I've never known anyone who serves our Lord more than you."

His face was kind, gentle, reassuring. I tried not to be too prideful in my thinking, but I had to admit, he was right—I was doing God's will. Those residents needed me.

Pastor Grexel inspired me, lifted me. I decided to call another prayer meeting at the church that weekend. I led the usual prayer warriors in prayer for all the residents at Mystic Hills, especially Rosa. Her suffering seemed so unnecessary.

Rosa's daughter-in-law, Cecelia, hadn't been in to visit for several weeks. Did it matter? Nothing about Rosa's demeanor ever changed these days. Like all the others, she was getting worse, not better. I couldn't help but feel angry, though, angry these poor failing people were left here, left to spend the remainder of their days with strangers.

It was Candy, one of the day shift aides, who brought me the news.

"Did you hear about Cecelia?" she asked, "Rosa's daughter-in-law?"

Of course, I knew who she was and asked Candy what she was talking about.

"They moved. Cecelia and her family moved. Florida. I guess she has a daughter there?"

"But what about Rosa?" I said. "They're just leaving her here?"

Candy shrugged. "Cecelia said something to Dylan about maybe calling in during their activities time on Fridays."

Dylan was our Activities Coordinator and had an iPad. Some residents got calls through FaceTime and Dylan used his iPad so they could see their loved ones. Much easier than a phone.

"But Rosa can't look at an iPad," I said. "What was she thinking?"

Candy just shrugged with indifference or acceptance and went about her duties that day. Such was life at Mystic Hills.

So Rosa was alone now. Well, she wasn't really alone. She still had me. And I knew what I needed to do. God was telling me it was time.

Months later Pastor Grexel asked me if I would stay after church that Sunday. He asked me to meet him in his office.

The church service concluded and I made my way past the church greeters, shaking hands and giving hugs. I walked into the pastor's dark paneled office, whose door was always open. I sat down in the chair across from his desk, adjusting the hem of my dress so my leg wouldn't brush up against the cracked green leather. I clasped my Bible on my lap, feeling the worn edges and softened cardboard bookmarks.

Pastor Grexel entered a few minutes later, his fingers loosening his vestment.

"Oh my, it's getting warm in here. I'm so sorry the air conditioning isn't working its best," he said. He slumped into his chair, a good-natured smile spreading on his perspiring face.

"Well," he began, clasping his hands on his desk and leaning forward. "I'm happy to tell you I have some good news."

I raised my eyebrows in anticipation. "Oh?"

He nodded. "You're a finalist. A finalist for our *Making a Difference Community Service Award*." He grinned at me, rocking back and forth in his chair. "I wanted to share the good news and of course, ensure that you'd be present at the awards ceremony Friday night."

My heart fluttered. "I'm honored, Pastor Grexel. And certainly I'll be at the ceremony! I was planning on it, of course, regardless of nomination."

We chatted for a few moments before I left the pastor to his work. I couldn't stop smiling. If only I could have shared the news with someone. The only ones I could think to share it with were the members of the congregation and in particular, my regulars at the prayer group. Perhaps some of them were also finalists for the award, so best not to bring it up.

On Friday night, I sat in the third pew. I wore my best dress: a green floral print with a mandarin collar. I smiled and nodded at others as I saw them file in. My hands were sweating, so much so that I needed to smooth out the program, which was beginning to curl at the corners. I read its contents yet again:

St. Michael's Lutheran Church *"Making A Difference Community Service Award"*

This award was created to honor members of the congregation who are making significant contributions to their community through their time, devotions, and dedication. The award will be presented to one individual who best serves his or her community by exemplifying what it means to be a Christian, and one who is a role model for compassion and helping those in the larger community.

Normally, in church, I am rapt with attention, but on this night, it was so hard to focus. I could barely hear the pastor's words until he said "...and this year's Making a Difference Community Service Award goes to..." He paused, smiled, and looked right at me. "Brenda Perry!"

Applause broke out and heads in front of me turned around, their faces smiling.

One of my hands went to my heart and the other to my Bible. I somehow managed to make my way to the pulpit, accepting my award and an embrace from Pastor Grexel.

I looked out over the congregation, so many smiling familiar faces. Men and women from my prayer groups. Older women who had brought so many meals to our house after my father had passed away. Younger women who were new to our congregation, new to Christ, women I took joy in mentoring. I took them all in.

"I am honored to be recognized by you all," I began, "but it's the Lord's work I do. As many of you know, I work as a nurse's aide at Mystic Hills. This award means the world to me, but the accolades are not mine alone. I am just a conduit and it's His hand that guides me. I am blessed to be one of the caretakers of our older population. A population who can no longer care for themselves, who can no longer even think for themselves. I care so deeply for them. All of them. Some still have family, but many do not. Many of them have families who visit regularly, and others do not. I understand this to some degree, I know how hard it is. But I don't understand abandonment. I don't understand how anyone could cast aside a loved one simply because it became too hard to even visit.

"My time at Mystic Hills has been the best years of my life. I know it's my calling to help these souls, to guide them, to see them safely into the Lord's hands." I paused now, the tears blurring my vision, but I had to continue.

"This has been my life's work," I told the congregation, holding up my well-tabbed Bible and smiling, "and I will never stop."

Corrina Malek (she/her) is the author of the novella The Ledger and other works. Her short story "Vacant" was included in the anthology House of Secrets (Ohio Writers' Association). She is retired from educational publishing and resides with her family in Worthington, Ohio. When she's not writing or thinking about writing, she volunteers with dog rescue groups in central Ohio.

DISPLACED PERSONS
by Leonard Kress

They say it was all my fault, my father spending the night in jail, then taking off to Canada. And things didn't work out in the end either. It cost my parents a lot of money—all because I was supposed to be minding my little sister.

I never let her completely out of my sight, though. I was sitting on our stoop, the one in front of our tiny grocery store in Fishtown where we live, trying to get a little color in my pale legs, at least below my cutoffs. Tommy Stankiewicz came by and started telling me about how Frankie Heston's brother got hit by an Amtrak train. I knew about it already, how Frankie and his brother went up there to sniff some paint thinner they found in a railroad shack, and what they really wanted to do was drop bricks off the Venango Street trestle bridge, onto car windshields. But I let Tommy go on and on because I wanted to know if Frankie's friend Jimmy Macko was there too. We were supposed to be going together—at least that's what all the kids were saying. But I hardly even talked to him, I just remember saying to my friend Liz one day that I thought he was kind of cute. That's all—so you can see why I'd be interested in whether or not he still had all of his arms and legs.

Anyway, Tommy was standing up, with the sun pouring down over his shoulders, so I was shielding my eyes with my hand and I couldn't see what was going on with my sister. It sounded to me like she was playing nicely with the little next-door kid. I gave her some colored chalk and they were making a hopscotch square on the sidewalk.

I didn't know what to do when his mom came over, hollering even louder than the el train. I couldn't understand a word she was saying—something about paying us back, but her voice was really high and cracking and she slurred her words. She was waving her arms all over the place and her robe kept opening and flashing her underwear and garter belt, which were black and lacy. I just stood there, speechless, trying to look pleasant, while my sister ran around behind me and stuck her head through my legs to peek out. We must have made a strange sight—this lady, her hair in juice-can rollers, wearing gold platform slippers, freaking out like some Polish DP you'd ordinarily see stumbling out of the White Eagle Club on Sundays, and my sister and me, two almost identical heads on one body!

My brother came up from the basement to see what was going on, but he just pushed up the metal doors, peered out, raised the visor from his welding mask, and stared. The same with Tommy Stankiewicz. He was looking only at her, waiting for her robe to open, so he could get a look at her big tits. I know that's what he was doing because one time he told me about how he was delivering a package to her house and from the doorway he saw a huge painted portrait of her hanging above the sofa. He described it to Liz and me in minute detail. Her bleach blond hair was pulled up and tied in some sort of knot, with little wispy curls falling in front of her eyes and around her ears. She was smiling and her lips were parted, with the tip of her tongue sticking out at the corner of her mouth. The painting only showed her from the chest up, and she seemed to be completely naked, except that you couldn't see her nipples because her arms were crossed in front of her, though maybe there was a tiny bit visible, in the crease of her elbow. Tommy wasn't sure. She was holding a rose in one hand and a champagne glass in the other. Tommy said she looked a little mad when she caught him peeking through the screen door, but then she laughed and even moved out of the way, pretending to be searching for a quarter. Tommy was sure he told Liz and me that she wanted to have it and that he was planning to go back, when her husband was at work, as soon as he could get hold of some champagne.

My parents were out. They're DPs, Displaced Persons, like a lot of the Polish people in our neighborhood and I guess they do act like typical DPs. Take now, for instance. They have to go out to stock our corner grocery. But do you think they could manage to do it like normal Americans? No, they have to shut down the store in the middle of the day, the second busiest time, right when all the workers from Craftex Mills and the carpet factory want to buy lunch. And do you think they could have gone down to City Hall and gotten a license to serve sandwiches? No, they refuse to pay the five dollars, so they have to slice meat and weigh it and wrap it and sell a roll separately. You should see how disgusted some of the men look when my father says to them, "No, got mooshtard."

So my parents were out when all this happened. My father was down at the wharf buying crate loads of tomatoes and lettuce. Then he drove all the way to Jersey to buy eggs from a lady who lived in the Pine Barren, an hour away. He insisted that they were better because of the pine-scented air, but I knew that she also came from his village in southeastern Poland, so he was interested in getting news about his sisters. After that, he drove to Czerw's Provisions for kielbasa and blood sausage.

My mother was even worse! She had her own business to attend to, so she had to take the elevated train downtown. Once she was there, she made the rounds to all the discount notions places, arguing with every single salesperson, all the way up to the owner. Their products were junk, she would say, or too dear, and she knew where to get it cheaper. She always had to get the best price for soap, paper towels, shampoo, and toothpaste, because she needed the leftover money to buy fabric and sequins and seed beads and trim, to make Polish vests to sell to all the children's dance groups in the area. She used to take me with her when I was younger—I remember one store that was so dusty I couldn't stop coughing. I even sneezed up a big gob of snot right on her sleeve, but she kept rummaging through cartons and talking and didn't notice. The owner was this short old man, completely bald, who wore plaid suspenders. They were yacking away in Polish for almost an hour. The way I understood it, this old man had saved her life once, back in her village, before the war. She must have been rushing home from the convent school during a blizzard and the bridge over the San River collapsed. He rescued her, but she ran away without thanking him. It was because she was afraid of Jews when she was young, she explained, to the man, probably thirty years later. He seemed to accept her explanation and shrugged his shoulders. Then they went back to bickering over prices and he pulled out a carton of flowered scarves he said just came in from Japan. Some of them she wanted to send to her sisters and their families back in Poland, but mostly, she wanted to sell them to Ukrainian women for three times what she paid.

The next-door lady left when her little son rushed out of their house calling for her. He was screaming his head off after he tripped over the cracked sidewalk on his way to her. He got so upset he stopped breathing and the lady had to pick him up, calm him down, and hug him back to life.

I thought the incident was over. My brother flipped down the visor on his welding mask and crawled back down into the basement. He turned up his stereo real loud and before he peeked out one last time and pulled down the iron doors behind him, I heard him chipping away a weld with a hammer and a pneumatic chisel. I knew that the next time I saw him he'd be covered in black soot and my mother would be hollering at him to keep his filthy black dupa off her sofa. Then she'd start screaming about how he looked and smelled like the devil because to her things that were black and smelly, especially people, were devils.

Tommy Stankiewicz left too. I saw him standing across the street, hanging out with some other kids on the barber shop stoop. It looked nice and cool over there. My friend Liz was hanging out with them, too, only she was leaning up against the wall and it looked like she was laughing while some guy was giving her rabbit punches. I'm sure she could've taken him if she wanted to, so it must've meant that she liked him.

I wanted to go join them, but I knew that my parents would kill me if I did—my mother thought they were all drug addicts and criminals, including Liz. They especially hated her because her mother was divorced and some guy with a beard was living with her. And they also thought that her whole family was dirty because one time I got crabs from swimming in their wading pool.

I was sure that Tommy and the other kids were badmouthing

me, and making fun of me, calling me little DP just like my parents. Only their DP didn't just mean Displaced Person or even Dumb Polak, but dirty pussy. If Liz wasn't so busy taking punches from that guy, I'm sure she would have stuck up for me.

If only my mother didn't make me wear braids tied with red ribbons until seventh grade, and if only they let me go to Assumption, which was right around the corner, instead of St. Stanislas. Even Tommy and the other Polish kid went to Assumption with all the Irish and German kids, because they weren't even Polish anymore. Their parents spoke English and got all flustered and embarrassed when they came into our store. They still called my mother Pani, but that was all they could manage. When they said please in Polish, it sounded more like the word for piglet.

When my mother came home, I didn't bother to tell her about the fight my sister was in. I would've gotten yelled at and punished more than usual. My mother was already hysterical because I parted my hair in the middle and was wearing it straight down my back. At least I didn't have to iron it to get it to look right.

"You look like Gypsy-girl," she yelled and she had that look on her face like she was going to go digging through her pocketbook for ribbons to tie it back.

I ran into the kitchen. "It won't stay back," I yelled. "You probably think I should slick it back with butter like you did when you were young."

Just then my father pulled into his parking space and began unloading supplies. He called to my mother and she went out to help. I unlocked the door to the store because I noticed some people headed our way.

It was the next-door lady along with her son. I think her name was Gloria, but I didn't know her last name because it was such a normal American-sounding name that it didn't sink in. She looked pissed and was dragging her kid behind her. He was still bawling and I thought she was going to yank his little arm out of its socket when she lifted him onto the stoop. Just like my little sister did to every single doll my mother bought her, only she didn't stop with the arms but ripped out the legs too, even the hair.

The lady got inside at the same time my father entered the store through our living room. My mother must have been all the way back in the kitchen because she didn't hear the chimes. My father was standing behind the cash register and the lady just charged right up, knocking down a whole stack of Campbell's soup cans and a display of Italian bread that the Amoroso man had just set up. She reminded me of the nun I had last year at Saint Stanislas who used to rush up and down the aisles, jabbing her sharp elbows hard into those students who didn't have their homework assignment showing.

It's lucky that my father was standing behind the deli case, because who knows what might've happened. He was holding the meat cleaver because he was getting ready to trim a soupbone for our dinner. My mother was going to make barley soup with some dried mushrooms her sister just mailed over from their native village in Poland. They came with a letter saying that the summer over there was so cold and damp that they were already planning to go out in the forest near Jaroslaw for more. "Prawdziki—like gold," my mother said, as she opened the package and swung them around. They were only little brown shriveled things, about a hundred of them, strung like beads. Then she put them around her neck and danced around the kitchen, doing this strange kind of stamping polka and twirling. She was whistling through her teeth and singing, "Look at my love beads, my love beads…" Only the way she pronounced it, it came out loff beets.

Tommy Stankiewicz came in, too, and he hoisted himself onto the Popsicle case and my father surely would've come after him with the cleaver, yelling and cursing if it wasn't for the lady and her kid. She was still wearing her pink robe and the gold platform slippers, but her hair was all combed out, the top teased in a real high pompadour, while the rest of it flowed down over her shoulders in big kielbasa curls, the kind my mother used to make me wear every Sunday to church.

"Keep your god-damn kid away from mine," she hollered. "If she so much as lays a finger on him, so help me God…"

"Huh?" my father mumbled. He raised his hand to cup his ear like he always did when talking to Americans, but it was all bloody from the roast he was pounding and trimming.

"God-damn DP!" she said. "I'm warning you. My brother-in-law's a cop. He'll close this fucking place down. All I gotta do is say the word."

My father straightened up and with all his concentration shouted, "You go vay now. I call po-leese, too." She just sneered at him and leaned over the counter. I had never realized just how short my father was—he barely came up to her chin. His eyes were at the level of her breasts.

Then her little kid, who was just sitting by her feet and sobbing, stood up by grabbing onto the cloth belt that was holding his mother's robe closed. Off it came and when she reached down to smack him with one hand and close the robe with her other, one of her platform slippers flew off and she tripped over a soup can. She was spread out on the floor, screaming in pain, and her robe was bunched up around her chest. I couldn't believe what I saw! She was wearing this fancy lacy pair of black panties that had a heart-shaped hole cut in the crotch. Her hair there was black and thick.

I don't think my father could see anything, because her legs were sort of tucked in under the meat case. Tommy Stankiewicz was standing on top of the Popsicle case, though, just staring like he'd seen a ghost.

The lady was only on the floor for a few seconds and she grabbed her son's arm and ran out the door with him flying up in the air behind her. "You're a dead man," she screamed, "D-E-A-D!" I guess she spelled the word out so her kid and my little sister couldn't understand.

My father must have understood more than I expected because that afternoon he went down into the basement and took one of my brother's long Phillips head screwdrivers. It used to be his, along with all the other tools down there, back from the time he used to work in a sheet metal factory. He was some kind of machinist there, long before my parents bought the store. Then the factory shut down and the workers were laid off. My father still loved his tools, though, and my mother always claimed that he treated them better than his own family—or at least his own family here in America. He was always soaking them in oil, polishing them and wrapping them in specially treated cloth. They were arranged perfectly down there, according to size and function. What he loved best was a set of micrometers that he got from another DP who worked in France before the War. They were metric, though, and I think he could never use them at the factory—all he could do was care for them. Besides, now that my father was busy running the store, which meant stocking the shelves, cutting meat, and handling customers who needed more credit, he didn't have any use for them. My brother, though, was sixteen and obsessed with rebuilding an old Triumph motorcycle he found in a ditch by the railroad yard. He inherited the tools, or I should say that he just took them over. And my father didn't say anything. It must have been strange for my father to be dreaming about tools and dyes and lathes when he was slicing Krakowska or head cheese. Especially when some of the picky old customers like Mrs. Marker or Pani Skawronska complained about their salceson being too thick and runny.

For the next few days, my father didn't go anywhere without that Phillips-head sticking out of his shirt pocket. It was there while he worked in the store, when he went out to tune up his Buick, and when he marched in the procession for the Feast of the Assumption, holding up a banner with gold fringe and the words *Matka Boska Czestochowa* on it. The procession was more than three blocks long and it stretched all the way around St. Stanislas—the priests first, the banners next, followed by all kinds of old ladies in Polish costumes. But the longest part of the procession by far were the children, hundreds of them, practically all the kids who attended St. Stanislas. They were all wearing their burgundy and gray spring uniforms, all lined up according to grade and class, led by their nun. Some of the kids, but not too many, were also wearing Polish costumes, dark embroidered vests, and thick flowered skirts.

I was one of them last year, and I even wore a wreath made of paper flowers. I vowed never to do it again. I was mortified when I spotted some of the kids I hang out with watching the procession from across the street. I don't think they recognized me, though, and that's why this year I ditched it and went to watch with my friend Liz. It was a real sight! All those priests wearing long black skirts and the banners flapping in the breeze, then all those kids marching in perfect order, the whole time the bells ringing out from the tower and everybody singing hymns to the blessed mother:

Mamo, nie placz, nie,
Niebos Przeczysta Krolowo,
Ty zawsze wspieraj mnie,
Zdrowas Mario.

You could even hear the organ music playing along through the propped-open doors. I could picture our organist, a little round guy named Jerry, all the way up in the loft. He also had his own polka band and played each week at the park. He must have been dripping sweat all over the keys, it was so hot up there in summer.

Everyone came out to watch, even people from the Italian, Lithuanian, and German churches whose processions had already ended. I stayed to watch the whole thing, even though Liz kept wanting to get water ices and pretzels and see who was hanging out at the playground. I was even a little sorry that I wasn't part of it, as I watched my father and my mother carrying my sister and then all my eighth-grade classmates. I could even spot that Phillips head sticking out of my father's white shirt pocket. Its handle had bright red and white stripes, just like all the banners and ribbons, much like that Polish flag that Mr. Kowalski, the city councilman carried. What else could you expect from a DP?

The next day it happened! My father was walking to his Buick, parked halfway down the block when the panty-lady's husband jumped him. Lots of people saw it happen, including me, the Greek lady who was scrubbing her stoop, and Tommy Stankiewicz who was hanging out across the street with Eddy, the neighborhood bum, drinking quarts of beer from paper bags. The man must have been waiting for my father because he flew out of the alley and tackled him. There's no way it could have been a fair fight, either, because the man was over six feet tall and, like I said, my father was a real shrimp. He wasn't much taller than me, but then all Polish men seemed short to me—at least the DPs that I came across. I never understood why everybody talked about Polak men like they were such giants. And there must have been some big Polaks who worked in the mines upstate and the steel mills. My father always said it was because of the Depression and War, that he never had enough food to eat when he was growing up. That and the fact that they all smoked since they were nine years old.

Everyone ran over to my father because they could see that he was in trouble. The man had a tire iron, but he wasn't using it yet. He was just standing over my father and kicking him in the stomach. It looked like my father was taking it, not trying to fight back, just curling up like a roly-poly. Then, all of a sudden, the man toppled over onto my father and my father pushed him off and ran to his car. He must have stabbed him with the Phillips head because the man was lying on the sidewalk howling. His pants were all soaked with blood.

I think the Greek lady must have called the cops, though I don't know how they could understand her. They pulled up with their lights flashing and their sirens screaming—two of them, coming from different directions, almost colliding. They blocked off the street like it was some kind of TV bust. They jumped out of their squad cars and a blue paddy wagon pulled up. Before anyone realized what was happening, two cops pulled my father out of his Buick, cuffed him, and threw him into the van. The man who attacked my father was still lying on the sidewalk and another cop was whispering something in his ear. Then the van and the cars zoomed off, sirens blaring. The Greek lady was jumping up and down screaming, "No right! No right!" She was waving her soapy rags and suds and bubbles were flying up all over the place.

My father spent the night in jail at the Roundhouse. He called in the morning and told my mother that he was charged with attempted murder. A trial date was set for the next month. He told my mother that she should take my sister and me and walk down the avenue toward St. Stanislas and hire the first Polish lawyer she could find. Only she should make sure not to hire any of the Jewish lawyers like Fiszman or Bialystocki, even if they advertised that they spoke Polish. It was only their secretaries who could speak it, my father explained. He also said that he wanted to be bailed out immediately.

The lawyer we found was a short, skinny, greasy man named Mr. Skora. He didn't even have a secretary and his office was in the back room of a barbershop. My mother rushed us through, kicking aside the hair all over the floor. Mr. Skora was pleasant, but his Polish wasn't so good and I had to translate. He said that he'd make some phone calls and that he was positive he could get the charges dropped. Or at least reduced. "You'll get your monsh back in no time, Pani," he told my mother and then he kissed her hand like all the DPs do. I don't think my mother understood anything he said, even when I translated for her. She was busy hugging my sister the whole time, wiping her tears in her hair and I thought she was going to smother her. "Don't worry, Pani," the lawyer repeated to me as we were leaving. "I'll get your daddy back for you." And even though I wasn't crying, he rubbed his fingers across my cheeks and said, "Nie placz, dear."

I think that if my father had just taken the time to listen to the lawyer and follow his advice, everything might have turned out okay. But he didn't. As soon as he was bailed out and Mr. Skora dropped him off at home, my father ran away. Just like that! He didn't even pack his suitcase, he just grabbed a carton of cigarettes from his room and a wad of tens and twenties that he kept in a little carved box and drove off. All the way to Canada, to northern Ontario, where we later found out, one of his cousins on his grandfather's side lived.

The lawyer was pissed that all this happened. He said that he could have handled everything, but that now it would have to go to court. We should have trusted him, he said. The attempted murder charge was just to scare him. The cops were only playing with him because he was an immigrant, a DP, and because his English was so bad. They were even ready to drop all the charges, but now, because my father had jumped bail, he couldn't promise anything. Plus, the neighbors wanted to introduce another charge—attempted rape. He had his work cut out for him; Mr. Skora explained. Also, he'd need more money because now he had to hire a private investigator to find out the real story and a person to translate for the Greek lady—because he couldn't trust the police version. "It'll go to court for sure," he said. "And you," he said to me, placing his arm around my shoulder, "are going to be my star witness."

My father returned a week later. He didn't say anything about his trip except that the mosquitoes and flies were terrible and that he felt like he had visited the moon. "I hate America," he said, when we visited him in the city jail. "I go back to Poland, only my Poland, not Poland no more, but Russia."

The trial wasn't scheduled to take place until the fall, but our lives still didn't return to normal, not even for a few hours—even though the lawyer somehow managed to get my father out of jail again. People stopped coming to our store to buy groceries. All those people who bought on credit and owed money never came to pay up. Only a few kids came in during the afternoon to buy popsicles and sodas when they got bored of waiting around for the Good Humor Man. I kind of liked it, though, because I got to stay inside the cool store all day. My parents even started to trust me with the cash register. They figured that they had nothing to lose since we had no customers. I remember that they spent a lot of time arguing about how they were ever going to come up with the money to pay the lawyer, and what would happen if my father actually went to jail. My father thought that they should go around to the neighbors' houses and try to collect the money they owed. But the neighbors all acted like they didn't know what he was talking about, even when he showed them the account book with their signatures next to the amount. It was strange to watch all these people who usually loved to gossip and gab act like they didn't understand basic arithmetic or money. My mother wanted to take out a second mortgage on the house, but the first one wasn't even close to being paid off and the bank wouldn't let us. Both of them refused to talk about it with the priest and St. Stanislas and my sister and I were forbidden to bring it up.

It was also strange that my little sister and the little next-door kid started playing together again. Every morning his mother would let him out of the house and he'd ride his big wheel over, along with a fistful of trucks and a squirt gun filled with kool-aid. My sister had her doll-babies in an old stroller and a carton of Legos. They always played nicely and I never heard any whining or yelling. It was the cutest thing to see them riding the big wheel together—him in front and her holding on in back, just like my brother and his girlfriend on his motorcycle. It made a real racket, though, bumping over the busted-up sidewalk and crunching over all the broken glass.

One night, right before school started up again, I even dressed both of them in little Polish costumes. My sister's was for the Pulaski Day Parade coming in October, and my mother made the vest for her by cutting down an old vest her grandmother had embroidered. The old vest was decorated with buttons that weren't bright and colorful enough, so my mother ripped them out and attached new sequins and beads. She wanted my sister to win the Little Miss Polonia contest sponsored by the White Eagle Club and I guess that was the only thing besides the trial that she was able to concentrate on. She would have been pissed if she knew that I also took a little boy's costume for the next-door kid to try on. He loved it—red and white striped pants and a bright blue kontusz. I practically had to rip it off him, though, because he wanted to wear it over to his house and show his mom.

Things weren't going too well for me either. I liked minding the store, but I didn't like minding my sister so much of the time. I was also having a hard time convincing my parents to send me to public high school in the fall. Everyone was against me—they all said I'd start taking drugs and dressing like a hippie and become some sort of radical if I did. What they were really afraid of, though, was that I'd stop going to church and that I'd start hanging out with Black people and maybe even Jews. Even my brother, who did go to public school before he dropped out, came up from the basement to agree with my parents. "It won't do her no good, "he said, "and I oughta know." My eighth-grade nun even refused to release my transcript so I could take the public school test. It wasn't until I started crying and made like I was going to throw myself out the third-floor window that she threw them at me and screamed in Polish that I was no better than a whore.

In a way, though, I think that I was lucky that this court case was upsetting my parents so much. I don't think they realized what I was doing. They must have thought that I was just talking nonsense, and that come the fall, I would be going on to St. Teresa's like all the good Catholic girls in the neighborhood. But I was through with Catholic school and all those mean-spirited and dried-up Polish nuns. That's why it was so weird that my father's lawyer, Mr. Skora, told me at a private meeting that I would have to wear my St. Stanislas uniform to court next month.

It was weird the way he put it, that I'd be capable of bewitching the judge with my angelic virginity or something hokey like that. I argued that I hated wearing that uniform. I hated having to iron those stupid pleats all the time and I hated the way it smelled because I only had one jumper and had to wear it every single day. It was gross, I told him, and besides, I was going to be attending public school in the fall. He got up from his desk and placed his arm around my shoulders, gripping me tight. "Trust me," he said, "I know this judge and I've been in contact with the other party's lawyer. You'll come back and thank me big time once I get your tatoosh off. I wasn't sure what he was talking about, but he scared me—and I decided that my father's fate was entirely in my hands. I told him that I would wear the uniform if he thought it would help. "Good girl," he said and released his grip. Then he took my hand, which was still sticky from a Popsicle that I was eating on the way over, and he kissed it, just like a real DP At least he didn't slobber all over it and leave a thin film of kielbasa and beer. "Ribbons, too," he yelled as I was leaving. "And pigtails, no braids."

The trial turned out to be a joke. It wasn't even in criminal court. We found out that it was scheduled to go to small claims court from the beginning. The neighbor was only suing us for medical bills. It turned out that the cops were only toying with my father because the lady's brother-in-law was a cop. And he hated DPs and Polaks because his beat was over near Belgrade Street and he was always breaking up fights. He even had a bottle of Zebrowska broken over his head during a wedding reception.

Even though I was supposed to be the star witness, I never even got to testify. I was ready, too. I had reviewed the entire case in my mind since I was the only one to see what happened from beginning to end. I even wrote down the events in a notebook, just in case the judge had questions. Tommy Stankiewicz was there too, only for some reason he was sitting on the neighbor's side, and he never once looked over at me. We were all shocked when the judge came in and it was a lady with bleach-blond hair and wearing high heels. She didn't even look over at us, she just called both lawyers up to her bench and they talked for at least ten minutes. Then the neighbor's lawyer told their version of what happened. It was all lies! He made it sound like my mother beat up their precious little boy, and that my father tried to rape the mother-right on the freezer case! Mr. Skora never even objected—not even when they said that my father chased the man down the block with a meat cleaver and not a Phillips head. I started to say something, but Mr. Skora gave me a dirty look and whispered that even though the judge was a lady, she'd still put me in jail for contempt if I didn't keep my mouth shut. "You'll get your chance," he promised. But I never did. After all those terrible things they accused my mother and father of doing, the judge asked Tommy Stankiewicz if it was true. Tommy said that it was. Then the judge told our lawyer to respond, and he just stood up and said, "I have nothing to add, your Honor."

I was furious, but my parents were just sitting there with these stupid, idiotic smiles on their faces, like they expected everything to turn out right. My mother was holding my sister on her lap and both of them were fiddling with her rosaries. My father was holding his hat real tight in his hands and gazing dreamily at the judge like she was some sort of movie star. I knew they didn't understand anything that was going on, not even when the judge ruled that we'd have to set up a monthly payment schedule to pay the neighbors the $2500 we now owed them.

So they could have parties on the first of each month. Big, noisy, wild parties that lasted the whole night. We could see them roll in kegs of beer and all the pizza deliveries. DP parties because they were all paid for by dumb Polaks. Drug Parties, too. I knew it because I always saw the lady walking over to the corner where Tommy Stankiewicz always hung out with his buddies. And I know she wasn't going over to him because she wanted him to do it to her—or anything like that—no matter what he said.

Leonard Kress (he/him) has published poetry, translations, and fiction in Missouri Review, Iowa Review, American Poetry Review, Harvard Review, etc. Among his collections are The Orpheus Complex, Walk Like Bo Diddley. Living in the Candy Store and Other Poems and his new verse translation of the Polish Romantic epic, Pan Tadeusz by Adam Mickiewicz. He currently teaches at Temple University.

BEEF SIGHTING
by Abby Taggart

Ex-Livestock Protection Act of 2035

Title I–Establishment of the Department of Livestock and Hunting
    This title requires all state governments to establish a Department of Livestock and Hunting. The members of this department will be voted on annually. The first vote must be completed by January 1st, 2036. Subtitle A–Duties of the Department of Livestock and Hunting…

weaving between evenly spaced trees, i hold my wide-brimmed hat against the breeze. sun-scorched leaves blanket the ground in shadow. but not enough. i cover my skin with long sleeves. i'd rather not end up like those yellow and brown summer leaves: victim to the unforgiving ultraviolet.

foliage rustles. shakes free a trickle of leaves and twigs. one catches the wind and catches my eye. my heart pumps, like i'm five years old again. giving in to the deep-rooted instinct, i run after it. it hits the ground before i can catch it. green bleeding into sickly, wilted yellow, still bright against my hand that's so pale and dull.

Title II–Termination of Mammal Farming

This title requires all farmers to release 5% of their mammal livestock [including cattle, swine, ovine, etc. Full list in Appendix A] into wildlife reserves [dependent on location as specified in Appendix B] and slaughter the remaining 95% of their mammal livestock. This must be completed between April 2nd, 2037 and August 31st, 2037…

the leaf leads me right to her. the brown cow. with the longest eyelashes I've ever seen. a startled giggle stumbles out of my mouth. i thought she'd be bigger, based on the pictures of cows i've seen before. she furiously rubs her neck against the trunk of a silver maple, scratching a tricky itch.

she came from the east, obviously. her hooves are bloated and spongy from wading through the standing water. maybe that's why she's so small. no undrowned grass to eat over there. a crack cleaves her front left hoof. ouch. they should make waders for cows. nose as big as my fist. her ears look soft.

Title III–Stipend for Affected Farmers
    Affected farmers will receive an amount equivalent to the amount of greenhouse gasses that would be released by their herds over 5 years [in $/ton as outlined in Appendix C]. This stipend will be distributed over the span of 5 years.
    Subtitle A–Further Compensation for Affected Farmers
    The United States government will buy a percentage of any farmer's uncooked meat. Purchase will only be initiated if Form XLPA 3 is submitted before March 31st, 2037.
Subtitle B–Compensation for Farmers that Produce Produce for Animal Feed…

impeccable lashes fan, and her brown eyes catch me. i freeze. she's still bigger than i am. taking her sweet time, her gate loping and unbothered. i expected her to charge. running of the heifers. the nervous breath trapped in my chest is released. i extend a cautious hand. she passes right by it,

Title IV–Protection for Released Livestock
    Livestock specified in Appendix A are protected under this title from any and all hunting until January 1st, 2137 (100 years after release). Hunting of these animals will be punished by fines and/or jail time as specified in Appendix D…

bumps her flat forehead against my chest, expelling another giggle. both hands scrub through short dun fur. her ears are soft. she eats a dandelion with all its greens from my flattened hand, square-looking lips and funny fat tongue leaving my palm a little slimy. "get outta here." my arms fit well around her blocky head. "the xlpa ended two years ago." you're lucky i'm the only one crazy enough to do my travel outside.

Title V–Transition to Hunting as Primary Source of Non-Fish and Non-Poultry Meat
This title allows citizens to participate in hunting of unprotected animals [specified in Appendix A]. All game captured for anything other than personal use must be registered with the Department of Livestock and Hunting before sale. Failure to register captured game or to attempt to register game without a valid hunting license will result in a fine and/or jail time as specified in Appendix D…

hungry hunters' eyes bore holes in my back. their mouths spill saliva like the rain that floods my basement when i want it the least. i can't help it: i wonder… what does she taste like? that thought must be physically shaken from my head. the taste of venison, gamey and metallic, sits in memoriam on my tongue. red meat is a delicacy, or so my grandma says.

grandma was alive during the festivals. when everyone ate meat for every meal. "bacon for breakfast. hamburgers for lunch. dinner was steak, pork chops, or lamb." my brother and i nodded over our mushrooms, pretending like we too understood the appeal of such things.

she noses at my hand, hoping for another dandelion. 102 years since humans kept cows in pastures with bells around their necks, but still, she's not even a little afraid of me. my fishing knife sits heavy in my bag. i could make a lot of money if i cut her throat.

"get out." I push her heavy head away. "get safe." my eyes dart, vulnerable; hers blink idly. she lips at my pocket. my heart wilts. *nowhere's safe for her, is it?*

Abby Taggart (she/her) is a senior at the University of Cincinnati studying mechanical engineering as well as English and creative writing. She has been writing since she was small, narrating stories to her mother before she could write and spending much of middle and high school at the Thurber Center. Passionate about queerness and the environment, she hopes to make the world a better place both through her work as an engineer and with her art.

COLOR

by C.L. Howard

I woke up in this skin. This tainted piece of flesh oozing with history that they want to rewrite or dispose of.

Never mind its purity, its tone screams hazardous therefore yellow tape covers its posture.

Out of place, they screech their spineless expressions.

Fingers flapping like swords professing terrain as a possession.

The homeland in which we all live. How dare they?

Devaluing equality, rewording the definition of quality, unwilling to follow me, stating this shade can't lead.

They follow leads of deceit begging for a path to get lost in because it makes them feel safe.

Safe from having to face the image, the mirror reflects,

Proud that the beast is shown, claws digging in a surface at a surface with no depth.

Still, they feel out of reach. Aren't you tired yet?

Because the Ritis in my knees will not be a part of a track team. The treads from the soles of my cleats are worn.

Off I tossed them, realizing that to keep up was to chase. So, I quit.

I'm chasing a belief in me, because I'm me, I forgot to be me because of you.

This beautiful piece of flesh oozing with a history I forgot to embrace.

A double-sided tape I allowed to define me, de-fined me. Til I found me.

Silencing the echoes of ignorance for protection, as my obsession is my possession.

Tell me, what is your question?

Because second-guessing my reflection will never lead to a connection,

Look at you flexion. A tendon of a temple caught in a tempest of hatred.

No longer will I be taking shelter in a sea of storms created by the same soil.

Tell me, what's to debate? Love doesn't equal hate.

Chanell Howard (she/her) is an author known for her poetry collections "Hibernation," "Explorations of a Woman," "Starvation," and "Exploration of a Woman." A resident of Cincinnati, Ohio, Howard 's literary journey began at the tender age of nine with poetry, sparked by the profound influence of Maya Angelou's 'I Know Why the Caged Bird Sings.' This early inspiration led her to craft verses for greeting cards, delve into songwriting, and eventually culminate in the publication of her own poetry collections. Beyond the pen, she takes pleasure in paddling through serene waterways, hiking picturesque paths, and embracing the splendor of visual arts.

MR. MUSIC
by John Sparks

Yesterday, my brother Tom came over from the hill country and told me that Mr. Music had died. I asked him if any of Mr. Music's former students had organized a memorial service. Tom just looked at me oddly and replied no, he'd only heard, secondhand himself, and besides, he supposed they'd buried him near wherever he'd been at last, and that was someplace back up north. Maybe close to Chicago, where he'd come from originally. I held up all right through the rest of Tommy's visit but last night after I went to bed I cried harder than I have since I was a kid. If there's one person in this world who shaped me and inspired me toward a vocation it was Mr. Music. In other words, I guess I was one of his compositions.

Mr. Music: that title was so fixed in all of his students' heads that even now I'd have to look through my old high school annuals to remind myself of his real name. It was something Eeastern European with C's and W's and Z's and S's all across it and a "ski" at the end and we used to laugh whenever the Principal or a secretary tried to pronounce it when they called him on the intercom. He'd laugh too, at least the times he wasn't in one of his bad moods, and he told them, and us, just to call him Mr. Music. That scandalized the other teachers even more than his hair and goatee and ponytail; but nobody better get the idea that Mr. Music didn't demand your respect. I've seen him shake majorettes till their hair snapped almost as loud as a whip after they'd mouthed off to him, and I lost count of the music stands he threw around and broke and the sheet music he scattered when any of his bands and choirs had trouble getting our parts right.

He never hit me with anything like that though he often threatened to "shake the liver out of" me and my band buddies after various things we'd done and mistakes we'd made. I guess maybe the first of the two times I was most scared of Mr. Music was when I was just getting used to the tenor sax and for some reason I'd put a bass clarinet reed on the mouthpiece rather than a sax reed and he saw it and screamed out at me that if mayhem was legal he'd have already had me on a slab.

Obviously he never murdered me, and very few that weren't around him could understand how dedicated to his band kids that he was. I don't know how to describe him: it was almost as if he was a force of nature like a hurricane or tornado that could mow anything down before his will. You might get your start in band by obeying him simply because you were terrified not to, but after a while, the care came shining through and then you wanted to please him. And although I watched some parents pull their kids out of band over the three years I knew him, I saw him cow other adults as easily as students, some mad enough at him even to fight him. He could get them right in line with what he wanted as well. They just don't make teachers like that anymore.

***

I was vulnerable at the time I first met Mr. Music. I needed a mentor at that stage of my life and it was good that it was a teacher like him. I'd been in grade-school band for a year or two before high school, and Mrs. Crum, the music teacher there, first started me on alto sax. But one day in my eighth-grade year, when the dam on the mine pond up the creek broke loose, my sisters went out to feed the chickens when it was raining and the littlest one, Isabel, chased a pullet toward the stream and slipped right into that heavy black headwater. The poor thing washed down to the river and it rained so hard that it took the rescue squad three days to find her. When they found her she had her arms wrapped so tight around a log that they had to pry her off with tire irons. Dad, Tom and I saw it ourselves and I still have nightmares about it.

Uncle Joe Maddox, the preacher at her funeral, explained to the family that when little Isabel grabbed onto that old rotten sawyer she was really grabbing the Lord Jesus who smiled at her and kissed her on the head and took her on home to be with Him and she'll never hurt or be sad or be scared again. And I loved Uncle Joe for showing us how it all made sense in the larger scheme of things, but still, our family went crazy. After the funera, Dad took an extra contract route from the Post Office, I think to try to work the pain away and maybe keep himself off the bottle. Mom lashed out at everybody around her but she blamed my sister Janie more than anybody for letting Isabel chase that pullet, keeping after her till Janie ran off and married a boy Mom despised, just to get out of the house. Tommy tried to be like Dad but wasn't the man yet for it; that summer I caught him crying more times than I can remember. I did the same thing. Then just before Labor Day he left for college.

At the time I started high school it was just me left at home with the ghost of a baby sister, a dad away at work six days a week running an enormous mail route, and a mother who wasn't only grieving for little Isabel but was so worn out from the change of life, Janie marrying a boy she considered worthless, and sending her other son away to college that she was depressed from sunup to sundown. On the days she didn't lock herself up in the bedroom with the light off, either smoking or crying or both, she was complaining about how bad everybody had always treated her, how she wished she'd never married and sometimes that she'd never even been born, nobody understood her, and I was the only one that hadn't failed her and if I failed her too, what would she do, God never had been good to her and now He'd taken Isabel and she might as well just kill herself. That scared me to death, though I know now that even before Isabel drowned nothing anybody ever did for Mom made her happy. I was always on edge trying to behave so she wouldn't commit suicide and burn in hell and it be my fault. Every weekday I'd get off the school bus afraid of what I'd find in the house. But I had to get out of that place sometimes, just like Janie had by marrying, Tom with college and Dad working himself to death, because, good Lord, Mom's mood swings could break through walls quicker than a wrecking ball. Seemed like they sucked all the energy out of the house like those black holes in the universe Tom talks about, no Heaven behind them.

So when I started high school the band and choir became my outlets more than they'd ever been before. It wasn't like I had a lot left to do at home to occupy my mind. After the funeral, Mom told

Dad he might as well get rid of his chickens because they reminded her too much of Isabel, and while he was at it sell the sow and forget the idea of raising any more big gardens either because she was too tired to help him out with any of it any more. Dad just went along with it, not only selling the sow and chickens but old Tony too and letting his tack and plows and rigging sit and gather dust. Never did I hear him contradict a single thing Mom accused him of doing or being, fair or not.

One thing that could cheer Mom up, though, was gossiping on the telephone. We had an eight-party line before everything went private, and I've seen her go at it for two and a half or three hours laughing as happy as a lark and then as soon as she hung up turning her depression back on just like a light switch. Dad and I would fix sandwiches out of leftovers, or he'd fry up day-old beans and we'd eat them with cornbread crumbled up in buttermilk or biscuits dipped in coffee. He called cornbread in buttermilk "shabby," and biscuits in coffee were "soaky," and once when Mom got on the phone he suggested we go and make us up some shabby I said back to him that shabby was a good name for it because it was a pretty shabby way to eat. But he replied with what I think was the most serious thing he ever said to me. He never was much of a talker, but he said then that he'd promised God that if He'd just let him get out of Korea alive he'd never again complain about any of the small stuff. Isabel's death had just made it all that more clear to him how small that most day-to-day stuff in this life was. I guess that outlook was how he tolerated a lot of things.

But it was over the phone that Mom first heard about the high school Band Director resigning over something I never quite got straight about a senior girl who left the county not too long after the ex-director did, and that they'd brought in a new Band Director from out of state. The reasons Mom and her friends were so interested were that the Superintendent rarely hired anybody that he wasn't kin to or could line up votes for him so he must be bringing this new man in like he did the football coach, with the hope of winning a big statewide reputation for the School District out of it—or at least to get one up on the City School District, which wasn't part of the County District and whose kids hated the County kids and we hated them just as much back. Nobody knew the newcomer's name yet, and like I said nobody could pronounce it after he started his job, but it turned out to be Mr. Music.

I met him on my first day of high school with everybody else who'd signed up for Concert Band. He told us his name and went on, in this flat Chicago accent that sounded sort of like Elwood Blues in the movie, that when he was at the Conservatory in Illinois he determined that one day he'd teach music to the poor children in the Appalachian mountains. He hoped we'd all have a good time learning and playing together, but at his last job his bands and choirs had won state and regional awards and he'd promised the Superintendent that he'd give him the best marching and concert bands and choirs in the state, so we better be ready to work too. And that was that: by the time he got us halfway along a B-flat major scale he'd already thrown two batons and a music stand and taught us a couple cuss words we'd never heard before, and the drummers along the back wall had turned pale.

Mr. Music was built solid like a bull and wiry, and that purple-red face, black-button eyes, and gritted teeth made him look like a crazy pirate. Now that I think about it, that was the first time he ever told me he was going to shake my liver out too. He caught me looking round at the drummers all trembling in their boots and roared out, "Boy, don't you know how to pay attention? I'll teach you a thing or two before I'm done with you, I'll shake the liver outa you…" and he stormed back scattering kids and horns and sheet music, and stands and grabbed me by the front of the shirt. I just hoped I didn't mess my britches, but he stopped short and then laughed. He looked around to a pretty little clarinet player who was about ready to cry and chuckled, "How'd you like to see this guy's liver flying out across the room?" He was funny like that; though he could stay mad even for days, sometimes his anger would disappear as soon as it came on him.

That question surprised everybody so suddenly that we all burst out laughing, even me as he dropped me back in my seat. And I don't know how it happened, but somehow he knew we'd play the B-flat major scale better after that, and we sure enough aced it and he smiled at us again. He was just magic like that.

When the bell rang and we were all putting up our horns he came back to me again and I guess I flinched. But he laid a friendly hand on my shoulder and said to me, "What's your name, son?" I told him.

"Well, no offense about your liver, I hope," he replied, smiling. "I just want you kids to do the best you can do." He winked at me and whispered "Purple nurple!" in my ear and before I knew it he had pinched my left nipple right through my shirt hard enough to make it go numb, and walked away looking back at me with another grin. I was pretty confused, but honored too in a way. Back before Isabel drowned, Dad and Tommy both teased me about my size, and Mom always came to my defense which was even worse than being teased. But now for the first time in my life, I felt like a grown man had treated me as his equal.

***

Long story short, for the next three years I worked my rear end off for Mr. Music. Freshman year I could do only Concert Band and Concert Choir because every time I had to go anywhere away from the house Mom would start crying and accusing me of deserting her along with everybody else and saying her cigarettes were the only friends she had left, and, those two programs were the only ones that met as classes with credit rather than after school. I had two electives that year so I switched one to get into choir even though both Mom and Dad grumbled that Concert Choir and Concert Band at the same time was too much music at once. But Mr. Music came to the house and told them that a university music scholarship was almost as good as an athletic scholarship and would pay a whole lot more for me to go to college than Tom could get for academics. He promised them, too, that he'd always make sure I kept at least a C average in all my courses, music or not, which was better than the athletes, who had to maintain just D's to play, and which most of the teachers would give them whether they earned them or not.

The next summer it got better at home, at least for me. Janie came back to the house with a baby girl but no husband, and although Mom would still throw up Isabel's death to her about once a week and they'd go at it fist-and-skull, Mom sort of adopted Janie's little Trinity Marie to replace Isabel and she and Janie bonded a lot talking all the time about how sorry as carrion Janie's ex was. Which worked out till Mom reminded her that she'd told Janie how worthless he was even before she married him, and then they'd go at it again for a while more.

But I could get out of the house then, and did I ever. Concert Band and Choir all year long for two periods in school and big recitals at Christmas and in the spring, Marching Band and all the home football games in the fall, Stage Band in winter and early spring at basketball halftimes—and then Summer Band and Marching Band Camp back at the high school, so I wouldn't lose my embouchure, as Mr. Music put it. I won't soon forget his explanation and demonstration to me of the French root word of embouchure, either. But never mind about that. He was just horsing around with me like men do. It wasn't everybody he horsed around with either, just me and a few other guys: stuff like, for example, when we were away on road trips to competitions and whatnot, he'd get with a few of us in our motel at night and play a game to see which of us had the biggest male equipment. When it looked like one guy was the winner he'd start talking about a majorette with a nice big bouncy rack or maybe how round and soft the ass of the lead flutist was and how would we like to feel her up—and then measure us again and we'd all be longer but often another guy would win. Just grown-man stuff, you know, mostly, but I'll admit some of the Music Ed students Mr. Music got in from college to do their practice teaching would take things farther than what he'd have liked if he'd ever found out what was going on.

The first beer I ever drank, the first toke I ever took from the first bong I ever made from a pop can, and the first valium I ever dropped were all on long-distance band trips, with the student teachers who sneaked the stuff along. There was a minor scandal when a senior football player got expelled for two weeks—it was after football season was over—for beating the crap out of one of them over a sophomore girl who was going out with him and the student teacher both. But I must say I feel sorry for the fellow who got fired at Ohio State that time. He got blamed for a lot of things that started way before his time as band director there because I know from experience that that kind of thing and more besides was going on with high school and college bands everywhere across the South and Midwest forty-odd years ago. He was just the fall guy, like Mr. Music turned out to be—but I'm getting ahead of myself.

Mr. Music had promised the Superintendent the best bands and choirs in the state within three years' time, and although we never got to prove it his final year with us I think he fulfilled the promise in two. We won second place at State both years running and we outdid the City Schools at every competition with them. During my third year in the high school band, I was never as close personally to Mr. Music as I'd been before, and I still feel bad because I'm to blame for it.

This was before I got either my driver's license or a car to drive, but Mr. Music was always good about coming out and giving me a ride whenever I needed one to get to Summer Band or Marching Band Camp or whatever. One other reason he offered all those rides to me, though, was his interest in what he called Appalachian Folk Music. Every year for the Choir concerts he'd have us work up an Appalachian Folk tune or two like "Blowin' in the Wind" or "If I Had a Hammer" or "Five Hundred Miles Away From Home." Mom's people were singers: some of my first memories are of Mamaw rocking me and singing "Shady Grove" and "Polly Put the Kettle On" and other of those real old tunes, and when you could get my uncles talked into singing they still remembered a lot of them too. So Mr. Music would ask me to sing some of Mom's family's old tunes on those rides, and he'd listen and nod and correct me when he saw that Mamaw or my uncles had gotten anything wrong about the melodies or the words.

So by the time this thing occurred, Mr. Music had already asked me more than once if I'd ever heard any dirty folk songs. The first time I told him, well, Mamaw would never sing a song like that but sometimes an uncle would, especially if they got to passing a bottle around on a summer evening.

I'd heard them do dirty songs but I'd be embarrassed to sing them myself. I suppose that was all right with Mr. Music to start with, but he kept pressing me so finally I sang him the one about the man who came home drunk five nights in a row and kept finding signs that his wife was cheating on him but was too soused to realize it. Mr. Music really liked that one, especially the verses where the drunk thinks it's only a cabbage head on his pillow but doesn't know why a cabbage head has a mustache and afterward the wife tells him it's only a rolling pin he sees, and then he asked if I knew any that were dirtier than that. I did know another, about a pretty young girl who marries a man and finds out on her wedding night that he doesn't have any balls. Lord, did Mr. Music ever laugh when I sang that last one, said he'd never heard it before at all, and when I got to the verse where the girl's mother tells her that she'd had the same problem with the girl's own dad he got so tickled I thought he was going to choke. So he's still driving along yet laughing so hard the tears are streaming down his cheeks, and he looks over and asks me if that's me I'm singing about, do I have any balls or not? Huh? Huh? Huh? Then he reaches between my legs and starts pinching and groping.

I know he was just horsing around like usual, but I guess it was where he was sticking his hand and pinching that I squealed and twisted and jumped and giggled just like a girl. All that motion back and forth made Mr. Music momentarily lose control of the wheel, and since we were on a curvy back road he swerved just a hair into the path of an oncoming car—which turned out to be the law, not just a deputy either, but the High Sheriff himself. Mr. Music corrected his course right away without so much as a side-swipe to the patrol car but the sheriff pulled a U-turn, his tires

squealing almost as loud as his siren, and he flashed his blue lights
behind us almost before we knew what was happening.

"Oh, shit," Mr. Music murmured, and he turned pale as a ghost
and got both his hands back on the wheel quickly. "I'm sorry," I
whispered back, but he just wiped his eyes and glared daggers at me
and then turned his head back around to smile at the Sheriff.

It turned out that the Sheriff wasn't in a good mood at all, and
he didn't smile back. After that near miss, maybe he wouldn't have
in any case. He looked at Mr. Music's license, asked him a bunch of
questions about if he had drunk anything, then made him get out
of the car and put him through about ten minutes of sobriety tests
before he finally wrote him a ticket for reckless driving. Made him
do a breathalyzer too. After Mr. Music got back in the driver's seat,
trying to hide it but I could tell he was so mad by now he wanted
to kill somebody, the Sheriff came round to the passenger window.
He rapped on it and I rolled it down.

Funny thing about the Sheriff: when he talked to me that day
he spoke louder than I ever heard him again, even when I saw him
arrest that crowd after the fight at the City-County Football Game
in October. "Ain't you one of Byron Stallard's boys?" he barked at
me, bending down to peer back in the car. I nodded my head yes.
He looked at me for a long time, then back at Mr. Music, then at
me again.

"Hmm," he finally grunted, scratching his chin. "Well, son, I'll
tell you," he continued as loud as before. "I thought the world of
your old granddaddy. He was my favorite teacher in school, taught
me more than every other teacher combined, and I served in Korea
at the same time as your daddy did and he's a fine man too. You
need me to give you a ride home, maybe?"

I blinked. Why would he think I needed a ride home? But I
remembered my manners. "No, thank you, sir," I answered after
I cleared my throat, "Mr. Music was taking me to Summer Band
practice."

The Sheriff nodded and didn't reply for another second or
two. "Well," he said finally, "you tell Byron I'll come see him

one day soon, and me and him can swap some stories about the characters we met in the service, and we met some oddballs, I tell you." He looked over at Mr. Music again, then back at me. "But you remember," he went on, "anything at all you ever need me for any time of day or night, I'm only a 911 call away, you hear me? Anything." He reached in and clapped a hand on my shoulder.

I looked down, confused about why he'd said all that. But I answered, "Yes, sir, thank you," and after the Sheriff gave Mr. Music another hard look he was on his way. It was only then I noticed that I was trembling almost as hard as Mr. Music was.

But if I'd been scared, Mr. Music was madder than hell. The whole time the sheriff talked to us he'd been as pale as a corpse, but he turned red around the neck and purple in the face fast now and every once in a while, he'd grit his teeth so loud and hard you'd think he was cracking a walnut in his mouth. He waited till the sheriff's car was gone before he pulled back onto the pavement, scattering gravel behind us, and then in a bass growl I never heard out of him before he started in: "Goddamn fuckin' country redneck cop, just because a man wears his hair longer... Boy, you've got some good friends and neighbors around here, don't you? Bunch of filthy stinkin' briar-hoppers all inbred and dumb as hell, the lot of ya, and that cracker son of a bitch Sheriff is the worst..."

I just sat and listened to him rant and rave, scared to death all over again, as we drove on into town: "'Walk the line,' he says to me. Who the hell does he think I am, fuckin' Johnny Cash? Who the hell does he think he is, some kinda goddamn Buford fuckin' Pusser?"

Finally, we pulled up to the Music Department door at the high school. There was a big bunch of kids already there waiting on Mr. Music to unlock it and I knew I should offer before anybody else heard: "I don't know how, but I'm gonna help you pay for that ticket, it was my fault for..."

I didn't get the last part of it out. He'd already opened his car door and he leaped up and spun back around and screamed loud enough at me for everybody to hear it and not miss a word, like the Sheriff had: "Shut up! You get your ass outta my car and get your horn into that bandroom and by God I better not hear you play one sour note today! Not another word! Just shut up! SHUT UP!" and he stalked off with the kids backing away out of his reach. He scared everybody so bad that they forgot to laugh and tease me about getting myself cussed out again, and I don't remember anybody even asking me what the whole thing was about. But we all set up to play and as soon as he came out and picked up his baton he was all smiles again and the rehearsal went well for once. I think we were all too scared of him that day to make a mistake.

After practice was over he came up to me friendly again but sounding very formal at the same time. He told me that the Presbyterian Church in town had offered him a job as Minister of Music, and although he was a Catholic he was going to take it because there were a lot of rich mine operators going to that church, and it paid well for a part-time gig. But he wouldn't have any time from now on to drive out to get me, and maybe I'd better catch a ride back home that day with Roy Dean and Jody Maddox if I could. He knew we lived fairly close to each other, Roy Dean always drove Jody to practice, and I could probably ride in the back of his truck in the future. I just nodded my head but I knew already that things had changed. I don't think he ever said one ill word to me after that, even for sour notes—but then again, all that next fall and winter I was always trying to play the best I could to redeem myself.

***

Though I made some progress, I never got back to the place with him I was before. Maybe it was my own stupidity over the summer, but somehow it just seemed like that whole third year was cursed, although all the bands and the choir were still doing as well as ever. If it wasn't the deal with the Sheriff, I guess it started when Teresa Salisbury bit her lip in Marching Band practice. By that I mean that she wasn't doing her job right as a majorette and Mr. Music was cursing at her and for some dumb reason she started crying she was going to quit so he grabbed her by the shoulders and shook her to calm her down and she bit her lower lip bad enough to need two or three stitches. It bled like a stuck hog, too.

The Superintendent and Principal tried to keep the thing hush-hush but I heard more details about it from Mom's Ma Bell gossip grapevine: Teresa's parents threatened to sue, but Mr. Music insisted he was only trying to calm her down, and finally the Superintendent got Miss Butler, this old, respected retired teacher whom they knew the Salisburys liked, to talk them out of suing. Miss Butler was one of Mom's best gossip friends, so I guess I got the story right from the horse's mouth. From all appearances it worked, although nobody ever could persuade Teresa to come back to the Marching Band, and there was still a cloud hanging over Mr. Music and the rest of us that hadn't been there before.

Other than that, football season was good that fall. Our team beat the City team on their own field, though there was a big fight afterward and the Sheriff had to haul a bunch off to the County Jail because the City Police wouldn't touch any of the town kids. Then the Christmas Concert was the best of all. We played "Sleigh Ride" so tight that Mr. Music actually walked down to the other end of the gym right in the middle of our final rehearsal, still waving his baton, so he could hear how it sounded that far away. But Christmas time was it, our swan song as a band and choir, you might say. That next spring three or four City High School boys that were in the Presbyterian Church choir that Mr. Music was directing on the side, started accusing him of sexual abuse. Of all things.

The radio station and newspapers never said a word about it, the whole evil story being too shameful even to print, but still, word got out and all the County District folks saw through it. It was obvious that the whole thing was the City School District's scheme to get rid of Mr. Music, and hurt our band and choir. The whole County School System knew those kids were simply put up to say what they did, and for some reason the only people I knew that didn't trust the most obvious answer were my Dad and Tom.

Right after all the gossip came out Dad called Tommy and asked him to come home the next weekend, and then that Friday night the two of them spent a long time together on the porch talking before they came in and Dad stood there looking worried and uncomfortable and Tom asked me if Mr. Music had ever tried any foolishness on me like he'd been accused of at the town church. I was insulted. I hollered out "NO! HOW CAN YOU ASK THAT?" Then Mom rushed in asking what was wrong and she and I started crying together and Mom gave them both pure hell over it till Tom left and went back to college on Sunday afternoon. Still, neither Tom nor Dad ever quite acted like they believed me, but at least they never brought it up to me again.

We were just crushed, the Band and Chorus members all. We had no one to turn to except the student teacher for that semester, so we just hunkered down and weathered the storm and waited to see what happened next. It didn't take long. For a couple or three days Mr. Music was gone and the Principal stayed in the Music Department supervising the student teacher as he rehearsed us, but just as suddenly Mr. Music was back—with his beard gone, his hair cut short, and nearly as pale as I'd seen him in front of the Sheriff. Truth be told, he looked so different that we didn't even recognize him at first.

It was at Choir practice that day he said goodbye to us. He didn't wait around to rehearse the Band one last time. He stood before us and, in a quiet voice I'd never heard from him before, he said he loved the time he'd spent teaching music to us Appalachian kids and didn't want any of us to bear a grudge against the City Schools or the boys that accused him, because he'd forgiven them himself. For some time now he'd been thinking a lot of things over and as a Catholic he felt like God was calling him to a vocation in the priesthood, so he was heading back north to talk to his old home parish priest there about seeing the Bishop and going to the Seminary and training for it.

I don't think there was a dry eye in the whole choir, and some of the girls just out and out bawled. He asked us if we'd like to sing one more song with him so we picked "May the Good Lord Bless and Keep You," which was what the choir always ended its Spring Recitals with. Mr. Music conducted it with his eyes shut tight and the tears streaming down all our faces—and then he was gone, out of our lives. There was some insensitive talk later on among the band guys, how did he think he was going to be a priest and cuss all the time? But I think Catholics have always been a little more tolerant of cursing than most Christians. I wish people were more tolerant, period.

***

In my senior year, we got another music teacher, but it just wasn't the same and both Band and Chorus that whole year were pretty much a bust. We didn't win a thing in Regional or State contests, although it sort of helped us feel better that the City District didn't either. Still, I stayed good enough at the sax and as a tenor in the chorus to try out for and win a music scholarship at a Methodist college up near Cumberland Gap where I could make a little additional stipend from singing in the choir and playing in the praise band for the town Methodist church there. I never heard from Mr. Music again, at least personally, but I guess you could say I still followed him: he became a priest back up north, and I joined the Methodists and went on to the Seminary in the Bluegrass and became a Christian School teacher and Minister of Music. And like him too, I've left the old home county behind, for good, I suppose now.

The thing with me, though—it was all such a big misunderstanding, it just kills me. I know attitudes have changed over the years, but I was only trying to inspire those kids the same way Mr. Music did with me so many years ago in the hills. That's all. And I never lost my temper or said so much as an ill word to them, that's just not in me, though they might have performed better if I had, just like we did for Mr. Music.

I was stupid about one thing: I had no business keeping all that junk on my hard drive in the church office, and I guess that's what they nailed me for more than anything else. I think that's about the same thing that happened to Mr. Music when his name came up along with all those other priests in the national news back about 2001 or 2002, I forget when exactly, with pretty much the same old accusations that those three sorry little town S.O.B.'s had leveled at him back twenty-odd years before. The law blamed him most for what they found on his computer, though. I was afraid his old accusers would try to get fifteen minutes of fame out of bringing up their moss-covered lies again too, but if that ever happened, Tom didn't tell me about it and I've not heard it from anyplace else. I think the Internet will be the downfall of us all. At least they showed Mr. Music—Father Music, rather, I guess—the mercy of letting him go to a monastery. The Methodists don't have 'em, of course, just my luck. And I guess, after all, that's where they buried Mr. Music, in that monastery graveyard, wherever it is. Probably not even a tombstone there.

Now I finally know what Mom felt like when she said she didn't have a friend in the world. The poor old thing smoked four or five packs of cigarettes a day for I don't know how long so I guess lung cancer was inevitable, but I suppose I should be glad that neither she nor Dad lived to see me in this place—betrayed not only by a bunch of kids who misunderstood me completely, and whose parents misunderstood me completely, but accused by my own sons after the whole thing started and then even condemned by my wife. Well, my ex-wife now since she served me with divorce papers in jail after I got arrested, pretty much the same way the Methodists pulled my ordination. That leaves Tom, who visits every couple months.

He's almost the only one from home who ever visits, not even Janie who married again to Roy Dean Maddox after he graduated high school although sometimes Roy Dean himself will tag along with Tom because he's got a brother of his own that nobody back home knows what to do about either. And we look at each other for fifteen or twenty minutes and Tom and I try to keep a civil conversation going. One time I asked him if anybody outside the family even knew where I was or what had happened to me, and he and Roy Dean just looked at each other and got up and cleared their throats and said they'd be back next month, or maybe the month after. I didn't press the question. What's the use?

So thanks for listening to me, Daddy K. You and your other guys are the only reason it's even safe for me to stay in the general Population rather than Administrative Segregation. You know how it is with people falsely accused of the stuff I've been accused of. If it weren't for you I'd likely get bullied to death.

John Sparks (he/him) is a writer, historian, healthcare professional, and former ordained minister who preached in years past at various churches of the United Baptist denomination in the Appalachian section of southeastern Ohio. His story is based on his experiences in dealing in a pastoral way with certain church scandals, and the self-deception he's seen used as a defense.

UNO
by L.L. Ford

I wasn't in that long. It was a short enough time that my throat still burned, and my stomach still hurt. Short enough that my mind still reeled with regret and the idea that this was my life still weighed heavy on my mind. That was much less time than the others. The others laughed and smiled and had figured out by now that they needed to make the best of their situation. I wasn't ready yet. I was still filled with shame—still hesitant. The other three—Danny, Trent, and Renee—seemed comfortable. Safe almost.

As I walked through the common area of the main room after the evening vitals check, I found it strange to see the three of them sitting at a table playing Uno. They were laughing with intense joy as they placed each card down. They shared a word amongst each other, laughed again, and then continued on in their triangle. I walked past them, my heart filled with excitement that the TV was open. Finally, I had the chance to play some music of my own off the TV. That was all it was good for anyway—they didn't let us watch anything other than music videos and game shows. I had begun writing lyrics to my favorite songs in my designated journal in desperation to feel something, but now it was time to just experience the music instead of thinking about it for hours on end.

Renee usually curled up on the couch before lights-out, watching music videos for hours. I appreciated her love for music. The gentle but sad tones that rolled from the TV when she was allowed to use the TV always felt chilling and heartbreaking but in an oddly comforting way. Her slowly unfurling dreadlocks were a sign of how long she had been stuck inside. The scabbing of the newer scars—which she made clear to anyone who would listen that they were usually kept covered up with bracelets that were confiscated when she got here—showed how little time she had actually been inside. She seemed well rehearsed in it all—maybe she had been here before—and the calm thoughtless gaze that she gifted the TV with was a familiar one to me. Renee seemed like someone who had seen it all and decided none of it was worth her time.

But now it was my turn. I took her spot on the couch while she played cards behind me at the table. I played my music but not too loud. I didn't want to be rude, but even more importantly, I didn't want anyone to comment on my taste. I don't think my fragile nerves could've handled the scar of something so intimately mine being forced to be exposed to the air of critique.

It never seemed cold or warm—the air, I mean. It smelled sterile. Everything felt so perfectly curated to be empty and meaningless. There was something dead about that. An illusion of the skin that's permitted to feel it. Like temperature was merely a creation of the outside. As though there was nothing to smell. Nothing I felt or experienced was real unless it was numbness, and this was it. This was the end.

Still. Calm. Thoughtless end.

It was inoffensive in the way that a white room was inoffensive. There was nothing to be upset by, but by that same margin, there was no joy either. This was the air of the dead—or the near dead at least. I heard the murmur of subtle laughs and stifled jokes better left unsaid behind me as the heavy bass of my music wafted through the air in front of my gently vibrating eyes.

I felt myself drifting away, imagining I was home in bed. It wasn't the most pleasant memory, but it felt better than this. I missed the darkness. The lights were always on here. I always sat in the dark at home. Maybe it helped me hide... or maybe it helped me feel like I was alone if I couldn't perceive what surrounded me. I missed the feeling of being alone, but that never happened at home anyway. I guess this was my chance to make a change. For me. For once. This could be a new beginning if I let it. Or a break before returning to familiar patterns.

A subtle uproar at the table followed quickly by several people flinching at the island counter in the center of the room left the open space dead silent. Other than the quiet and steady flow of my music which acted as an undertone to the tension between the employees monitoring us and those of us trapped in this cage. Before it could drag on any longer, Danny spoke up,

"Sorry!" The scrawny boy who slept two doors down from me called in a high-pitched voice to the island. A nurse shook her head with a smile and a technician shrugged, returning to his computer. He could've been playing a computer game for all I knew. The trio returned to their game, but the disruption had shifted the mood. I felt eyes on me now. Their whispers weren't playful, but conspiratorial. I felt my deepest anxieties kick in. No one had spoken to me in days, no one acknowledged my existence aside from the nurse who checked my vitals. Now I couldn't escape the horrible feeling of being noticed in that too bright room.

"Hey!" Trent called. I felt my body run cold and I stiffened, sitting completely still as I waited for him to lose interest in me. "Hello?" Trent added with impatience.

"Maybe his implants are off." Renee pondered.

"He doesn't have implants, just you, Re." Danny chimed in. I slowly turned my head and looked over my shoulder,

"Me?" They all tried not to laugh.

"Who else?" Trent said with a chuckle. I would think with the way his mouth was rounded out with piercings, they would've made him remove them, but here he was, a smile full of metal.

A smile.

A rare commodity in this place. I felt embarrassed, but there was something sort of special about knowing I was giving them the chance to laugh. That felt so rare here. So terrifying to acknowledge that you could find joy in a place like this.

"Wanna play Uno?" Renee asked.

"Oh, I don't know. I haven't played in years, and I'm not very good, and I—"

"Oh, come on, we're not trying to win," Danny said with a jeer. "Besides, Trent's been cleaning us out all night."

"I wish I was cleaning you out. Too bad all our money was left at the door." Trent added.

"Come on, just play with us!" Renee said with a smile. I

shrugged,

"Okay, but I warned you." My words felt like gravel in my throat. I guess I hadn't talked much to anyone here. My voice felt like the first wails of a newborn trying to find their voice for the first time. It made me feel sick to think I couldn't even speak like a normal person.

With anxiety welling up inside me and the voice in the back of my mind telling me it wasn't too late to run away and go get in bed with my journal, I went to the table. There was already a fourth chair at the table. That made it a lot easier—like I was supposed to be there. Trent dealt the cards out and without hesitation, the game began.

"I remember the last time I played Uno," Trent said with a small laugh. Nobody responded. I looked around then said in a ginger whisper,

"How was it?"

"Well, my dad was still alive, and my mom wasn't an addict, so it was pretty good."

"Oh…" I almost said I was sorry, but you don't apologize for a person's situation here. You say nothing, or if you knew the person well enough, you matched.

"Last time I played, I was with my first foster family," Danny said with a laugh through his ever-growing facial hair. When I first got here it was short and spindly, as though it grew from his sideburns down and not all at once. Now there thick patches were forming all around his chin and upper lip. He put down a card, "Draw 4. Red." He gave Renee a wink and she groaned. "Next day…" Danny said, putting his cards down on the table and making eye contact with me on the other side. "Got picked up by a guy on the side of the road. Didn't see that 'home' again." He didn't break eye contact with me. I was afraid to look away.

"Hey." Renee tapped the table gently in front of me. You never know what somebody's triggers might be, don't want to touch a stranger. "Your turn." I snapped away from Danny.

"Right. Thanks." A red 3. A silence went over the table again.

Trent put another card down. He wasn't necessarily the oldest of the four of us. Well—he might've been. I'm not sure. He was certainly the tallest. He was a bigger guy who dressed in band tees and all black. If we weren't here, he probably would have chains on his black ripped jeans. His skin was pale like he was used to the inside and the iridescent lights that it took me a full day to acclimate to. For all I knew, this was the only home he ever knew.

Trent dropped a blue 3.

"Fuck, Trent really?" Danny said with a glare as he looked at his cards to see if he had any blues.

"Nothing personal, man," Trent said with a wicked smile.

Danny's thin features clung to his V-neck tee and revealed a heartbeat tattoo on his collarbone. Interesting to see the number of flatlines. Danny drew a card before passing his turn.

"You know, usually when I play…" Renee said as she dropped a card down—a blue draw 2—"We draw til we get a playable card."

"Are you trying to actually make me kill myself?" I blurted out without thinking. Immediately my heart dropped into my stomach and the air felt hot around me. My ears burned and I felt the sweat building up under my blue scrubs—no one had brought me clothes from home like the others. There was a silence in the air as I felt the eyes of the table on me. Further still, there were medical eyes watching with concern. I'm sure that would be noted down for review later.

Then Danny burst into a raucous laugh. He couldn't stop as he leaned on the table, his thin frame crumbling down onto itself. He lifted his head, his face scrunched in a fit of laughter. Renee cracked a beaming smile, and Trent let out a chuckle and clapped his hands with an echoing boom. The island of healthcare professionals looked across at us, but none of my new friends stopped their show of acknowledging what I said.

The mood immediately lifted, and I cracked a smile of pride as well. I made everyone laugh again and this time it was because I was funny, not because I said something stupid. Gallows humor meant something when everyone you were speaking to had brushes with death in their recent memory and needed to escape it with a smile.

After a few minutes, the laughter died down and we continued the game in a much lighter mood. The color had changed back to red by then and it had become a relatively inoffensive game—if only briefly.

"Shit man," Trent said with a chuckle as he dropped a red draw 2. "You know, I'm not trying to make this harder on you, Danny."

"Fuck you, Trent. I thought you loved me," Danny said with a well-rehearsed seductive eyebrow raise. Trent laughed,

"I love you enough to agree to share a room with you in this shithole. Don't mean I love you enough not to make you draw."

"No friends in Uno, boys," Renee reminded them. Danny drew two and Renee dropped a red reverse. Danny put down a wild card,

"You're right. But I don't have any friends outside of Uno either. Yellow," Danny said with a smile and a wink.

"Is it like… the rules go further then so all you have is enemies in Uno?" I asked. Maybe I was trying a little too hard. Trent gave me a courtesy laugh,

"I hope not." He put down a yellow 8.

"Why not?" I asked.

"Cuz, he knows if we're enemies, then I'm coming for you," Danny said with a smile, covering his playful threat.

"And he's a biter," Trent said with a nod. Renee laughed,

"Danny bit Trent right on the forearm his first week."

"Wow, really?"

"I don't like waking up with strange men in my room," Danny said with a shake of his head.

"It's our room now," Trent said. "You got yellows or what?" Trent had turned his attention on me.

"Oh, right. Sorry," I said, fumbling to get my yellow skip card out and down. It fell onto the table and Trent and Danny gasped,

"Damn! Bye, Renee!" Danny cackled. Renee slowly looked up at me,

"I'll never forgive you for this," She whispered.

"No friends in Uno, right…?" Danny gasped.

"Oooh, girl, they're using your own words against you!" Renee smiled.

"You're right."

"Wow, no blood…" Trent jeered.

"I'm not much of a fighter anyways…" I said with a sigh. In a way that's what got me here instead of in a tasteful casket at a cheap funeral. I thought of saying so out loud but decided I'd rather keep it to myself.

"That's too bad," Danny said as he dropped a yellow 2. "I was hoping to get a beating from you before the visit was over."

Trent shot Danny a look.

"Danny come on, don't make 'em uncomfortable."

Danny shrugged. "Sorry."

"You're fine. It's not weird. Or at least if it is, it doesn't really bother me," I said.

"So," Trent said, dropping down a reverse to Danny, "you seem pretty chill…"

"Thanks…" I mumbled out.

"Is it your first time in a place like this?" He asked.

"Yep, first time."

"You're lucky." Renee said.

"I am?"

"Oh yeah," Trent answered. "This is the best one in the state. I've been in way worse. Facility-wide riots, no outside time, overdoses in facilities, employees who can't keep their hands to themselves. Worse. Way worse."

"Damn…"

"Yeah. Damn," Danny added, "Yellow," putting down a draw 4. Renee grumbled as she drew. I put down a card absentmindedly. A yellow 5.

"So… How many times have you guys been in places like this?"

"5 or 6 times, easy," Trent said, putting down a green 5.

"Fuck, green, really?" Danny said as he drew a card. He moved down his v-neck in the same movement, fully revealing his tattoo,

"4 times. Once for each try." I nodded. Renee put down a green draw 2,

"A few," she said, with a blank face. "I stopped counting a long time ago."

Some time passed with a few laughs, cursing at our own misfortune. The nurses were starting to look more closely at us with a looming concern that they knew it was almost time to tell us lights-out. All that meant was that the overhead lights would be slightly dimmer, and we wouldn't be allowed to do anything other than lay in bed and wake up every 10 minutes when someone clumsily did their check-ins throughout the night.

We had gotten braver as they watched us. Louder. We were a little more comfortable in our own bodies. A little is all that could ever be asked of us. When you looked like, lived like, and were born like us, that's the best anyone could ever ask. Just a little extra. It wasn't about who won—that much was true—but I felt like I had won by just being part of it.

As Danny dealt out a new set—our final game, because we all knew this was the last round and they wouldn't tell us twice—he asked me a simple but stressful question, "So, why are you in here?"

I felt the faint feeling of dinner trying to force its way back up my throat and onto the table, but I swallowed it back down as the acid burned the back of my throat. Why was I here? How could I answer that question? How could I possibly tell the truth?

I played the first card of the last round and shrugged,

"Oh, you know…"

"It's okay. You don't have to say," Renee added. Danny nodded along then added,

"But if you're comfortable sharing, we're here to listen."

"Yeah," Trent added. "We're in this shithole together. Even if it's for different reasons."

I smiled and wondered how this moment could go on forever. How many draw 4s would it take to never reach the end? How many times could we forget to call Uno and have to draw extra cards before the nurses knew we were up to something? If I could stretch that moment in time for miles and wrap it in a blanket of acceptance and understanding that kept me warm at night, I'd hold it tight and cry tears of joy before sleeping better than I ever had before. I'd never let this moment go. I'd let it replay over and over and over again because all I could ever ask for was someone to understand. And they did. God, they did.

But instead, when it was time, I placed down a green 3. "Uno."

L.L. Ford (he/him) has been writing for as long as he can remember. He started out writing on the walls of his childhood home but finds that a computer does just fine these days. From grand worlds beyond his own understanding, to the simple fears of everyday life, L.L. faces it all through the words he puts out into the world. When he isn't doing mental health research as a neuroscientist, he's serializing stories on the internet, writing poetry, seeing the world, and trying to catch up on sleep.

WHILE SHE IS BRAIDING MY HAIR
by Samantha Stanich

I sit with my Pumpkin Spice vanilla latte,
my perfectly manicured hands are wrapped around
the ceramic cup that that signifies a thoughtful
lessening of my carbon footprint,

I am making a difference.

A stylist pets my ever-fragile hair ego, saying
she can't find a single gray. I know she's
patronizing me since I see them every day but
I won't dye it, won't give into the industry.

I am making a difference.

The stylist drones on about her husband and
children, how she's on her feet all day
making money, But you're strong, independent,
I say, holding your own. She quips, I would trade
independence for stay-at-home, while I think

She is making a difference.

I want to believe her, sitting in her swivel chair,
I wonder how any woman could not want control?
Not me, I am a strong, independent woman, whose
parents pay her phone bill and boyfriend pays
the rent, but I pay my car lease and credit card bill…

I AM AN INDEPENDENT WOMAN.

The stylist pulls my hair into a tight boxer braid:
I am paying for a service that little girls learn
from their older sister because their mom works
the night shift and the kids are making sure they look like
they have it all together, even when the third eviction notice
has been stapled to the door and the only thing
in the fridge is CheeseWhiz and stale saltines.

My perfectly manicured feet sport sandals
that could feed a family of four, comfortably.
My mom bought them for me because I work oh, so hard.

I am making a difference.

My college educated, whiteness hits me in
the face as another hair is pulled to my scalp.
My Pumpkin Spice vanilla latte burns
my tongue, privilege
is not a burden I carry
because privilege
is not a burden.

Privilege is thinking something isn't a problem because it's not a
problem for you.
Privilege is walking into a job interview and not being judged on
your name.
Privilege is walking down the street and not seeing people cross to
the other side.
Privilege is not being followed around at CVS because they assume
you are stealing.

As someone with it, I should point it out. I *should*
hold up a vanity mirror and illuminate it to those who
"don't see color." Who think the world is safe.

They live in a world that wants them there.
Not one where they are stopped in their own neighborhood because
the local George Zimmerman thinks they are lost.
Not one where a knee to the turf causes so much upheaval.
Not one where they have to tell their children how to speak to a
cop
because "Yes sir," "No mam," doesn't work when you can't breathe.

As I sit with my Pumpkin Spice Privilege in hand,
I vow to speak up even if it is easier
        to sip quietly.

Samantha Stanich (she/her) is a poet originally from Poland, Ohio. She earned her MA and MFA from Wilkes University and currently resides in St. Petersburg, Florida. Her poetry explores themes of motherhood, self-realization, and the complexities of politics and women, and she is currently working on her collection Don't Tell Me I'm Pretty.

DIABOLUS

by Katherine Hedrick

A demon sits in quiet contemplation on the porch of her downtown apartment, snuffing out the glow of her cigarette and letting the early morning snowfall shine without contest. She does not shiver, as much as she would kill to. While only trace amounts of hellfire burn in her veins, they burn just hot enough to forbid her from feeling any semblance of the cold. She reaches out a hand to catch a stray snowflake and sighs as it melts before even touching her skin. The demon, Mary, cannot sleep. She had arranged a meeting with a friend of hers that was to take place in the nearby church, and while she knew it was in her best interest to get some rest beforehand, something in her chest rattled around just enough to keep her conscious. This restlessness plagues her on most holy days of obligation. Today, she recalls, is the Feast of the Immaculate Conception. The Virgin Mary was born without sin, so the church says. She wonders what it must be like, to be sinless—she has always been more Magdalene than Virgin.

Rising from her stoop and carrying freshly bought wine and plastic cups with her, Mary makes her way through the night to the stone steps of Saint Jude's—the church only five or so minutes away from her city apartment. She climbs the snow-brushed steps and pushes open the church's heavy wooden doors, seeking refuge from the wind and snow (she cannot feel the cold, but the frost bites her skin all the same) and an audience with one Father James Altomare.

She had promised him the usual: a drink and conversation, most often of the theological sort. James would find it amusing (if not slightly unnerving) for a demon to take such an interest in the scriptures if it were any demon other than Mary. His fellow Benedictines never quite approved of him taking any course of action other than immediate exorcism, but the sole belief he held closer to his chest than God's unconditional love and mercy was Mary's capacity to be really, truly good. At least, that's what he told her during their very first of these late-night meetings, wine glass in hand and a softness to his gaze that she tries even still not to let her thoughts linger on.

Last winter, when they first met, Mary had sought out the aid of the church almost immediately after she learned of her true nature. When the devil began sending demons to earth to live alongside humans, it was understood that there would be those whose humanity rubbed off on them, and thereby those who would rebel against their purpose. She was among the unfortunate few whose demonic nature never made itself apparent, those who lived their lives in blissful ignorance. As a girl, she was frequently seized by night terrors that left her in tears of burning sulfur. She frequently complained of phantom pains in her temples after telling lies or getting up to childish mischief, and with age came to realize that those were the stubs of horns threatening to burst forth from her skin should she continue with her sinful ways.

Mary never considered herself to be particularly religious, but going the route of the church felt like her only real choice. After all, if God and the Devil were unambiguously real and she was unambiguously a pawn in their never-ending war game, it felt wrong to remain a conscientious objector.

Mary enters the sanctuary to find James already inside, rosary draped across his hands as he prays. He recites the Hail Mary-fitting, given the occasion. The rosary's silver beads glimmer softly in the candlelight, candles that James himself must have lit before she arrived. He handles the beads delicately, moving them almost so as not to hurt them on their way down the rosary's cord. Mary has always known him to have a soft touch, treating everything around him with something that reads to her as reverence. She supposes it's only natural for a priest to possess such a quality, and does not allow herself to think of the way he ever so gently takes her hand when he really, truly wants her to take in what he says. Mary stands by in silence as he finishes his prayer, unwilling to interrupt him in a moment where he seems so utterly in tune with the divine. She almost envies him.

James breaks from his almost-trance, eyes sparkling like

snowflakes against the quiet, peaceful dark of the sky as soon as he registers Mary's presence.

"Sorry," he says, his expression an apologetic half-smile, "I didn't notice you were already here. You know how I am when I'm in prayer."

"No, I get it- the other Mary takes precedence. It's a pretty important day for her, so I hear."

James nods.

"Yes, today is the day when the Virgin Mary was conceived, her soul free of the original sin that permeates the hearts of man," He says, playing up the drama as though he were delivering a particularly gripping sermon.

Mary can't help but laugh as she uncorks the merlot she bought earlier that day. It's been exactly a year since their first meeting, after all, and she knows James has a taste for red wine. He almost has to, with all the leftover Eucharist wine he's made to drink each Sunday. She wonders if it ever bores him to perform the same miracle time and time again, if it ever exhausts him to extend such genuine goodwill and grace to everyone he meets, to embody such virtue. She wonders if it ever hurts to be so saintlike.

"Really, it's fine. If anything, I should be the one apologizing for bringing red solo cups instead of real glasses," Mary jokes, "glass doesn't exactly travel well."

James takes an eager sip from his cup all the same.

"No need- it's the wine that makes the drink, not the cup. It's like-"

"-The church," she interjects with a self-satisfied smile, "the church is the people in it, not the building itself. See? I do pay attention during your homilies."

James laughs, his dark eyes sparking to life yet again. Mary prays he doesn't notice as she averts her gaze. She can't allow herself to feel this, not around him. She decides she'll blame the flush on the wine and pray that he believes her—not that he'd ever ask. She prays even through the searing pain—demons are not capable of prayer without it. The devil has never taken kindly to his creations aligning themselves with the divine.

"Speaking of homilies, I want to ask you something. This isn't a trick question, I'm just curious."

"Shoot," Mary says, taking another drink.

"Do you like being here? In church, I mean. I know it's more of a necessity for you than anything, and I can't say I'd blame you for resenting it. Obligations are easy to resent."

"Isn't this an obligation for you, too?"

James goes quiet, and Mary curses herself for asking such an obvious question. Of course it's an obligation, it's been an obligation since the day he set foot in seminary, it's been an obligation long before he ever donned the cassock and clerical collar. James is lucky, she thinks. He knows his purpose. He doesn't have to go looking for it elsewhere, and he certainly doesn't have to try and find it in the outstretched hand and sacred promises of a man he knows he could never have. She knows it's a sin to covet what isn't hers, and yet she finds herself indulging in that same sin every time her gaze falls upon James. If God were here now, Mary would swear that it's not her fault, that she couldn't help it even if she tried, not when James holds all the world's stars in his eyes and has all of heaven's wisdom flowing forth from every damn word he says. She knows now that the scriptures were right—God made man in his own image, the man sitting beside her most of all.

Mary stammers out the beginnings of an apology, but James silences her with a hand laid on top of hers. Her heart thrashes against the prison of her ribs, making enough noise to break both of their silences.

"Yes, it's an obligation," James says, voice softer than before, "but look around. It's beautiful, isn't it?"

Mary shifts her gaze to the stained glass windows upon the walls. Even if she hasn't always bought into the idea of a God, she's always loved art like this, always been fascinated by it. Images of divinity, of saints and angels and everything she is not, lovingly rendered by human hands. As her humanity stares in awe, the demon within her burns with rage. She inflames with jealousy for real people, real humans who can pray without ceasing and clutch rosaries close to their real human hearts and kneel before God in real human reverence without every fiber of their being screaming for them to stop, crying out for relief as it feels itself being torn apart. Her desire for a body that does not rebel against her imitation soul is so fervent that it borders on obsession. Hot tears well up in the corners of her eyes, streaming down her cheeks like liquid flame. To want is to burn, she now knows.

"I want to be human," Mary says suddenly, her eyes aglow with a light so close to holy fire she thinks she sees James flinch, "I want a real soul."

"You're human enough already," James offers, reaching out a hand to dry her tears. Mary recoils on impulse, nerves like a wounded animal, as yet more tears roll down her cheeks.

"To you, maybe, but not to God."

James draws in a breath. To Mary, he looks almost ready to shed tears of his own, his expression painted with the sort of sorrow and pity that wouldn't look out of place in the portrait of a martyred saint. Mary fights back the urge to recoil once again. She hates evoking pity, and she hates that James of all people is being forced to pity her.

"Mary, I'm afraid I can't help you the way you want. In any case, you're more virtuous than half of my congregation-."

"Just perform an exorcism," she says, tone on the precipice of begging, "that's how you normally deal with things like this, right?"

"An exorcism? That won't give you a human soul, it's only meant to banish demons-"

"I want the demon banished. It seems perfectly reasonable to me."

"I can't-"

"Of course, you can, doesn't God act through you?"

James puts his hands on Mary's shoulders, looking at her through pleading eyes.

"I can't do it because I don't know if you'll be the same afterward."

The beast of Mary's heart roars to life once more, flush spreading over her skin like wildfire. She forces it back into its cage, biting back the sickly rush of feeling and forcing herself up onto her feet. She makes her way toward the looming wooden doors. James follows close behind as he grabs her shoulder, unwilling to see her go.

"Mary, please, you are the demon, I don't want to end up sending all of you away—I don't want to end up hurting you."

Mary tenses her shoulders and grits her teeth, imagining wings unfurling and fangs bursting through her gums. The inferno in her blood sparks to life, flooding her senses with heat and rage and fire.

"Do you have any idea how much it hurts, James? To try your absolute fucking hardest to be good and pure and holy, but to live with the knowledge that you were made to do evil, and that there's not a damn thing you can do about it? Do you have any idea of how much it eats at you? I just want to live without feeling like that. I thought you would want that for me too."

James reaches out for her as she leaves, shutting the doors of the church behind her and leaving him in perfect silence. He does not chastise her for profane speech in the sanctuary- he cannot bring himself to, as he so often must. He tells himself that God would allow her this if nothing else.

He resigns himself to solemn prayer until the sun comes up.

In the silent hours, James reminds himself of who and what he is, what responsibilities he holds as a holy man.

He reminds himself that for a priest, an exorcism is an honor to perform. He reminds himself that demons are agents of Satan, that Mary is far nobler than him for wanting her soul made clean, made pure. He asks himself what he would do if he were the one whose soul had been touched by darkness, darkness that he had no way of agreeing to, darkness that he actively fought against.

James reminds himself that he is a human, and as such, he is as susceptible to Satan's temptations and influence as anyone else. Of course he would react with such horror to Mary's request for an exorcism- in that moment, his heart betrayed him- betrayed Mary.

He loves Mary, and reminds himself that he is only to love her as God loves all his creations. He curses himself for not yet being able to love unselfishly.

James prays until his fragile human body, sinful and woefully imperfect, forces itself to sleep.

***

Father James Altomare's first and only exorcism takes place not even a week after Mary first begged for it. In the ensuing days, it was James' turn to feel the guilt Mary spoke of—her tears and rage and leaving were etched into his memory like a nightmare that lingers long past waking. The prior week's rain has cooled into snow, and the precious few daylight hours continue to dwindle. By the time he arrives at the church, the sun has long since faded. He has already recited the requisite prayers, and all that is left for him to do is fulfill what he has every reason to believe will be one last promise to her.

The stark white alb draped with a violet stole is tight around his neck, the material just itchy enough to cause discomfort. The ornate golden crucifix he holds is cold to the touch. He feels almost unworthy to be playing the part of exorcist, knowing that God has borne witness to both his sleepless nights spent in premature mourning of a demon and the days spent reassuring himself that this was good, this was right, this was the natural order of things. Nevertheless, doubt sleeps soundly in the back of his mind, ready to awaken.

He finds Mary in prayer, clutching a votive candle in her hands despite the pain he knows it must be causing her. She's surrounded by a ring of smaller candles, undoubtedly lit with the now-extinguished lighter that sits on the floor beside her.

"Are you ready?" James asks, knowing that the question is unnecessary, knowing that she has likely been ready to be purged of her demonic nature since she first learned of it. Who would want to live as something unholy? Who would want to hold that guilt, that shame?

Mary only nods.

James calls her to rise, taking her hands in his and stepping within the ring as prayers fall from his lips. Mary listens, reciting prayers back when she must. She listens despite the wrongness of it, despite the pain that her preemptively taken migraine medication is doing little to dull, despite her shaky breaths and trembling. He can hardly bear to keep the ritual going, but he pushes onward.

Litanies, psalms, intercessions on behalf of saints and angels and God himself. Each and every one of them makes Mary wince in growing agony, but she utters not a word. It hurts beyond hurt for him to see her in this state.

Minute after grueling minute passes until James forces himself to the final step, the bearing of the crucifix and final expulsion of all demonic entities. He knows it will be Mary's undoing, but cannot stop. With a shaking hand and wavering voice, he raises the crucifix, and readies to recite the final prayer.

Before he can say even a word, Mary doubles over in agony. She cries out as her soul is ripped into, as blinding pain tears through her and almost renders her unconscious. He knows God is looking down upon him in rage, he knows he has no better way to ease the ache deep within her soul, but he refuses to let her die by his hand. To him, she is, has always been, and will always be human- always be Mary. James throws away the crucifix on instinct, as though it burns to touch, as though he himself is the demon. With all of his strength, he pulls Mary out from her ring of candles, snuffing each and every single one of them out with the bottom of his shoe. The flames lick at and singe the edge of his pant leg, but he cannot bring himself to care. Ever so gently, ever so reverently, James lays Mary on the floor as silent tears stream down his cheeks. Such heresy, he thinks, to be weeping for a demon.

Mary regains her strength little by little in the ensuing calm. She stares up at the church's vaulted ceiling, looks here and there at the stained glass windows once again. Nothing seems to have changed—she remains a demon. However, her heart seems lighter, more content. She glances over at James. In this moment, he is not the saintly Father he has spent so long molding himself into- no saint would interrupt a ritual as sacred as exorcism. What he is, however, is beautifully vulnerable, beautifully human.

Mary tugs on the sleeve of his alb to draw his attention. She has only one request.

"Hold me," she asks, and so he does.

He holds her to his chest, and hugs her tightly as if to apologize.

They remain like this for a long, long time, until James' tears dry and Mary has drifted off into a merciful sleep. The shadows born from the snuffed-out candles embrace them just as they embrace one another.

This, James knows, is a holiness all its own.

Katherine Hedrick (she/her) is a sophomore at Otterbein University studying creative writing. She has previously been published in Quiz & Quill and Flip the Page, Otterbein and Thurber House's literary journals respectively. She was born and raised in Columbus, Ohio.

TICKET TO NOWHERE
by Mary Moody Hunt

I'm sitting here with a winning lottery ticket in my hand and I don't know what to do with it. I was going to go wake my parents and jump up and down screaming, "We won!" But then I thought about who my parents are. That's why I don't know what to do with it.

It's not my ticket. I'm not old enough to buy lottery tickets. My parents buy them. They won $5,000 once but didn't know it for a month because they never take care of anything. I found the ticket when I was cleaning out the car. That's something I started doing last summer because I was embarrassed by the trash and stuff they let pile up in it.

After they pissed through their winnings, they decided I should be in charge of checking the tickets. They give them to me, and I check the numbers in the mornings after a drawing while they're still in bed sleeping. If it's not a winner, I tear it up and throw it in the trash. If it's worth anything, I give it to my dad, and he cashes it in. And then he buys more tickets with the money.

Here's the thing. My parents aren't very good with money, and they don't take care of anything. That includes me. Sometimes I overhear my grandmother telling people that I'm the only adult in my house. It makes me mad when she says that because I don't like to hear other people bashing my parents. But it makes me feel good too because it means I know how to take care of myself. I'm just glad I don't have any little brothers and sisters to look after. At least they realized they aren't very good at this parenting thing and stopped with me.

My parents met in a rehab center for addicts in Marietta. My grandmother took my mother there because she'd had, "just about enough." My mom is a crack addict. Drug addicts lie and steal all the time. She stole from my grandparents many times and lied about it. One day Grandma caught her taking money from her purse and gave her two choices: get the hell out or go to rehab. She chose rehab.

The police escorted my dad to rehab. He's a heroin addict. He was caught breaking into someone's house. He got probation because it was his first offense, but he had to go to rehab before his probation started.

I get this sick feeling in my stomach when they talk about how they met. I want to scream at them to shut up because they tell everyone. So everybody knows, including some of the kids at school who like to tease me about it. I can't tell you how many times one of them has said to me, "Well, at least my parents didn't meet in rehab." I got so sick of it that I snarked back the last time it happened. It was this scrawny little bitch named Zara who's not too bright.

"Even though my parents met in rehab, I still get straight As," I told her. "And you're on the dishonor roll." She didn't like it much, but it made me feel good to stand up for myself and she hasn't said anything about my parents since.

I know the story of how they met by heart because I've heard my Mom tell it so many times.

"I went out on a smoke break and there was this absolutely gorgeous new guy out there. He only had one cigarette so when he finished it, I gave him one of mine because we still had ten minutes left. We started talking and I just fell in love with him. We got married two months after we got out."

I guess I'm surprised they're still married because they fight all the time, sometimes even physically, especially when they're out of money and can't get drugs. I just go to my room, put on my headphones, and blast my music when they get like that.

Oh, the way they talk, you would think they're clean. They talk about the 12-step program all the time and even go to Narcotics Anonymous meetings, but I know they're still using. They just don't do it in front of me anymore, but I know the signs. I can even tell what drugs they're using because they can't always get their drug of choice. When Daddy shoots heroin, all he does is sleep. When Mom smokes crack, she never shuts up but a lot of what she says doesn't make any sense. Sometimes they snort cocaine and stay awake for what seems like days binge-watching television. To be honest, I wish they'd just smoke pot because when they do that, they're almost happy.

So anyways, I've got this ticket worth a million dollars. It doesn't have the Powerball number, but it has all the other five numbers that were drawn. I looked it up online and it says that's worth a million dollars. I'll bet they would piss through the money in less than a year. Oh, I'm sure they'd buy new cars and a new house, but they wouldn't take care of any of it. The drug man would probably get most of it like he did when they won the $5,000.

My dog, Rascal, just saw me eating cereal. He came over and nudged my arm and made me decide what to do with the ticket. Rascal was a present from my parents on my tenth birthday. He was a puppy someone gave them, so they gave him to me so they wouldn't have to spend any money on a present.

Rascal's just a mutt but he's a good dog. When I was twelve, I went on vacation for two weeks with my grandparents. When I got home, they told me Rascal ran away and they couldn't find him. I talked my grandmother into taking me to the dog shelter and that's where I found him. They described the people who brought him in, and I knew right away it was my parents. See what I mean about not taking care of anything? They couldn't even take care of my dog for two weeks.

So, I'm going to write "Humane Society of the Ohio Valley" on the back of the ticket where the name goes and mail it to them. I follow them on Facebook, and they always need money for animal food, vet bills, and lots of other things. They're always having some kind of fundraiser. If I give them the ticket, they won't have to do that anymore. I'll bet it will even be on the six o'clock news in Parkersburg and no one will ever know I'm the one who did it.

Maybe that's a stupid thing to do with a million-dollar lottery ticket. Sure, maybe my life would end up easier if I told my parents and gave them the ticket, but I don't think that would last. In the end, it would just end up worse. Sometimes I worry about coming home and finding them dead from overdoses. Both of them have OD'd before. I think if I gave them the ticket, they would both end up dead.

Besides, I can take care of myself. I'm not like them. I have my future planned. I'm going to go to college, get a good job, and have a loft apartment in a city someplace where no one knows about my parents. And I'm never, ever going to need a winning lottery ticket.

Mary Moody Hunt (she/her) is a writer and poet who emphasizes social issues in her work, which has appeared in Mobius: The Journal of Social Change and Rat's Ass Review. Hunt is a veteran and former military journalist who also worked as a news writer and columnist for a small weekly paper. A native of Maryland, Hunt lived in West Virginia for nearly four decades before settling in central Ohio.

RESISTANCE TO DISPOSABLENESS
by Amy Randall-McSorley

There's a bare space on my neck where my hair used to lie
Narrow silver blades
Snip, snip
Lobbed
Chopped
Floating baby soft curls
Harmonized with
Cascading
Bitter, silent tears
Salty stings down
Cherub chipmunk cheeks
But I am still a girl

There's an empty box where pink ballet slippers once were kept
Pointing
Twirling
Spinning nightmares into thin air
Dreams slashed
Hand smashed
Shredded pink ribbons
But I am still a girl

There's a compression where my spine was once spaced
Like raindrops on dewdrops
Piercing sun on burnt petals
Brandy on a scorching summer night
Blistering pavement to bare feet
No matter the beatings
Dew is still cool
Petals are still flowers
Night is still peaceful
I will still walk

And I am still a girl

There is a whispered cry where my voice once spoke
"I am here. I am right in front of you."
Eyes pierce
Over my head
To my side
Circuitous
Bypassed
Water thicker than blood
Clear stream muddied
Stirred with steps unseen
Unseeming
Never enough
Freckled face, runner's thighs, ugly girl
Stupid girl
PhD, just a
Framed paper
Nothing more
Moving across the room, tying a shoe, pouring a drink
Not even the smallest of tasks
Done in a satisfactory manner
But I am still a daughter

There is a flaw where there once was perfection
It manifested before I had even learned
To put one foot in front of the other
And it grew like an ugly wound
Deep, red, crust that flaked with every grimace
Like fire beat out with a rake
No salve would ever heal and make it pretty again
And the hair grown rebelliously long
Weaponized against me
Hands grabbed and twisted my locks
Drug me across the hot asphalt

Up the porch
To the kitchen floor
Where I laid
Flawed and disposable
Ugly rag doll
But I am still a daughter

There is a broken string where my fiddle once played
Frets added
Where there should be none
The man's metrical goals
Doubled for me
The man's salary
Halved for me
The man's future limitless
Concrete ceiling for me
Footprints on my neck
Double standards racing
Stripes down my back
But I am still a woman

There's a hole in my body where there once was a womb
Now I'm chattel that yearns for the return of Roe
And I remember
When the window
Was shattered
The door splintered
Me—belly down on the floor
As he exercised his right to rape
Smugly grunting of his future paternal rights
But Roe had not left the room yet
And my body
Still had a small voice
I am human

There's a hole where the years have flowed from my bloodstream
Soft ripples feeding a hidden creek
Twinkling in the dancing shadows
Of the trees in the deep woods of my heart
Thick with protective tangled vines
The air dense and moist
Soft and rich with pine
I lick my wounds
With mouth closed,
I scream
I dry my tears
I carry on
Because

I am still a girl
I am still a woman
I am still human

There's a hole
There's a hole
I am whole
I am whole
I am woman
I am whole

Amy Randall-McSorley (she/her) resides with her husband, Gary, and their rescue dogs in beautiful south-central Ohio. She holds a bachelor's degree in organizational communications with a minor in psychology, a master's degree in marketing and communications, and a doctorate degree in education. She is a newspaper columnist, the author of several books, some under her former name Amy Cooper, and is currently working on another collection of poetry. When not writing, she and her husband enjoy spending time outdoors hiking, star-gazing, and riding their motorcycles.

THE GULF

by Charles Derry

Although Theresa still carried her key, she no longer felt welcome to use it. She peered through the front door window of the home she had grown up in, called out "Hi, Mom, are you there?" a little too boisterously, and when there was no response, rang the bell like some door-to-door salesman hoping for the big sale of the day but feeling more dread than anticipation. Finally, she saw a figure shuffling toward her.

Her mother seemed tired to Theresa, her gait slow. Although Polly James had moved away from the Texas panhandle over fifty years ago to marry Giovanni Russo and settle in an Italian neighborhood in Cleveland she looked now like an old farmer's wife, skin weathered and freckled, the lines in her neck like a freshly plowed field. Giovanni had died exactly one year ago tomorrow of a particularly virulent colon cancer. During the course of his illness, Polly had looked at Theresa through more compassionate eyes, and all had been forgiven.

Well, not forgiven exactly—but at least mulched over, like weeds buried deep enough for crops to become established. In any case, when your husband is dead and unable to walk the shopping malls with you, companionship may now be more important than whether your daughter is lesbian. At least, that was Theresa's theory as to why she was now welcome in Cleveland, when for so long she had not been. The war between them had never really ended, although her mother had consented to a cease-fire of sorts. Theresa had been surprised, because her mother was a stubborn woman, and eight years of silence were several fewer than she had expected. But now was not a time to obsess on the humiliations of those years, on all the overtures rebuffed. *Not now,* thought Theresa, *put them aside*. Still, the eight years had almost destroyed her.

"So how long did it take you to get here?" asked Polly as she held open the door.

"About two-and-a-half hours."

Fifteen years earlier, when Theresa was an Ohio State student commuting between Columbus and Cleveland at least six times a year, the trip had taken two-and-a-half hours; now, after she had been long settled in Columbus, the trip still took two-and-a-half hours.

"That long?" said Polly, who had always seemed surprised by the answer. "And how was the traffic?"

The inane ritual of arrival conversation was only somewhat reassuring, because Theresa was inordinately aware of feeling like a stranger: *how peculiar to put your overnight bag in the kitchen because you're not certain whether your "old room" is still yours.* Her mother seemed oblivious to Theresa's hesitation.

"Look what I brought," said Theresa, trying to change her own mood and raising the flute case she carried in her left hand.

"Is that a new one?" said Polly.

"Yes, from China. Hong Kong, actually. It's been very difficult to get the franchise on this line."

Certainly, Theresa was proud of her business: the flutes which she made, sold, repaired, imported, wrote about, and sometimes—though with far less frequency these days—even played.

"It looks small," said Polly.

"Not really. Do you want to hear its tone? I could play it for you."

"Maybe later. Did I tell you about Audrey?"

Although stung, Theresa was prepared for the slight, surprised only by how quickly it had come. Audrey, her older sister, had made choices that always pleased her mother: Audrey had a husband, a child, a part-time job as a nurse, and a home only fifteen minutes away. Theresa had already consented to take her mother to visit there tomorrow, and Theresa would have to cluck appreciatively over Audrey's pretty daughter, Audrey's well-appointed home, Audrey's providing husband. Although Audrey had accepted Theresa's interest in women, she had never been willing to represent Theresa's case in the court of their parents' opinion. And since both parents had always doted on Audrey, even a word from her could have made a significant difference in the quality of all of their lives.

"Will Audrey be meeting us at the cemetery?" asked Theresa.

"No," said Polly, "it's too hard with the baby. Anyway, she took her family last week. But I know your father wanted you to visit him on his first anniversary."

"And you wanted it?"

"Well I asked you, didn't I?" said Polly, turning to the TV, where Patriot Missiles were downing the Iraqi SCUDs. The Gulf War, adding to Theresa's edginess, had begun only days earlier.

"But not Anna," said Theresa after a pause, referring to her lover, a Chinese-American who worked as a social worker.

"What are you saying?"

"But you didn't ask Anna."

"Oh. I don't know," said Polly, moving to the sofa, and then added solemnly, "These bombs are something. Have you been watching?"

Theresa followed into the family room and started to take her father's chair, then left it vacant when she saw her mother cringe. She sat instead on the floor against the sofa. The two of them looked at each other, and Theresa realized that neither of them, for the moment, could think of anything to say. Perhaps to ease the tension, her mother let out a long sigh.

"You know," she said, stretching out her legs, "It's harder and harder to get around. These feet of mine ache all day and I don't know why, all I do is sleep."

"My knees hurt since I turned thirty."

"Is that arthritis you think?"

"Is that what you have in your feet?"

They fell silent again and listened to the TV. After a moment (*was she being too familiar, too soon?*) Theresa started massaging her mother's feet, like in the old days, before their war.

"I'm so glad you've come back," said her mother, but Theresa noted that she said it with no apparent feeling.

"Thank you, Mom."

"And I wish your Dad was here. Having a meal with us."

When Theresa was growing up, her father had always come home late from work, and no one watched much TV. Her mother had always been a lonely woman, grateful for her daughter and eager for Theresa and Audrey to come home from school to provide the company and family she so needed. Yet paradoxically, the longer she lived in Cleveland, the more she dedicated herself to her Texas-based Church of Christ, purposely estranging herself from her Italian Catholic in-laws, who were unable to get close to her. Giovanni had at first fought Polly's isolation from his family, but eventually found it easier to surrender to his wife's desires and started building his own walls in respons—both to his Italian family and to his wife. Every evening, with a casserole bubbling in the oven, Theresa, Audrey, and their mother would wait for Dad to get home, but separately: Mom in the family room working on a Sunday school lesson, Audrey in her bedroom listening to WHK's Greatest Hits Countdown, and Theresa in the kitchen preparing the next day's lunchboxes. (Years later, when Theresa graduated from college and her parents were unable to come to her commencement, she finally exploded with rage over her earlier household responsibilities. Audrey, who attended the event without her husband, only laughed and said, "Well, you always volunteered to do the work around the house, and your lunches were terrific, so why are you complaining now?" And Theresa was stunned because it was true.) Around 9 p.m., Dad would finally arrive home, and the four of them would eat. At dinner, no one would speak much, in part because they all knew that a controversial opinion could upset Mother. (Once at the age of twenty-two, Theresa had revealed that she had drunk a bottle of beer after four sets of tennis, and her mother—shocked by this Biblical transgression—had burst into tears and walked around their long block at least twenty times.) It was odd, now, that the silence Theresa had so long remembered should be punctured by silent images of exploding bombs from the television.

Theresa was not a fan of the President. Her friends were dying of AIDS, the recession was pushing her business to the brink of bankruptcy and creating stress, and her own personal demons were committing terrorist acts upon her relationship with Anna.

"Go to Cleveland, go!" Anna had screamed at her the day before, her new spike of auburn hair a shock to her Chinese features. "I don't need to go with you, then. We need some time apart 'cause we both have to think."

"Think about what?"

"About whether we want this."

Both had been afraid to continue the argument, so Theresa had resignedly packed her overnight bag and driven the two-and-a-half hours ("That long? And how was the traffic?") from Columbus to Cleveland. And did they really want this... what? This argument? This relationship? This life?

"Do we have to watch this?" said Theresa.

"Mrs. Ventura's daughter is actually over there, fighting."

Mrs. Ventura was a neighbor, recently divorced by her husband after thirty-four years of marriage. For most of the years the two families had lived side-by-side, Polly had kept her distance, disapproving because Mrs. Ventura didn't believe that baptism required total immersion. (Undoubtedly this woman was headed for hell.) Since being abandoned, however, Mrs. Ventura had stopped going to Sunday Mass, a fact which had somehow allowed a friendship between the two women finally to bloom.

"Your father fought in a war, too," continued Polly. "In the Pacific. That's just the way of the world. But he wasn't in the desert or in sand. Not like Iraq. Can anything grow there? I think I'd like the heat, myself. He never wanted to see pictures of himself in that uniform, I don't know why. But we all have to do our duty now, even the women. They should have thought of that before they burned their brassieres. There may be some children without mothers. But that's the way life is. I haven't watched soap operas in a week. It's about time we had some Presidents who believed in principles."

Some primal need propelled Theresa to push it: she was

suddenly a teenager again, smoking her first cigarette (it had made her sick to her stomach and she never smoked a second, though she had let her mother discover the pack in her room). "You know, Mom, your beloved Bush and Reagan were responsible for all the foreign aid to Iraq that allowed Saddam Hussein to do all of this in the first place. I'd rather not have to watch this every minute I'm here."

Her mother didn't take the bait quite as commandingly as she would have in the old days. "Oh, I don't want to hear any criticism of the President. In a one-newspaper town, that's all you get. Don't you know that?"

"Yes, Saddam is a monster who doesn't have a chance and George and Barbara will be elected again, I'm sure," snapped Theresa, "but it still doesn't make any of this right."

They sat without speaking for a few minutes, and then Polly turned off the TV.

"How's Anna?"

Her mother had never before asked about Anna (and in twelve years had met her only once, at Giovanni's funeral, when Anna had driven in for the service, sat discreetly in the last pew so as not to offend, and then driven back immediately to avoid being snubbed at the family home). Theresa was suddenly so close to tears that she could hardly speak.

"She's... fine, just fine," she said in a measured tone, but really wanting to let it all out—that Anna was so very far away; that with every day, Theresa was coming closer to losing her, losing her forever; and did her mother know (*of course she had to know, she had been married*) that even a solid relationship could be traumatically destroyed by a few perfect, venomous words—fired into the air like a heat-seeking missile. Had their official life together begun differently—with a gift registry at the May Company and an actual wedding ceremony (*that'll be the day!*), and with in-laws wishing them well from appropriate sides of the church—perhaps neither Theresa nor Anna would have found themselves thinking the unthinkable: how, now, to be alone; how, only perhaps, to stay together.

One day recently, an argument over the laundry had escalated into something horrible and scary. "Do you have to be so moody?" Anna had shouted at her. "And so controlling and so rigid and so critical!"

"I am not rigid!" Theresa had shouted back; and then they had both laughed because the other accusations were true.

More quietly, Anna had pressed on: "Sometimes I'm not sure you love me."

"I don't think I do," said Theresa abruptly, immediately regretting saying it, not even believing it, but seeing a wound open up in front of her, Anna struck silent.

"Maybe next time Anna can come and visit, too," said Polly. "I think the two of you could be very comfortable in the Ramada Inn, and we could see each other every day."

Theresa was flabbergasted that her mother had finally issued an invitation for Anna to visit and recognized that this gesture took an enormous effort. Of course, Theresa picked up on her mother's ambivalence, too: that Anna would be welcome, but only if the two of them stayed in a hotel and didn't destroy the sanctity of the family home by sleeping together (heaven forbid!) in Theresa's childhood bed. At least her mother was trying.

"I sit here, on the couch like this, every day when I'm sad, and I look out into the backyard. The grass is so nice, and I love the flowers way out back, but I wish I had a little herb garden, and maybe a brick deck, like that picture you sent of your backyard."

"So you looked at the pictures I sent all those years?" said Theresa, both startled and moved.

"Well, yes."

"Wait a minute," said Theresa, and she ran to the kitchen and returned with a silver framed photograph from her overnight bag. "Look at this, Mom."

Theresa handed her mother the photograph of her Dad, taken in 1945 at a navy base in California. Handsome in his navy uniform and standing in front of a beautiful saguaro cactus, he looked like a young Caesar Romero. His mouth was open in laughter, which is why Theresa liked the photo: she couldn't remember having ever heard her father laugh.

"He gave it to me when I graduated from high school. It's what I wanted."

Polly suddenly started sobbing and threw her arms around Theresa. "Thank you for coming back to me, thank you for coming." Theresa was shocked. Even at her father's funeral, her mother had not embraced her, and now her mother's clasp was so tight that Theresa felt smothered. And yet, the bones in her mother's shoulders and back seemed brittle, like dead perennials in late autumn, and Theresa was afraid that if she hugged her mother back too fervently, her mother would break into pieces entirely and crumble to dust.

Later, when Theresa took her mother to the cemetery, her mother was not as effusive, but reserved as she brushed away an errant blood-red leaf from her husband's headstone.

"I loved him so much, but he was a quiet man. Sometimes, when I'm blue, I drive out here and talk to your father."

And he still doesn't answer, thought Theresa. *Nothing has changed.*

"Last year, before he got really sick, we went back to Texas to look for Nanny's old farm."

"Did you find it?"

"I appreciated that he came. He only did it for me, he had no interest at all. But he wouldn't fly, we took the train."

"And did you find it?"

"No, it was like that movie. Nothing was left. I think we found the land, but the house was gone. Like it had been bombed or something. Nothing was growing. And no matter where your Dad went, he wouldn't take off his hat. Self-conscious about losing his hair, I think."

"From the radiation."

"No. From getting old. He babied that hair for the last ten years."

"Did Dad and Nanny like each other?"

"He didn't know her really. But I should never have let your father take me to Cleveland and get married. Never. I see that now. But the man does have dominion, that should be. You treat your mother right, you hear? Not how I treated mine..."

They stood there some moments without speaking.

"So did you enjoy the trip, or no?"

Polly shrugged, her mind already somewhere else. "I always wondered what divorce would be like, and I think it's easier to get through a death than a divorce. At least with death, you know that your husband is not having any more experiences, you know that there's no alternative for you. With a divorce, imagine how horrible it would be to know that you were unhappy and he was out having a new life somewhere. I would prefer being a widow to that. Better him dead, than that. At least I get comfort from my Bible. Yes, I get lots of comfort."

They drove back home in silence. Theresa was appalled by her mother's self-centered sentiments, which seemed monstrous because they had been delivered so matter-of-factly. But Theresa's mind kept wandering to Anna, too, for reasons which were all too clear. Was Theresa herself turning into a monster? Would she rather Anna be dead than gone?

Still, it had generally been a good day; and Theresa felt closer to her mother and almost happy. Very late in the evening, after her mother had gone to bed, Theresa decided to act out her autonomy from her mother by going out to a gay bar. Although Theresa had never sought out other lesbians in Cleveland, she did know where at least one bar was located: she and Anna had gone there a few times early in their relationship when Theresa was still bringing Anna into town in one failed attempt after another to convince her mother to meet her. Mingling with other lesbians in this city was always a startling adventure: what a surprise, it had always seemed to Theresa, that there were any other lesbians here at all.

This time, Theresa did not feel that sense of home she had felt the first time she had stepped into a gay bar. The smoke irritated her eyes, and her nostrils ached. What she really wanted was to be part of a cheerful family sitting on the floor around a fire in the family room, a Monopoly board in front of Mom's early American sofa and Dad's La-Z-Boy; now that would be home. If only her father and mother could have provided it! Once, at the beginning of her relationship with Anna, Theresa had insisted they play Monopoly. Anna went through the motions of playing the game, but dumbly, the whole idea of the friendly competition clearly eluding her. "What part of this is supposed to be fun?" Anna had said afterward, shortly before Theresa had packed the game away in the furthest corner of their attic.

Although the women in the bar were laughing and smiling, the liquor was flowing too freely for Theresa (who had exactly one Coke), and she was surprised by her own wave of moral disapproval—which she thought of as a genetic inheritance from her mother.

"And I can tell that you must be from out of town," said a young woman with short blond hair and a turquoise necklace, approaching Theresa.

"I what?" said Theresa, a bit startled.

"From out of town," said the woman. "You're reading the posters on the walls."

Actually, Theresa had been merely squinting into the near distance.

"And sensible shoes," said the woman. "So you're not here on business, but visiting. I'm Jane. Are you drinking something here? Visiting your mother maybe, or an ex-lover. Am I right?" she said and touched Theresa's shoulder, her hand lingering an extra moment in a clear invitation. "I pride myself on reading people. It's real turquoise. Do you want anything?"

Theresa smiled broadly. "Well I do, I guess," she answered, looking into the woman's green eyes, but then after a pause, thinking of Anna, stood up from the stool. "But I'm not drinking anything here. No. Not really."

"Not even another coke?"

"But thanks for asking," said Theresa, and then walked to the door, turning back just long enough to see that the woman was still looking at her and smiling.

When Theresa returned to her mother's home that evening (Theresa having purposely left the front door unlocked, so she would neither have to use her key nor ring the bell), she sniffed at her clothes and knew that her mother would be able to tell that she had gone out to a bar. At two o'clock in the morning, Theresa first showered, then stood in the cold basement, nearly naked, waiting impatiently for her smoky clothes to come out of the washing machine so she could put them in the dryer. Afterward, she picked up her overnight bag from the kitchen and finally took it into her old room. The bed there seemed softer and more comfortable than she remembered, and before she could even begin her characteristic habit of analyzing and re-analyzing her day, she was sinking into the desert sand, now floating above it, now sinking.

***

"So are you ready to go or not," Polly said bitterly the next morning, standing in the bedroom doorway and glaring at Theresa like a marksman training a target in his sights.

"What?" Theresa was still in bed, a little groggy.

"I've been up for several hours and I've been waiting. I'm sick and tired of all this bullcrap you put me through."

"We said ten o'clock," said Theresa, on guard by her mother's reversion to the vulgar language of the Texas farm. "It's not even nine thirty."

Her mother sniffed at the air, her arms folded in front, her mouth tense and twisted. Was the faintest smell of smoke lingering in Theresa's hair? Theresa felt like a blip locked in by her mother's radar.

"Audrey is expecting us, and Audrey always gets up at a reasonable hour."

"Well, okay," said Theresa. "Let me just brush my teeth and throw something on."

"I already told you. I'm ready now."

"Are you a little cranky this morning?" said Theresa gently.

Polly threw her purse to the floor, its contents spilling.

"Yes, I'm cranky. And I'm allowed to be. This is my house. Now pick up my purse."

She stormed out the front door, slamming it behind her.

Theresa threw on some clothes, ran to the bathroom, and brushed her teeth. Her mother's moods had always been inscrutable, her rages and tranquilities equally capricious. After briefly debating whether to put on lipstick for Audrey (no), Theresa picked up her mother's purse. The wallet had tumbled open, containing her mother's special photographs: one showing Giovanni—tight-lipped and defeated— shortly before he died; one showing Polly's favorite view of her backyard; one showing Audrey flanked by her husband and cradling her newborn Paula (named after Polly, they claimed); one, taken several years later at the K-Mart, showing the beloved granddaughter holding a teddy bear; but none showing either Theresa or Anna, not even the wallet-sized photo in front of the Christmas tree that Theresa had sent after her father's death when she had been so hopeful that everything had finally begun to change.

There was no sound in the house, save the whir of the ceiling fan, which sounded like a faraway reconnaissance helicopter. Was the TV news still on? From outside in the driveway, came the sharp honk of the car horn: once, twice, ("Alert, alert"), then again silence. The drive to Audrey's home would take only fifteen minutes, and Theresa knew that she and her mother would not speak, that the trip would carry their whole lifetime of silence together... and their father's silence, and some of the newer silence with Anna. Looking through the front-door window, Theresa could see her mother in the car: her squat figure stolidly in the passenger seat, her arms still crossed, her head shrouded in a farmer's straw hat, her gaze directed not at Theresa at the front door, but at Mrs. Ventura's maple tree next door, festooned with yellow ribbons. For eight years, Theresa had sent cheery Christmas cards, although her own heart was breaking. ("Dear Mom, I still love you and think about you. I so hope we can figure out how to come together again.") For eight years Theresa had called once a month, leaving messages on the answering machine which her mother never returned. ("Hi, Mom, I just called... well, to say I love you.") For eight years Theresa had remembered birthdays and Mother's Days (dozens of yellow roses, boxes of camellia-scented soap). For eight years Theresa had sent photographs (of herself, of Anna, and of their home together) in the hope that one day, with a shock of recognition, her mother would actually see her as a human being and Theresa's life would *matter*. And now, finally, after years of battle plans, longing, and regret, the enemy she had been stalking was in her car and it was suddenly unclear as to which of them had been trapped.

A horrible insight hit like a SCUD from Saddam Hussein: Theresa didn't like her mother and she never would.

The morning with Audrey was awful. Her four-year-old, Paula, ran about the house shrieking, which inexplicably Theresa's mother found charming.

"Don't you love her energy?" said the proud grandmother, "We're going to sign her up for swimming lessons soon." And then pointedly to Theresa: "Too bad you're not going to have children of your own."

Theresa would not be goaded into a confrontation, not even when they discussed politics, nor when her mother asked Theresa whether she and Anna had a lot of "chink" friends. That particular uncomfortable silence ended when Audrey hurried to the kitchen to serve a lunch salad with balsamic vinegar.

"Balsamic, you say?" said Polly to Audrey.

"Yeah, Mom, I bought you a bottle. It's something new. Don't let me forget to give it to you."

By the time lunch was almost finished, the precocious Paula had sensed that Theresa didn't like her and so had begun climbing onto her aunt's lap to apparently wrestle her off her chair. The first two times this happened, Audrey interceded and physically put her daughter in her baby chair on the opposite side of the table. The third time, an exasperated Audrey looked at Theresa pointedly, as if the roughhousing were Theresa's fault.

"What?" said Theresa.

"Can you stop already?" said Audrey.

"What are you talking about?"

"Do you have to let her be touching you like that?" said Audrey, who was now protectively holding Paula tightly on her lap, and then, when she saw a humiliated Theresa look away tearfully, quickly retracted. "No, not that. Not because you're that. I mean, just that without ever having children of your own, it's hard for you to know how to behave."

"No one knows how to behave these days," said Polly. "All these kooks on the talk shows. Everyone seems to think they can do whatever they want. No common sense anymore. But some ways are better than others, no matter what the media tell you."

"Oh, Mom," said Audrey, "Don't be picking on Terry like that." And then to Theresa: "Oh, did Paula show you the dolls that Grammy gave her? Maybe we can play tennis, later, Terry, would you like that? You know, I think you look younger than me. Tell me your secret."

Later that afternoon, after they had returned to the house and her mother had taken a nap, Theresa sat down in her mother's spot on the sofa and plotted her escape. She could wait until after dinner and then announce that Anna had made an emergency phone call summoning her back to Columbus. Or perhaps Theresa could make her retreat now, while her mother was still asleep, and neither of them would have to confront their feelings ever again. As she pondered, she gazed through the sliding glass door at the garden landscape beyond. The yard looked attractive, if imperfect. Though the meadow was certainly lovely, it was incredibly wet because of the drainage problem that Theresa's father had never been able to correct. The big oak tree needed a bench to set it off and give it scale. Theresa retrieved pencil and paper and started sketching a redesigned garden as a final gift for her mother. She drew the lines skillfully: first the drainage tiles, then the bench. Multi-colored brick on the cold patio would give warmth to the backyard—and then a curved brick walkway to the bench and back flowerbed, and perhaps here they could put the herb garden her mother had always wanted, and flank it with perennials, and even some roses. Here could be some bulbs: yellow daffodils to remind her mother of her old Texas home, and some grape hyacinths, favorites of her father. And in the mornings, with the sun rising, her mother could sit on the bench and finish her coffee while Theresa serenaded her with the Chinese flute, its melodies calling to the birds. Engrossed in her work, Theresa had hardly been aware that three hours had passed until her mother called suddenly from the doorway.

"What are you doing?"

Theresa whirled her head, feeling for a moment as if caught in some forbidden act. Relaxing, she offered her mother the sketches.

"Maybe next spring I can do it for you if you like. Anna and I can come down and do it for you."

Her mother looked at the drawings carefully without saying anything, and then, when Theresa moved aside, sat down in her usual spot on the sofa and looked out at the backyard, staring for a long time, as if in a trance.

"Yes, I can see it," said her mother slowly, "It could be very beautiful."

Charles Derry (he/him) born in Cleveland, taught film studies at Wright State University in Dayton for over 30 years. His books include Dark Dreams 2.0: A Psychological History of the Modern Horror Film and The Suspense Thriller: Films in the Shadow of Alfred Hitchcock. Derry's fiction/memoir include works in The Portland Literary Review, Writers' Forum, Harrington Gay Men's Fiction Quarterly, and the anthologies Contra/Dictions, Reclaiming the Heartland, and Our Naked Lives. "Ten Memories of My Mother, in the Order I Think of Them," a Pushcart Prize nominee and Heidemann Award finalist, appeared in The Chattahoochee Review. He is especially proud of his cancer memoir, "A Year Like Any Other," in The Sun. He has also directed and written plays and films.

RAPTURE
by Ed Davis

Ruth shuddered and clutched Serenity's waist tighter, fearing that her friend, now emitting tiny wails, might crumple to the sidewalk if she let go. Fortunately, few people were out and about in Shawnee Springs on this nippy late-September overcast Friday morning to stare. Ruth was furious at the shopkeeper who'd just gone off on the girl—at twenty-five, that's what Serenity seemed, compared to Ruth, almost sixty.

Steering Serenity toward her apartment, Ruth recalled how, back in April, she'd met her in Glenora Wood's pine forest. The girl had become too paralyzed by grief to walk the rest of the way to the site of her husband's suicide. She'd trusted Ruth enough to guide her the rest of the way. After that, Ruth had practically adopted the waif whose body she was now holding as close as she would've her own pre-teen daughter poised on womanhood. If she'd had a daughter.

Yes, the old hippie at Arjuna Imports had lost his lover, but it'd been three decades ago! The guy acted like it had happened yesterday. He'd minimized Serenity's losses by exalting his own— never acceptable.

Ruth had been widowed 18 months ago and on good days, she felt progress; on bad, the loss hissed like a fuse from her gut to her head, laying her out in bed or sometimes even on the floor, for hours, maybe the rest of the day. Why did the experts she'd read insist on calling grief that lasted more than a year "extreme?" Why was there a limit?

Finally, they were only steps away from Ruth's building across from the elementary school. Kids' gleeful shrieks grated against the memory of the Grief Monster they'd just encountered. Up the stairs and they'd be safe.

Inside the apartment, Ruth helped Serenity out of her jacket. On the way, she'd decided on a course of action to bring her friend out of her shell-shocked stupor.

"Sweetie, how about a nice hot bath? Doesn't that sound good?"

The girl shrugged, eyes on the rug. The shopkeeper's verbal assault seemed to have temporarily robbed her of speech. Soap and water would help; it sure couldn't hurt. She helped Serenity into the bathroom, closing the door to lock in the heat, and began running hot water.

"Go ahead and undress," she said. Within moments, the girl stepped into the shallow pool and sat down.

"I feel like that guy spit on me," she murmured. "Would you wash my hair, Ruth?"

Yes! That sounded like the Serenity she'd come to know the past five months. Since meeting, they'd gotten together often at restaurants, cafes, and parks. But she'd never invited her new friend here. Ruth's love-hate relationship with solitude couldn't be explained; before widowhood, she'd been outgoing. These days she mostly wanted to be alone.

"You bet, hon."

After nudging the girl's head forward, Ruth scooped palmfuls of water onto her thick strawberry-blonde mane. The sound Serenity made could've been a sob or a sigh. Plucking up the Sweet Annie shampoo she'd bought yesterday at Herbal Solutions—on a whim because she liked the kick-ass-looking granny on the tube—she applied a huge glob. Within moments, the air was redolent of spice. Whatever herb was in the shampoo had to be the most wondrous substance on the planet. It allowed Ruth to enter an altered state, not her first experience with things not actually present since her husband's death. Once, before she'd left forever the home they'd shared, Mike had appeared over her shoulder while she stood at the bathroom mirror brushing her hair, his big hands poised to grasp her shoulders as he used to, telling her what he had planned for that day. Then he'd vanished. It hadn't happened since she'd moved here and she was mostly glad.

While Ruth's fingers did their job, she closed her eyes and saw another face, hair, and eyes: a laughing girl with auburn curls and threads of green in her eyes. Nanette O'Brien. Something in this steamy bathroom had returned Ruth to the night at the abandoned garage, when she and her best friend had smoked the joint Nan had stolen from her brother. Nan's family was moving to Oregon in two days. Both seventeen, she and Nan had been inseparable all summer. At first, the weed seemed to have no effect, but when her friend started giggling, Ruth did, too, which led to Nan snorting, cracking Ruth up. The night was drenched in an aroma she'd hardly noticed earlier. It rose and filled her head as if she'd entered a glorious garden. Sweet Annie! It had to've been the same herb in the shampoo she was now kneading into Serenity's scalp.

Closing her eyes, Ruth saw herself impossibly young, with a long life ahead of her, huddled with Nan in the shadows of that old garage. After they'd smoked the joint to a nub, things took a more serious turn. Pre-empting memory, Ruth grabbed the plastic cup she kept on the tub and began filling and dousing until the soap was gone, leaving the girl before her gasping and, Ruth hoped, returning from where she'd been since the shopkeeper's tirade.

"I'll leave you to it now," Ruth said. "Take as much time as you need."

After drying her hands, she opened the door and stepped into the hallway's cooler air. Touching her own cheek, she felt the humidity, like warm tears. Something big had just happened. Its presence gleamed deep within. Following Mike's funeral, she'd returned to their old country house, collapsed onto the oriental rug in the living room, and pleaded to die. Now she forced her mind away from the ghastly memory and back to the girl—no, woman—in her bathroom and wondered, for the first time, what Nan O'Brien would look like now. Imagination failed her. Her childhood friend remained in her memory a teenager forever, making fun of every adult in their tiny town, devouring hot dogs slathered in ketchup and sprinkled with a thick coating of pepper, drinking Mr. Mistys at Dairy Queen.

Food! She would feed Serenity. A good veggie soup, that's what her own mother, dead these last 15 years, would make in such a situation. Thank God Ruth had shopped yesterday and had

everything she'd need. But first, she walked to the bathroom door
and knocked. "I'm going to make soup. Why don't you lie down in
the bedroom when you're finished? I'll call you when it's ready."

The girl's cheerful voice echoed loudly through the door: "That
sounds awesome! I can't thank you enough."

Ruth leaned against the wall, shakily. Even though this day's
events were wreaking havoc with her solitude, she wouldn't trade it
for the emptier ones preceding it.

While she cooked, the memory of Nanette O'Brien returned.
After their giggles fizzled out on their last night together, Nan had
seized Ruth's hand and with her other pointed up to the huge rosy-
gold moon. Gazing skyward, lips parted in a gasp, she felt Nan's
breath on her cheek just before her best friend's lips brushed hers
and she inhaled the Juicy Fruit Nan had chewed earlier to mask
the weed. Nan's eyes, when she stepped back, flashed a challenge.
Although Ruth didn't speak, she must've somehow conveyed assent.
Coming closer, Nan covered Ruth's mouth with her own. They held
the illicit kiss for a long time while katydids kicked up a ruckus and
Sweet Annie perfumed the night.

It ended too soon.

Afterward, they'd talked a little more, cried, hugged, and finally
parted. Within days, the best person Ruth had ever known was
gone forever. Now, forty-five years later, had the steam rising from
Serenity's bathwater, possessing the exact scent of that August night,
revived what she'd felt? And what had she felt? Excitement at doing
something her parents would name taboo, yes—but . . . something
more? She couldn't remember.

She'd married a good man and lived more or less happily, except
for not having children. His reasons—not in this hard world, not
given the rough childhood he'd had, blah blah blah—weren't
Ruth's. She'd let him decide for them both. At thirty, he'd gotten
a vasectomy. Her uterus had been cut out years ago. Why hadn't
she stood up to him? Was it guilt that made her enduring grief
extreme—because she'd felt oppressed in her marriage? But while
she may have been oppressed, she hadn't felt oppressed—the

distinction mattered. And now here was this girl reminding her of her first real kiss. What might it mean? Passion?

"Give me a break!" she muttered. Her knife thunked hard on the cutting board, severing the carrot she gripped with the other hand as if it had tried to escape. She glanced around to see if Mike might be lurking nearby, judging. But no. Whatever this was about, she didn't need his help. And she would not let her memory affect her relationship with the girl in the bathroom, her first real female friendship in years—no, decades.

By the time Ruth heard the bedroom door creak open, the soup was emitting thick aromatic steam, fogging the windows. Also, the timer was ticking for the serviceberry pie in the oven, made with frozen fruit she'd plucked last summer from trees at the edge of the schoolyard. She'd been aware when Serenity had left the bathroom and padded softly into the bedroom. Now, bending toward the stove to ensure the crust wasn't getting overdone, Ruth sensed movement behind her, shut the oven door, and half-turned. When arms surrounded her from behind, she stiffened. Had Serenity overheard her thoughts? Stifling the fear before it could sink roots into her heart, she turned to face her friend.

"Feeling better, hon?"

"Yes! Lots." Serenity grinned mischievously. "What do you call the color of your bedroom wall?"

Ruth reddened. She'd grown so used to it that she'd forgotten that, right after moving in, she'd painted her bedroom orangey-yellow in a doomed attempt to cheer herself upon awakening. She'd've warned the girl but didn't even notice the color anymore.

"Rapture," she confessed. "To distract me from dark thoughts."

Serenity studied the kitchen tile.

"What that guy in the store said . . ."

"Forget it, hon. He's a selfish prick."

Disengaging, Ruth leaned against the stove. Serenity's cheeks glowed, her wet hair gleaming in the late-morning light. It had felt silken in Ruth's hands; she would've liked to touch it again.

"Can you imagine," the girl marveled, "still having that much pain after thirty years?"

Amazingly, Ruth could. She heard the shopkeeper's voice, "What if you'd found your lover in his dorm room spread out on the bed like Christ on the cross, totally bled out?"—and felt her face burn as she imagined a comeback: What if the world had denied you the possibility of even naming your lover?

"Then he should've gotten professional help years ago," Ruth said.

When Serenity smiled, it was a sight to behold. Without her glasses, her eyes weren't brown but hazel, exactly the color of Nan's, whose green flecks had complimented her auburn curls.

"That's the therapist speaking."

"Ex-therapist," Ruth retorted, stirring the pot. She hated when her counselor side showed up, unbidden, reminding her of her failure to save everyone in her last job as an addiction counselor.

"Well, he should've, yeah, but you know how most men are. Brian wouldn't, either. Only wimps get therapy, not real war veterans."

Serenity stood close enough to touch Ruth's shoulder, the scent of Sweet Annie lingering in the girl's hair. When she leaned forward, Ruth flinched, half-expecting to feel lips on her cheek. Serenity bent close to the stove, removed the lid, and inhaled deeply, eyes closed.

"Therapy in a pot!" Serenity reopened her eyes and grinned. "What's in the oven?"

"Serviceberry pie. My grandmother's recipe."

"I love berry pie!"

Her enthusiasm sounded exactly like Nan's.

While they'd eaten, Serenity confided a lot that she hadn't before. Because Brian had committed suicide, there was no insurance money. She had zero job skills, had never worked, dropping out of high school to marry. She was taking classes to get a GED so she could attend community college. If she didn't get a job, a real job—waitressing at Country Kitchen didn't cut it—she'd have to find somewhere cheaper to live, maybe get a roommate.

She'd already told Ruth many times about her dead father and estranged mother who'd wanted "Frilly Frou-Frou but got a tomboy instead." They hadn't spoken in years.

While Serenity talked, Ruth had another crazy thought: You can stay here. For now, though, she kept it to herself and kept listening.

"We were trying to have a baby before Brian offed himself." Serenity dabbed at her eyes. "I'd already started buying baby clothes—what was I thinking!? Then there's Brian's clothes in the closet. I thought I'd taken them all to Goodwill but found the old brown suit he'd worn to his granddad's funeral blended in with my dresses. It smelled like the cologne he used—El Diablo. I pitch things and pitch things, but they never go away! How can that be, Ruth?"

"I know, sweetie, I know."

Ruth hadn't been able to touch Mike's teal Telecaster sitting on its stand in his study for weeks. The vintage guitar was too valuable to give away. In its case, it took up way too much space in her one tiny closet. She'd piled all his clothes into several large garbage bags and hauled them away, only to find his hiking boots in the garage the next day. She'd broken down and had to go sleep it off. Serenity sniffed into a tissue and spoke.

"At the morgue when I had to identify the body, I thought he'd look awful. But they had his head all wrapped, so I couldn't see where the bullet entered, and the rest of him looked so young, so perfect. He didn't have much body hair. Naked, he looked like a little boy."

Now, as Serenity cried in earnest, Ruth stroked her hand.

"Do you want to stay here tonight, hon?" She whispered as if someone might overhear and disapprove. Screw that. She sat up straighter. "You can have the bed and I'll take the couch."

"That's so sweet of you! But I can't miss class tonight. Actually—" She glanced at the clock above the stove. "I should probably get going."

"Not yet. You've just had a glass of wine. Go in the living room and put something on the stereo while I clean up. I'll join you in just a few."

She expected the girl to argue, and took it for a good sign when she didn't. Maybe, Ruth thought, she could work up the courage to offer her more than an overnighter. Was she actually willing to surrender her solitude? She would see . . .

While she washed the dishes, the sound of Cyndi Lauper's "Time After Time" wafted into the kitchen. At the chorus, Ruth smiled: being lost, being found; falling, and being caught just then seemed the aural equivalent of what Sweet Annie promised.

Walking into the living room, Ruth found her guest gazing out the window.

"You know," the girl said, "I could imagine that shopkeeper wanting to kill himself after we left."

"Nah," Ruth replied as casually as possible. "He probably gobsmacks people like that with his grief all the time."

Turning, Serenity wore a determined look. "No, I think he recognized us as fellow survivors. His words were almost religious."

Ha! Blasphemy was more like it. But Ruth didn't say it. Maybe if the girl kept talking, she'd find something healing in this new take. Meanwhile, maybe Ruth could screw up the courage to make her offer, shaky as it made her feel. Serenity's chin drooped as she studied the faded oriental rug. Weak sunlight leaked between the curtains, illuminating a patch that looked like crossed scimitars. When, after many seconds, the girl lifted her head, the bottom of her face was illuminated, her jaw tight.

"I've made it all about me, Ruth. I thought the guy only wanted to wield his pain as power. So, I weaponized my own grief against him—even after he apologized." Ruth was startled when Serenity slammed her fist into her other palm. "Dammit, I may have killed another man!"

The words transported Ruth back to One Day House, huddled up with yet another PTSD victim whose chronic pain no drug, legal or illegal, could reach, regardless of the amount ingested: a human being between whose death and some semblance of acceptance she'd stood. This time, though, she knew better than to trust words alone.

Approaching Serenity as if she were a feral kitten that might run, Ruth laid hands on her slight shoulders, guided her to the flowered couch and coaxed her to sit. After a moment, she stroked the silky golden hair, eventually touching her downy cheek. The delicate hairs seemed to rise as if magnetically to meet Ruth's fingers.

A tingling had begun deep within her belly—her womb, if she'd had one. The girl laid her head against Ruth's thigh as she continued to stroke. Outside, a distant chainsaw, toot of a semi out on Route 86, crow's distant squawk, said that life went on out there, while in here everything waited, like a water droplet gathering enough substance to fall from the faucet.

At last, gravity did what it does. Serenity moved over and drew Ruth down beside her, sharing the widening shaft of light now dissolving the girl's features except for a glimmer of smile, on her parted lips. A great patience had descended (more gravity). Ruth saw them as children in a garden at serious play, dolls abandoned in favor of what was rising within, impossible to name since, in her fantasy, they were too young to have ever felt anything like it. Without adult intervention, they were free to explore this new enchantment in the surreal pale light.

When Serenity extended her hand to touch Ruth's face, she let both of hers relax into her lap. Her friend's fingers smelled sweetly of Merlot and serviceberries. Ruth's abdominal tingle had moved higher into her stomach, now glowing warmly. She banished the impulse to define what she felt, intuiting that, for what was happening to unfold, she'd need to proceed without labels, without language. Serenity's hand retreated into shadow as she moved closer, her thighs hard against Ruth's.

Leaning in, the girl touched her winey lips to the tip of Ruth's ear: a puff of breath, then gone. Ruth shuddered and closed her eyes, whether, from ecstasy or fear, she hardly knew which. Blessedly, Mike was nowhere to be seen. Serenity drew back a few inches. Ruth recalled how, back in April, standing on the Horace Mann statue's pedestal together, the girl had trusted her enough to let Ruth seize her hand and leap into the air. They'd landed where she'd've never predicted.

Ruth's hands now rose as if on puppeteer's strings to draw Serenity closer, the girl's silhouette blocking the sun. Ruth's lips found hers and their breath mingled, in, out, to exactly the same rhythm. As their tongues conjoined, the tingle now flared inside Ruth's mind, igniting every cell and synapse. The meeting of flesh and nerve lasted a lifetime or two before the girl finally retreated. The kiss left Ruth nearly blinded. Serenity suddenly stood.

"I gotta get to class, Ruthie."

A new name! Ruth liked it a lot. Somehow it implied a future in which she found what, in her solitude, she'd been missing. She rose to hug her friend before closing the door and turning to face emptiness. She promised herself she'd ask Serenity to move in when they met again.

When her cell phone buzzed a few days later, Ruth was breathlessly ascending one of the limestone cliffs in Glenora Wood. Answering, she heard unrestrained excitement in Serenity's voice.

"I can't make it tonight."

Well damn. The girl had put her off for over a week. Tonight, Ruth had planned to cook her veggie lasagna that Mike had so loved and pop the question, inviting her to move in.

"You won't believe who called me," the girl added in that voice of innocence and awe that made her smile. But now Ruth found herself suddenly breathless and unable to speak, though she'd been fine a moment ago. She struggled to the summit and gazed into the valley, wondering, perversely, how it would feel to fall and smash onto the rocks. She sucked down a shallow breath.

"So . . . who called you?"

"Would you believe it—my mom!"

"But I thought you—"

"Yes, yes we were—but she's gotten sober, and she apologized for, like, everything! And she says I can live with her as long as I need to."

"But when—"

"I'm already here, in Cincinnati! Her condo's huge."

Widening her stance, Ruth put the hand not holding the phone on her waist to steady herself. She strove to keep her voice from shaking.

"But . . . your GED?"

"I'm pretty sure I can finish down here. Meantime, Mom thinks I can get a good job while I decide what to do next."

Has Mom not heard about the recession?

"Sweetheart, I'm so happy for you," Ruth lied.

"Thanks! I told Mom about you, and she wants to meet you sometime. Maybe we could meet halfway and have lunch?"

Meet the alkie who'd abandoned her daughter and would probably do so again when she relapsed? Fortunately, Ruth's inner therapist stepped up.

"That'd be great, sweetie."

"Oh goody!"

Ruth could almost imagine Serenity, in her excitement, falling off the chair she was sitting on. But maybe it was a couch. She imagined the girl beside her on her couch, lips still wet, sliding away to the other end, out of the sunlight, into shadow.

"Listen, Ruth, I've gotta go—Mom and I are going shopping—but I'll call again. Before I go, though, I want to say that you helped me so much. You brought me back from the edge."

The creek below gleamed like a big curling snake of fire. Though the light was blinding, Ruth didn't avert her gaze.

"I love you, Ruth."

Ruth dropped to the ground like a sack of potatoes. Finally, she found her voice:

"Not in the way I need." The words had emerged without her permission. But there they were. A long pause before the girl spoke again in her tiniest voice, coming from deep space:

"I realize that . . . and I'm sorry."

"Don't be. We pooled our grief for a time. We moved forward—how lucky is that?"

Then Ruth segued into absolution mode. The path of parental

reconciliation, she knew from her clients' experience, was a perilous one. Her job as a counselor was now to wish her "client" Godspeed. Which she did. But she needed to end this conversation before she melted down completely. When the call ended, Ruth hoped she hadn't sounded as insincere, cold even, to Serenity as she'd sounded to herself. But she was pretty sure the girl knew there'd be no reason to call again. One mother was enough.

Ruth half-expected Mike to be waiting for her at home, to point a finger and say young girls are fickle, but he was nowhere to be seen. After eating a carrot with a spoonful of peanut butter, Ruth fell into a deep, thankfully dreamless sleep.

She woke to find early dawn light leaking through the blinds, illuminating the bright wall. Rapture. Yeah, right. Getting up to pee, she glanced into the living room at the couch, where, for a minute or two, she'd felt so alive. Returning to bed, she pulled the blinds tighter and slept again until almost noon.

After eating a bowl of leftover oatmeal, Ruth roamed the apartment, standing at the front window, unseeing; pacing from kitchen to living room, to bedroom and back, then beginning again. At one point, she aimlessly turned on the stereo, but when Cyndi Lauper started singing, she quickly shut it off. Finally, she dragged herself to the computer, unable to put it off any longer, and began the Google search.

As soon as she typed in Nanette Aileen O'Brien, she stopped. Surely, her old mate had a different last name now? Ruth hit return anyway and there it was, the past beckoning.

She moved to the couch, phone in hand, breathing fast, sinuses burning. With quivering fingers, she punched in the numbers she'd memorized.

"Hello?"

How could you know from just that one word? But she did.

"Nan? This is Ruth—"

"Ruth Ferguson! Oh my God!"

"Your name hasn't changed?"

"Nope. I'm the same old Mick. I've waited a long time to hear from you, girl."

"Almost a lifetime."

Nan's laugh soared. "We may be old, but we're not dead!"

In the silence after, Ruth heard through the liquid hiss of their distant connection the sound of the ocean. Plus, she thought she smelled stolen weed and Sweet Annie rising up from the cushions. Before she could speak, Nan did.

"So, when are you coming to see me?"

It was all happening so fast, Ruth felt light-headed.

"Where are you?"

"Louisville, Kentucky."

"Just three hours away!"

"Imagine that."

The watery hiss continued. Static interference, of course, but it sounded like Nan was drawing a bath or washing dishes, maybe even frying chicken in an iron skillet. Ruth spoke louder to be heard above the noise.

"Actually, I was thinking more along the lines of a joint?"

Nan snorted, just like she used to. "You mean a doobie, ganja, Mary Jane . . . boo!"

"You remember?"

For a few heart-stopped moments, Ruth heard no more sea sounds, nothing. Finally, just when she felt herself being sucked beneath the surf . . .

"Yeah, I remember. God, I remember!"

Ruth exhaled in a rush.

"Are you single, Nan?"

"Yes. You?"

"Widowed. Eighteen months ago."

A big sigh. "Oh, honey. I'll hold you, you can cry."

She hadn't said get over it. But the hiss was back, a mystery how it came and went, carrying them along like two kayaks in a creek. Now, in the pause between their voices, as she concentrated, Ruth realized it was not the ocean she'd been hearing but the braided waterfall at the end of the lower bridge in Glenora Wood. Her beloved had always been that close.

"I'm cried out," Ruth finally said. "I want to laugh."

"Not a problem, hon. We'll have everything we need to make you laugh. So, when are you coming?"

"Tomorrow?"

"The wine will be chilled and waiting. Red or white?"

Their connection was now as clear as prayer in a hushed church.

"Red," Ruth whispered, then louder so even the walls could hear: "Definitely red."

Ed Davis' (he/him) novel The Psalms of Israel Jones (West Virginia University Press 2014) won the Hackney Award for an unpublished novel in 2010. Many of his stories, essays, and poems have appeared in anthologies and journals such as Write Launch, Hawaii Pacific Review, The Plenitudes, and Slippery Elm. His story "Secret o' Life" appeared in the Ohio Writers' Association's 2023 House of Secrets anthology. He lives with his wife in the village of Yellow Springs, Ohio.

HER FAVORITE TIME OF YEAR
by Emily Jones

They say that love can overcome anything, and I believe it. Martha and I are living proof of that. Through all the hardships of the past few years, our love has sustained us, given succor to our weary spirits, and we needed every bit of it to get us through since the accident.

I looked up from a hearty pile of scrambled eggs and bacon, courtesy of Mitch Connell's farm down the road, and smiled warmly at Martha across the kitchen table. She was just as beautiful as the day we had met four years ago, maybe more so. The fresh, country air agreed with her.

"The fall colors are really exploding right now. Maybe we could go for a drive later," I suggested.

She didn't respond. She couldn't. The accident had robbed her of her speech, but I could still see the twinkle of excitement in her eyes at my words. I reached across the table and gave her hand a gentle squeeze. "Great! We'll head out in a bit." I released her hand and used my fork to pick up a steaming bite of egg. "I need to do some work after breakfast, but then I promise you I'm yours the rest of the day."

When I had cleaned my plate, I sat back in my chair, shooting a meaningful look at Martha's plate. "Can we try the toast again?"

Martha could make feeding time very difficult when she wanted to, and it seemed that lately, she always wanted to. We were down to toast as the only acceptable option for most meals, and even then, it was a struggle. I picked up the plain, scratchy bread and brought it up to her mouth, but my hopes were quickly dashed. I could tell from the rigid set of her lips that this was one of those times when she wanted to be difficult. It wouldn't do any good to try to change her mind. When she didn't want to eat, she didn't want to eat.

I dropped the toast back on her plate and held my hands up in surrender. "Alright. Alright. I'll give up, but you need to start eating more."

I studied her face, looking for a muscle twitch or something to indicate she had heard and understood me. Nothing. The only sound in the room was the ticking of the rooster clock over the kitchen sink, and a sense of helplessness stabbed my gut.

I stood up and grabbed both of our plates before heading to the kitchen. After I had cleaned up, I got Martha into her favorite easy chair in the living room positioned where she could both look outside the picture window and at our modest-sized television, although she didn't seem to pay much attention to either these days. Once I had her settled, I put on her shows and gave her a peck on the cheek.

"I'll be as fast as I can, and then we'll go for that drive," I said as I pulled a blanket from the nearby couch and draped it over her lap. I had done what I could to keep her comfortable and entertained, and so I left to tend to the farm.

The dimly lit barn with its sweet smell of dry hay was a welcome change from the somber mood in the house. I took a moment to close my eyes and listen to the world around me, the buzz of insects, the chirping of birds, the sounds of life connecting me to something larger, something greater than the struggles Martha and I faced in the private sanctuary of our home. Reluctantly, I opened my eyes. I couldn't treat Martha later if I didn't get my chores done, and there were so many chores. I had cover crops to plant and winter squash to harvest, and I would have to do it all with the ATV because I still hadn't gotten the damn tractor fixed.

I'm ashamed to admit it, but I didn't think of Martha again until well after lunchtime. When I realized what I had done, mostly because the gurgling of my own stomach had become impossible to ignore, I quickly packed up and ran to the house.

She was just as I had left her. It was difficult to tell if she was distressed by my extended absence, and I assumed the worst. I got down on my knees and held her flaccid hand in mine. I promised I would never leave her for so long again. I made several heartfelt apologies. Finally, I realized she probably wanted food more than she wanted an, "I'm sorry," and I got busy making lunch.

I quickly checked the weather on my phone to confirm that there was still no rain in the forecast this afternoon. You can never be too careful. In Martha's condition, moisture is the enemy. I chatted while I made sandwiches, keeping my voice light and upbeat. "We should grab some pumpkins while we're out today. What do you think we should carve?" I paused, giving her time to think. "What about a werewolf this year? I think the kids would really like that."

We put a lot of effort into our jack-o-lanterns, and it made our home a popular spot on Beggar's Night. Our full-sized candy bars didn't hurt either. It was one of the few joys Martha had, watching through the picture window in the living room as kids paraded up to our doorstep in their bright, festive costumes, their voices filled with excitement as they shouted, "Trick or treat!"

This was Martha's favorite time of year, and we were going to do what we always did, make the most of it. I settled Martha in the car, tucking a pair of sunglasses over her ears to protect her sensitive eyes from the sun before shutting her door. Once we were both settled, I drove down the long, gravel driveway and pulled out onto the highway headed toward town.

On the way, we passed the truck stop where Martha and I first met, and I felt a surge of bittersweet nostalgia. The first time I saw her she had been passed out in a patch of grass near the edge of the parking lot, plastic cups and wrappers scattered irreverently around her unconscious body from the overflowing trash can nearby. While sitting in my car observing the scene, I witnessed several men glance over at the unfortunate woman before continuing to their vehicles. It had been clear to me that no one cared about her, and so I decided to do something about it.

After pulling the brim of my ballcap down to obscure my face, I walked nonchalantly to the edge of the parking lot, picked her up, and put her in the backseat of my car. I had kept expecting someone to yell at me or say something, but no one did. To this day, I am still shocked that no one stopped me, a guy carrying an unconscious woman to his car.

Things were difficult at first. I wasn't prepared for the ugliness of detox, and sometimes, she seemed to be completely out of her mind. It took two full days before she would even tell me her name. Martha. Years later, I can still remember the rush of elation I felt in that moment when she spoke her name to me for the first time. I had gone to bed that night knowing that she was the only woman for me.

Not long after the high of that moment, the accident happened. I had thought we were past the worst of the mania and delusions. I had let my guard down. And I had been wrong. Martha had an episode in the middle of the night, one of the worst ones yet. We struggled, and she was left in her current condition. In trying to save her, I had left her entombed in her own body. The road to hell is paved with good intentions.

I glanced over at her to see if there was any flicker of recognition or reaction as we passed, but it was too hard to read her when I was driving. I focused my eyes back on the road and made a promise to myself yet again that I would give her the best life possible. So, we got caramel apple milkshakes, and I described the flavors to her as her own milkshake sat untouched. We drove through the countryside, basking in the splendor of autumn. Toward the end of our journey, we stopped at a farm stand to buy some pumpkins, and I presented each one to Martha for her inspection before loading them in the back.

Satisfied, we drove home, and her silence felt lighter, happier. Hopeful to continue this sense of goodwill, I placed a few of the pumpkins on the kitchen island and made dinner while Martha sat at the table watching me cook. Although she refused the mashed potatoes and Salisbury steak I had whipped up, I was pleased to see she made more an effort with her toast. It was progress.

When our shows ended for the night, I carefully placed Martha on the seat of the chair lift and strapped her in, waiting until she had traveled all the way to the bottom of the basement steps before following her down. With an efficiency that comes with practice, I got her into the wheelchair and rolled her over to the custom-built freezer. Bracing my aching back, I lifted her up and gently placed her in her icy bed atop the gingham quilt my mother gave to me long ago. Once she was safely nestled inside, I brushed a few stray hairs out of her face and kissed her forehead.

"Sleep well, my love," I whispered before closing the lid. Modern embalming techniques have come a long way, but I still felt it was best for Martha to sleep down here, even though that left me alone in our bed, staring at the space she should have occupied. It was a minor discomfort. We had already proven that our love could burn through the darkest of times. I could and would bear any discomfort for the privilege of getting another day with Martha.

Alone in my room that night as my thoughts drifted closer and closer to the absurdity of dreams, I thought of Martha. Martha and I, we were going to stand the test of time. Nothing, and I mean nothing, could ever tear us apart.

Emily Jones (she/her) lives in Ohio with her husband and three children. She received her B.A. in philosophy from The Ohio State University. Emily has been published in Altered Reality Magazine, Dark Fire Fiction, and the Ohio Writers' Association, and she produced, contributed to, and developmentally edited the award-winning Outcasts: An Anthology through the Ohio Writers' Association. On occasion, she has dabbled in the darker arts known as horror with "Her Favorite Time of Year" on Day 26 of the Creepy Podcast's 2024 31 Days of Horror. You can learn more about Emily and her work with the online fantasy and science fiction blog The Worlds Within at theworldswithin.net.

DAISY

by Brienne Daugherty

I'm high as fuck the first time I see her. That's why I mistake that whole "world stops turning" feeling. It's like everything in my periphery slows to a crawl and my eyes can only focus on her.

They slide up her slender legs, tan from too much time outside. She's tall, narrow-waisted with a harsh face. There's something different about her and at first, I can't put my finger on it. Then it comes to me—there's a certain pluckiness about her. A childlike joy glimmering in her eyes and cheeks. I can't tear my eyes away from it.

I can tell she's a punk like me, her black combat boots a dead giveaway, but she's paired them with an ill-fitting pale pink dress dotted with daisies. Her crimson hair frames her face in long, loose curls, but there's something just a little bit off about it.

This is a girl who knows The Ramones, The Clash, The Dead Kennedys. This kind of girl could kick it with the guys and meet your parents. She smiles.

When we make eye contact, I swear I can see into her soul. It's not the pot, I promise. She's just—everything I have ever wanted. I know, I know that sounds like a lot for a first glance, but I'm telling you. You just know.

We stand there like that, the two of us connected for I don't know how long. Occasionally she tucks a strand of hair behind her ear or smooths her dress with her palms. I move this way and that, soaking in every angle of her. Somehow, I know this'll be my only encounter with her for a long time. I have to say something.

She moves closer.

I smile.

Annoyed footsteps stomp down the hall outside my room.

I open my mouth to speak.

She extends her hand toward me.

"Hi, I'm Daisy," I whisper.

My fingertips gently brush against the glass.

"Robert!" Mom calls up the stairs in an exasperated voice, "Have you seen your sister's Easter dress?"

I hang my head. This was always gonna be the outcome. I just wanted a little longer. I hang my head knowing what I have to do.

Unzipping, I step out of the dress and remove my sister's old Ariel wig. My fingertips glide over the smooth, synthetic strands as I indulge myself in a single, lingering moment. I yank my jeans back on and toss a tee shirt over my head.

"Robert!" my mother calls again.

It'll be a long time before I see her again. But I'm looking forward to the next time we meet.

Two sets of feet march up the stairs followed by an angry knock. I place the mattress back down and wad the dress up in my fist.

"Come in," I say, remembering to snuff out my joint at the last second and tossing it into the drawer of my nightstand.

Mom enters, followed closely by Angela.

"He does have my dress!" she wails, pointing over Mom's shoulder.

"Why do you have her dress, Robert?" Mom asks, pinching the space between her eyes.

"We were out of toilet paper in the bathroom!" I shout.

I mime wiping my ass with the dress, tossing it in Angela's direction.

She hops back instinctively before realizing it was a joke as I clutch my sides with fake laughter. Angela glares at me and we exchange fingers.

"That's enough," Mom says, "Robert you're the older brother I expect you to be more mature than this. Quit harassing your sister."

I roll my eyes but agree that I will.

After they've gone I lay down on my bed, smiling to myself as the lyrics to Sheena is a Punk Rocker weave their way through my brain.

I close my eyes, recalling the memory of her.

She had to break away

I start to drift off into the best dream I've had in a while.

Sheena is a punk rocker
Sheena is a punk rocker

The music follows me into my dream where Joey Ramone is giving the concert of his life from the center of a stage that seems to have been planted in a field full of waving daisies.

Sheena is a punk rocker, now

I spread my arms wide, and dance.

Brienne Daugherty (she/her) received her B.A. in English literature from Ohio Dominican University. Her goal is to craft stories that either heal or traumatize the reader. She self-published her first novel, a body-horror called Fat Phobia, in 2023. She lives in rural Ohio with her husband, two kiddos, and three grumpy cats. To see more of her work visit www.briennedaugherty.com.

NAKED AF

by Paisha Thomas

…is how he answered the door. Here's what happened:

When I got to the motel room that Elder Cooper had rented to meet with me, I knocked on the door. I should have stopped right then and gone home, but there I was. He opened the door. He was butt-ass naked.

Now I had to screw. I would leave that night, pregnant by my pastor with my second daughter Christian, and having contracted bacterial vaginosis.

I somehow felt it was my fault that he opened the door naked. Like I had caused him to believe I would consent to sex with him just because we were meeting at the Knights Inn. Yes, any mature adult should be able to surmise that meeting a man in a hotel room means that they are expecting sex.

I had just imagined a little more nuance. I assumed we would sit down and talk and then I would be able to make a decision after I assessed my best chance to leave there with as little conflict as possible. There was a time when I blamed myself for thinking it would be easy for me to choose whether or not I wanted to follow through but in the moment I felt obligated.

When I was young, and maybe also still now as a full-grown granny, I sought validation and acceptance in each and every way. Church seemed to do something for me back then. I was faithful. We went to church damn near every day.

I was a young woman with a sex drive. This reality did not fit well with the one in which I was saved and sanctified. Filled with the holy ghost, fire baptized, etc. No. The Lord wants you to save yourself for marriage. Be a shame if he came back in the middle of the night and I'm laid up on top of some guy getting my orgasm. And you know that he don't forgive unconfessed sin. I drove myself crazy in the cycle of sin and confession. Getting married didn't stop me from sinning, though. I was messed up. Broken. Naive.

In 1994, Né and I finally had our first apartment, and I was
ready to find her a new dad since she had asked me if she had one.
Tony Williams was fresh out of his first marriage, and this was the
first one for me. We had met at a district church council young
people's meeting. Tony was the youth president for the Southern
Ohio district.

I was singing in the district choir which was seated on the stage
and Tony sat in one of the pastoral seats in front of the choir. I was
near him, and he was flirting with me. I was somewhat surprised,
because being Black in Piqua where no potential prospects were
around to validate me in this way, I didn't feel desirable. And being
desirable was frowned upon. Desirability as a way of being was dirty
and lascivious.

Tony and I started dating in April 1994 when Né was four years
old. We got married four months later in August to avoid going
to hell for fornicating. It's easy as a semi-developed adult to know
in hindsight that this relationship was not set up to succeed. I was
nineteen and Tony was thirty-one. I had no idea who I was, and
who I wanted to be seemed ridiculous. Laughable, if you please.
Tony was hurting, fresh from a divorce where his wife had been
unfaithful.

Back then, I couldn't conceive of how this could be. In my
scarcity, I assumed that having one man who loved me would
be plenty for me. My concept of love came from what I saw on
television and the relationships at my church. I would later fuck
around and find out though.

Marrying Tony Williams meant we had to travel the fifty miles
back and forth to Lima from Piqua for church because that's where
Tony had been living and where he went to church. Elder Michael
Cooper was able to use the fact that he, too, commuted and his
commute was all the way to Lima from Springfield. Cooper had a
strong influence over Tony's decisions.

Tony was also young and had a troubled past relationship with
his father. His mother had passed away. So, he was also vulnerable.
Tony was hopeful that one day he would pastor the church in Lima. It

seemed that Elder Cooper had given Tony reason to believe that this would be his future. So, for Tony, this was an investment.

If I wanted to be in the Lima church choir, that meant I had to drive up there by myself one extra time per week for rehearsals. But that choir was not really trying to have me in it. They had their circle of trust, and I wasn't about to walk up in there thinking I'd have the same political luxuries that I had developed over time back at the Piqua church.

We were traveling back and forth about 100 miles round trip, two or three times a week. I once wrecked my car with Né in the front seat trying to drive up there on some please everybody else bullshit. Luckily Né wasn't hurt, and neither was I. I just now owed a white lady a lot of money for the damage to her minivan. That accident ended up landing me in jail. Not for the accident itself, but for the fact that I didn't have car insurance. So, my license was suspended for driving without insurance and would remain suspended until I was able to pay off that woman's car repairs at about three thousand dollars.

Later on that summer, I was pulled over on 25A where the highway patrol used to conduct random traffic stops. Driving under suspension earned me one hundred twenty hours of community service work which I never completed it. After five years of not doing the community service, they issued a warrant for my arrest. I was arrested on the Market St. Bridge in Troy around the corner from where I lived then. I had my three small kids with me. It was a week before Christmas.

Since Judge Kessler was deeply racist, he was interested in giving me the maximum sentence which was six months in jail. His preferential treatment was notable in the way that the blonde who was chained to me on the (literal) chain gang on which we walked over from the jail to the courthouse had the same charges as I did, and he let her off with "time served." I would have spent that Christmas in jail but Sister Collier—the pastor's wife of my church in Piqua—pled my case to her husband. Elder Collier went to Judge Kessler and petitioned for my release. I spent the weekend and got to go home on Monday.

We called Elder Collier Pops. His benevolent and caring nature, mixed with his deep voice and love of counseling made him very much a father figure. Pops also set it up for me to finish my community service at the church. This kept me from working on the side of the highway picking up trash and litter. I can imagine having a stroke out there on 25A after accidentally coming into contact with a dead bird while trying to pick up litter. But thanks to Pops, I could do office work instead. I think I ended up transcribing sermons from cassette tapes into Word documents.

In our transition to the Lima church with Michael back in 1994, I switched from confessing to Elder Collier in Piqua to confessing to Elder Cooper. I don't call him that anymore. But I also don't call him. I think my confessions turned him on because it wasn't long before he started giving us money and I started projecting this provider/father thing onto him that I hadn't resolved yet.

One afternoon during a regional conference in Toledo, I ended up confessing some shit that I had thought or said. I was looking more amazing that day than I ever knew at that time in a navy blue suit and cranberry red lipstick.

How do I know this? Because Cooper said, "I wish we were in this car alone."

"Why?" I asked, semi-unwilling to see that he was flirting.

"Because I'd smear that lipstick all over your face," he answered.

Someone found me attractive. I loved that. We soon started talking non-stop in secret. He even called me at work. He seemed to always hand us money after church services and other random times. The first time I agreed to meet him he showed me exactly what was about to happen by opening that door butt ass naked.

The news spread across the country within our church organization overnight. I had earned myself the reputation of a treacherous woman who brings down great men. Rumor had it that I had seduced Elder Michael Cooper and I was a homewrecker. One lady told me sometime after Christian was born that she had once offered to push me down the stairs so that I could miscarry. She would do this for her beloved "Uncle Mike" (Cooper).

I didn't really ever live down most of the widespread rumors within the organization. When Christian was five or six years old, I met a man named Aaron who might have been a really good fit were it not for purity culture. He knew my story. He liked me anyway, but he couldn't afford to tarnish his life by being with me.

He told me once during one of our frequent all-night phone conversations that after Christian was born, he couldn't believe that I had the audacity to bring her to church. My response was something having to do with why wouldn't I bring her to church? I think people tend to have Jesus all the way twisted. Becoming a person of no religion has been a healing place for me and for my kids.

The news of Bill Cosby's overturned rape convictions was cause for celebration for some of the Black men with whom I used to fellowship. "The law worked for a Black man," was the premise for one of those praising the moment.

Sadly, these men completely avoided caring for the women whom he had raped. They dismissed all possibility that he had raped these women. One commenter insisted the women had consented to sex with Cosby, even after he admitted he had given them quaaludes to make it easier to have sex with them. The testimonies of these women meant nothing to my former co-laborers in the faith.

When I think about how unfair my choices have been for my kids, in a river of miseducation, I mourn for them. Looking back, I would tell my twenty-two-year-old self I didn't owe Michael Cooper anything. I would let that young hard-working single mother know that she was right to stand up for herself. That she didn't actually need Tony or Michael. The patriarchy, manipulation, and sexual assault are rampant in many churches.

I was broken and searching. I wanted to believe in a potter who would put me back together again. I was a perfect candidate for salvation. But allowing myself to be selected came with a cost, because apparently "he that findeth a wife findeth a good thing" (read: let 'em chase you down even after you say or suggest no, club ya 'cross the head and drag ya into their cave.) I guess I accepted that predator preacher's advances because I thought I was a wretch who couldn't do any better.

Paisha Thomas is descendant of the Randolph Freed People—a group of 383 freed slaves who traveled by foot from Roanoke, Virginia to their promised land in Ohio in 1846 only to be met by violent white mobs. Their land was seized and sold from under them—they scattered throughout Ohio. Paisha's music and writing preserves not only her family history but addresses the current social and racial injustices in our country. Learn more at www.paishathomasart.com

HALLOWED BE THY NAMES

by Stephen Kraynak

…of course
loss is the great lesson.
Mary Oliver, "Poppies"

***

These days I visit with those dead men, my friends and lovers, though on
my terms, not theirs.
Fenton Johnson, Geography Of The Heart

***

It rained the morning we left. Our beloved Old Beechwold home of ten years, with its bay window view of the wooded ravine and stream, was empty now, broom clean. My husband and I stayed overnight in the guest bedroom of our friends, Ken and Jim, and set out early, the back seat and trunk of my Camry crammed with our possessions we would not entrust to Mayflower. Toast and coffee breakfast, last-minute key check, "Come see us in the Grand Canyon State," hugs and kisses around. We waved goodbye as I reset the trip odometer to zero. I didn't have time to clean my car. Serendipitous, that redemptive rain. All the sins of my past— washed away.

Mile 0—Tuesday, May 24, 2011: Columbus, Ohio.

What is it about the open road that frees one's mind to wander, prods it to play, and invites it to spin in a grand pirouette enticing one's muse to dance?

Breathe in… Breathe out…We had lived a whirlwind since the previous January 31. On our way to Tucson International, we closed on our Sabino Vista foothills home with its panorama of the Santa Catalina Mountains. We bought the house where the coyotes howled after dark under the spreading mesquite tree in the backyard. I was the one who suggested that we move to Tucson saying, "Let's go look at real estate while we're here on vacation."

Back to Columbus to put that house on the market. Sonoran sunshine, here we come.

Mile 418—May 24: First overnight, just west of St. Louis.

Breathe in… Breathe out… Clean out that basement! Kids get first choice of unneeded furniture, kitchenware, and excess linens. Truckloads to auctions. We left the rusty snow shovels, the ones with corners bent from slamming them against packed ice, arrayed in the garage for the new owners. We donated the snow blower to our church.

Mile 916—May 25: Second night out—a Holiday Inn beyond Oklahoma City.

Breathe in… Breathe out… Bob had ongoing sinus infection issues. Medication first. Then a roto-till surgery. In consultation afterward, Dr. Massick asked, "Have you ever thought about moving to a dry climate? Like Arizona? Could help." "Yes! Yes!" I cheered to myself.

We had made room for Ruth, Bob's aging mother, in her declining years. Ruth, of the, "In those days…" Ruth of the gnarled hands and scoliosis. Ruth, of the home hospice care. Ruth, of ashes scattered in the memorial garden by Rev. Mark.

Mile 1458—May 26: Third overnight—Albuquerque, New Mexico.

Breathe in… Breathe out… On my first day at McKinley School in Mrs. Martlock's kindergarten class, I knew I would be a teacher. Thirty-five years teaching in the Columbus City Schools, and loving it. Where did those years go?

It was when I attended St. Vincent de Paul Elementary School that I began to notice the eighth-grade boys. Coming out in my thirties. Carrying our church banner in the Columbus Pride Parade. First time kissing a man. First time sleeping with a man. First HIV test. First negative. First former lover.

We take the route 26 cut-off from I-25 toward Deming and I-10 west, and stop for lunch at the Hot Damn Chili Parlor in

Hatch. Outside, we marvel at the vivid clear blueness overhead.

Mile 1775—May 27: New Mexico—Arizona border

As we cross the Arizona border heading for Texas Canyon, my cell phone rings. Janet, our Columbus realtor, relays the news: "Successful closing. Best wishes for the next part of your life!" A high five. "We did it!"

The final miles blur, lost in a mélange of anticipation and conversation. "Mayflower comes next Tuesday. We need air mattresses. Remember to stop at Walmart. That kitchen needs remodeling. What day is trash pick-up?"

Musings diminish: my Cleveland roots, teaching, our years together in Columbus, house hunting, sorting and packing, bridge loan. Memories fade: good friends, coming out, past lovers, former partners, safer sex, AIDS, the years of living dangerously. All of that, all of that, left far, far behind. We are Arizonans now. People of the desert.

Mile 1886—Friday, May 27, 2011: Breathe in…Tucson. Breathe out…Home.

***

John died alone. On his kitchen floor. He put the handgun in his mouth and pointed it upward. The building manager called the police and hired a crew to clean his blood and brains off the ceiling, walls, floor and appliances, and to disinfect the apartment before it could be advertised as vacant. John was in violation of his lease and owed back rent, but he had no money, no estate. His sense of aesthetics was of no value now. The police even took his gun. John lost his job because of his illness. He had no access to medical care for his compounding afflictions. He had no hope. He chose to end his misery his own way, by his own hand, instantly. Official cause of death: self-inflicted gunshot wound to the head.

John's friends designed a panel in his memory for the NAMES Project AIDS Memorial Quilt, stitching in the words: "Where are you? JOHN Are you making it pretty?" It was among the hundreds of AIDS Quilt panels displayed at the Woody Hayes Athletic Center indoor football field in Columbus.

Where are you?
JOHN
Are you making it pretty?

***

Jim proudly talked about his sex partners. When he went to the home of a man he met in a Key West bar, the man entrapped him as a sex slave, refusing to let him leave until Jim convinced him that he was a Catholic priest who had told his parishioners where he was going for vacation and when to expect his return. Jim convinced the man the police would be looking for him.

Jim pulled two plastic bags over his head and tied them securely around his neck after he had consumed a bottle of sleeping pills with a fifth of whiskey. He had lost his job at Kroger's, too weak to work. Without income or medical insurance, he despaired. His body had begun to decompose, its odor bringing an inquiry. They found him alone, in his bedroom. In lieu of ongoing suffering, he chose asphyxiation. He was buried at St. Joseph's Cemetery on the south side of Columbus.

Trick   Trick   Trick
JIM
Love in the Time of AIDS

***

Zack and I were teachers on the same school staff and learned that we were born in the same year. Both gay and single. And available. He loved to cook; I loved to dine. When I heard he was going to New Mexico for spring break I offered to join him. We both agreed to get HIV tests at the City of Columbus Public Health Clinic. Both negative. Zack referred to these results as "getting a new lease on life." We left for a week together in The Land of Enchantment.

In Santa Fe, we did our own art walk of the galleries and, on our first evening, reserved an upstairs table for two at the fashionable Coyote Café where I became annoyed by the tittering gaggle of people hovering nearby. Zack explained that they were autograph hunting because Linda Gray was seated directly behind me. "Linda who?" I quipped. (I had never watched Dallas and had only a vague memory of Sue Ellen Ewing having been mentioned in the teachers' lounge.) Zack never let me forget this moment and 'Linda who?' became the first of many entries in our collection of private jokes. We toured the Taos Pueblo and Chaco Canyon. At a family-owned restaurant on the road to Mesa Verde, I learned I didn't like huevos rancheros.

Zack took me to New York for my fortieth birthday. The hotel. Tickets to Phantom and Les Mis. Dinners at Windows on The World atop the World Trade Center and at Café Un Deux Trois, writing love notes with crayons on the white butcher block paper table covering. A stroll through Central Park. MOMA. The guided walking tour up inside the Statue of Liberty. Two footloose gay men in the Big Apple for a weekend on the town. NYC was our oyster. The very stuff of Broadway. I got my man; he got his. Who could ask for anything more? Best birthday gift ever. We were an item for two years before Zack decided our time together had run its course. He recentered his life on his long-standing group of friends. He wanted to socialize and travel with them, saying "I want to go" on short notice and without any encumbrances. Our primary relationship hindered his freedom.

Some years later, two of these same friends went to Zack's home when he did not return their repeated phone calls. They found him, alone, in his garage inside his convertible, windows and top down. The garage door was closed and the car's engine running, exhaust fumes permeating. The anti-depressants prescribed by his doctor had not eased his cries for help. Zack, always stylishly preppy, was a gay man 'born to clean.' He chose a clean and quiet death, carbon monoxide poisoning. Except for an empty pill bottle, he left no mess. Against the wishes of his family, one of his sisters secreted some of his ashes to those friends who had found his corpse. They scattered him in the Atlantic at Nags Head with a toast of Kendall Jackson chardonnay, Zack's favorite.

I Love New York
Zack
Give My Regards to Broadway

***

AIDS was killing us. First reported in the coastal meccas of New York, San Francisco, and Los Angeles, and in Washington, D.C., it soon arrived in Columbus, Ohio. Through our loving, we were unknowingly infecting each other. In the 1980s and 1990s, symptomatic gay men were abandoned, ignored, shamed, and shunned. Evicted by owners and rejected by biological family. Condemned by Christians. Vilified. During the Columbus Gay Pride Parade a single-engine plane circled overhead pulling a banner that read: "AIDS—God's curse on the homo's." (sic)

Political leaders and power brokers made us invisible. In 1985 Edgar T. Wolfe III, scion of the wealthy family that owned the then local evening newspaper, The Columbus Dispatch, died of AIDS in San Francisco. Eddie's death was reported by the Columbus Citizen Journal, the non-Wolfe-owned morning daily.

Our truth was denied in death notices. Families did not allow the word gay or the term AIDS to be used in print about their sons and brothers. We were pariahs. Untouchables. Thrown out in body bags next to the trash.

The yellow brick road terminated in a morass of human blood, bodily fluids, pus, and the stench of feces, all drenched in tears. AIDS taught us that we, gay men, ourselves, must assume the responsibility to care for ourselves and our brothers.

***

Robin, the piano accompanist for the Columbus Gay Men's Chorus, was able to perform until a few months before his death from AIDS. At its December holiday shows, the Chorus displayed a poinsettia at the front of the stage for each former Chorus member who died from AIDS and listed their names in the programs. The number of potted poinsettias and names increased annually.

> *Columbus Gay Men's Chorus*
> *Robin*
> *Voices Raised. Lives Changed*

***

Robert, never Bob, always Robert, was a classified staff secretary in the Board of Education building of the Columbus City Schools. In my interactions with Robert, he was courteous, efficient, meticulous, and respectful. He never made small talk; I never saw him smile. One Saturday night I noticed him near the dance floor in the testosterone-soaked back room of Kismet, a downtown gay bar. He stood alone against a wall holding a drink, not speaking with anyone. When I stepped toward him, he did not acknowledge me, a gay bar signal of 'not interested.'

My long-time friend, Rita, also a Board classified secretary, befriended Robert when she was transferred to the administration building, assigned to the office of an assistant superintendent. During our regular dinners together, she told me about him. Robert loved his work and always received positive evaluations. His work was his life. He was lonely and wanted to meet other gay men, but his family and his AME church did not approve of his homosexuality. Rita asked me if I could help him meet other gay men.

I had met Black men at the downtown YMCA weight room, locker room, and showers, and at the Ward Y on Woodland Avenue. Robert was not a gym rat, and I did not know where Columbus Black men met other Black men living on the down low. Rita cried through one dinner about Robert's deteriorating physical condition, how gaunt he was from wasting. Months later she told me about Robert's memorial service at his AME church. She was one of the few white people in attendance.

Sometimes I Feel
Like A Motherless Child
Robert
I Am Who I Am

***

One summer afternoon in 1982 I drove south on High Street for an appointment with Fr. Paul Robichaud, a Paulist priest serving at St. Thomas More Newman Center adjacent to The Ohio State University (OSU) campus. My car radio tuned to NPR, I heard Patti Neighmond speak about the yet-to-be-named fatal illness—although some termed it the 'gay cancer'—affecting many gay men in major U.S. cities. I was in my early thirties, and I chose Fr. Paul to be the first person to whom I would say the words, "I'm gay." As I was about to come out, the first of many times, NPR was telling me I was doing so in a time of uncertainty, anxiety, suffering, and death of what would eventually be named human immunodeficiency virus infection and acquired immunodeficiency syndrome or HIV/AIDS. By September 1982 the CDC began to refer to this disease as AIDS.

Fr. Paul welcomed me with a hug. After I outed myself, he said, "That's great, because I'm gay too." He invited me to attend the newly formed Gay Men's Support Group at Newman which he facilitated. Through meeting other gay men there and at the Gay Parents' Group which included both women and men, I became more comfortable with my orientation, began to see gays and lesbians, and myself, as normal, and made some life-long friends. Coming out and actively participating for several years in these support groups proved to be life-changing for me.

On October 1, 1986, Joseph Cardinal Ratzinger, Prefect for The Vatican Office of the Congregation of the Doctrine of the Faith issued a Letter to the Bishops of the Catholic Church on the Pastoral Care of Homosexual Persons which instructed the bishops to withdraw all support, or even the semblance of support, from any group vague on the immorality of homogenital acts. We, the gay men from Newman, were not vague about the morality of homogenital acts. They were an intimate part of our loving.

Columbus Diocese Bishop James Griffin evicted us from the Newman Center. He owned the Newman Center building and its land, and he alone decided who was welcome to gather on his real estate. We, the Catholic gay men, were children of a lesser god and not among the righteous and just. The hierarchy of the one, holy, catholic, and apostolic church dismissed and abandoned us at a critical time in our lives. We had to minister to ourselves.

I found my way to the local Unitarian Universalist Church.

***

I met Craig at the First Unitarian Universalist Church of Columbus and got to know him better through our monthly discussions in the Whitman Circle, a gay men's support group at that church. Craig acknowledged being HIV+ and bipolar. While in a manic phase, he was garrulous and loquacious, and often overbearing to the point of insolence.

Craig was arrested one evening on suspicion of arson which destroyed the Boob-B-Trap, a strip club on Olentangy River Road west of the OSU campus. Police found him with a loaded gun in his possession and exhibiting erratic behavior. He was taken to the Franklin County Jail. A corrections officer subsequently noticed that Craig was unresponsive in his cell. Allegedly the penal system did not consistently dispense his HIV medication. His mother refused to allow the words 'gay' or 'AIDS' to be used during his memorial service at First Church.

> *Worth and Dignity of All*
> *Craig*
> *The Whitman Circle*

***

In the summer of 1994, I attended the first all-gay men's workshop at the Omega Institute in Rhinebeck, New York. Psychologist, Peter Hendrickson facilitated the group of thirty men from around the country. Peter told us of his HIV+ status. We spent time together processing the effects of AIDS in our lives, including survivor's guilt and methods of coping with it, and learned ways of celebrating life, such as meditating, chanting, and Sufi dancing.

One of the men from the Midwest cried us through the crushing, deadening loneliness of his life in the closet, hiding his love of men from his kith and kin, his employer, and the faithful of his church. He reasoned that if he intentionally contracted HIV, he could request a support team from the local AIDS task force which would provide him the contacts he craved. In his desperation, he valued these potential human connections more than his lonely life, more than life itself.

For an evening group session, Peter asked us to stand shoulder to shoulder and face each other in two lines. He then invited all who so wanted, to pass through the tight space between us, one by one, and offered the man from the Midwest the opportunity to go first, eyes closed in trust. As he walked down the line, men from both sides moved in to lay their hands on him, guiding him down the path, speaking his name, and affirming him. Others followed. This was my first experience with the 'Walk of the Angels.' Peter died in 1996.

> *Teacher   Counselor   Guru*
> *Peter Hendrickson*
> *Omega Institute*

***

To help fight the spread of HIV/AIDS and reduce its rate of transmission in central Ohio, local leaders in the Columbus medical, counseling, education, mental health, and social services fields joined efforts to create the Columbus AIDS Task Force. I was one of its initial volunteers, serving as a team leader of five people who coordinated and provided services to a Columbus man, our HIV+ 'buddy.' We visited him in his home, offered transportation to medical and counseling appointments, and performed basic tasks such as grocery shopping or doing laundry. Periodically I reported to Howard Fradkin, a local psychologist, about the status of the team and our 'buddy.' All team leaders met regularly to discuss their respective team efforts and learn about recent developments in HIV/AIDS treatment and advocacy.

This method of providing team services to individuals was multiplied many times during the duration of the AIDS pandemic. The Task Force grew into an organization with thirty-five staff and a base of over five hundred volunteers. The vision of the Task Force was a world free of AIDS, and we worked toward it by empowering individuals to make their own choices.

Our sisters, particularly our lesbian sisters, were instrumental in the planning, organization, operation, and success of the Task Force. Without them, the men would not have been able to manage the overwhelming needs of those infected with HIV, and the level of suffering in the Columbus and central Ohio gay community would have been intolerable. These women were our Angels in America.

***

Jack, an Ohio State University professor, was one of the first gay men in Columbus who admitted having symptoms of an HIV infection. He reached out to the local gay community for assistance. In response, the Columbus AIDS Task Force was formed and implemented.

The Ohio State University
Jack
Columbus AIDS Task Force

***

Chris, a fellow Task Force team leader, had a degree in social work and counseled HIV+ men. We were about the same age and height. He was a hunk who pumped iron at a local gym. I developed a crush on him. Chris openly spoke about his feelings, an attribute I found endearing and alluring.

After coming out to his parents, they abandoned him, saying they would "pray for him."

Because Chris missed many Task Force team leaders' meetings, I got copies of handouts for him. One afternoon I delivered them to him at his apartment. After talking business for a while, we began kissing. When I offered him a massage, we found ourselves in his bed with our shirts off. As Chris lay on his back, I began to rub my fingers across his muscular chest. While I massaged down his abs toward his crotch, his phone rang. Chris answered and I listened to a one-sided conversation. It was his gym buddy, a man whom Chris said he was 'kind of' involved with, and who was coming to see him. I left.

Chris informed the Task Force leadership that he was moving to Washington, D.C. with his partner who had found a job there. About six months later when I saw Chris across High Street during the Short North gallery hop, I jaywalked to go talk with him. A small group of friends gathered around him as he explained that his partner had died of complications of AIDS shortly after they arrived in D.C. When I asked Chris about his own HIV status, he replied, "I can't talk about that now." That was our last conversation.

> *Counselor   Pump Fe*
> *Chris*
> *Columbus AIDS Task Force*

***

James, born with clubfoot, endured many surgeries during his youth to improve his mobility. He was a spotless housekeeper. He confided to me that as he aged, at times, he crawled on his hands and knees when he was home alone to ease recurring pain in his feet. He was active in the Metropolitan Community Church of Columbus and a long-term member of a gay bowling league. Many attended his viewing and memorial service. James died ten days prior to the death of our mutual gay friend, David, in the summer of 1995.

> *Columbus Gay Bowling League*
> *James*
> *Metropolitan Community Church*

***

When I first entered Kobacker House, an inpatient Columbus hospice, to see a teaching colleague with terminal pancreatic cancer, I found it quiet and peaceful. I interviewed and received training as a volunteer, hoping it would offer me some respite amid the turmoil of superstorm AIDS. On Friday evenings I served at the information desk where I accessed the names and room numbers of all patients so I could assist visitors, family, and friends. Soon after I first began this task, I saw names of gay men whom I knew on the roster.

***

David, who taught Spanish at Lancaster High School, was an avid art collector and regularly attended the Park West Galleries auctions in Columbus. To display his purchases, he had his hallway ceiling lined with track lights and welcomed his friends for casual wine and cheese.

Two of these friends transported David, in a medical crisis, to Kobacker House. As they helped him inside, David went into spasms and his body stiffened. He appeared to be unconscious when I visited him, and he was unaware of my presence. Staff members entered to change the sheets on his bed. I sat on a chair and watched his Adam's apple slowly move with his shallow and belabored breathing while they carefully turned him. His chest stopped moving. "Did he just stop breathing?" I whispered. Both staff slowly rolled David onto his back, rested his head on the pillow, and silently left his room. I sat with him for a while before I called his aged mother and aunt.

At his memorial service at the First Spiritualist Church, I read the passage, Love is patient, love is kind… from I Corinthians and later attended another memorial at his family's Lutheran Church in Thornville, Ohio. I accompanied David's family to the cemetery and watched as his urn was placed in the family plot. His elderly mother did not understand how her only child had died so young of "cancer." His aunt, who knew David died of AIDS, could not console her. David had asked me to serve as a trustee for his estate, which he put into a trust for his two pre-school granddaughters whom he had never met. From his art collection, he left me two framed, signed, and numbered prints of Paris street scenes, both now on my living room wall, remembrances of our friendship.

> *Son, Nephew, Father, Grandfather*
> *David*
> *Love Never Fails*

***

I knew Richie from the Newman Gay Men's Support Group. He was a quiet, unassuming person, who rarely spoke in the circle. Twice he filed for bankruptcy and sometimes needed financial assistance from the other men. Richie was alone in his room at Kobacker House as I pulled a chair close. As I spoke to him, he gurgled and babbled incoherently, staring blankly, vapidly gazing into the emptiness above his bed, acknowledging nothing, including my presence. Dementia and Richie were now an exclusive item. I quietly sat at his bedside, trying to breathe in tandem with him. Richie died quietly. At his viewing, his family members would neither look at nor speak to any of his gay friends from Newman. They ignored us as we stood together offering our final respects.

> *Say His Name*
> *Richie*
> *Newman Men's Support Group*

***

Bob and I met at an informal gathering for those from Columbus going to the Second National March on Washington for Lesbian and Gay Rights on October 11, 1987. The AIDS Memorial Quilt would be displayed for the first time on the National Mall during the six days of protest.

We had a few casual dinner dates prior to D.C. Both of us were teachers. I taught middle school English in Columbus, and Bob was a professor of theater at OSU. Bob said he knew Derek Jacobi from summer stock theater in Wales, and that Jacobi would perform the lead role of Alan Turing in Breaking The Code at the Kennedy Center during the National March weekend. He asked me if I wanted to meet Jacobi. That sealed the deal. We would "do" D.C. together: attend the play, see The Quilt, walk in The March, room together at the Hotel Congressional, and share a bed.

On our first date, Bob acknowledged his HIV+ status. He wanted to have sex, assuring me that we could use safer sex practices. This would be my first time having sex with an HIV+ man. I wanted time to ponder initiating a relationship with someone whose life may be short-lived.

In D.C. we attended the Saturday matinee of Breaking The Code, my first time at the Kennedy Center. Jacobi performed a stellar Alan Turing, including replicating his stammer. After the show, we approached the 'No Admittance' doors to the backstage. When Bob gave our names to the guard, he opened the doors for us. Jacobi's dresser answered our knock, and we entered the dressing room. Bob introduced me to Derek Jacobi who extended his hand in greeting, one of the few times in my life I was speechless.

Sunday morning, we were among the half a million people who viewed the AIDS Memorial Quilt. In 1987, the stigma associated with AIDS precluded many of its victims from having funerals because some funeral homes declined to deal with the remains of the decedents. The Quilt was their only memorial. We silently listened as a series of volunteers at a microphone read aloud the names of all those whose Quilt panels were unfolded before us, an overwhelming visual array of the nationwide suffering and death from AIDS.

Bob and I joined the Columbus contingent for "The Great March." Jesse Jackson and Whoopi Goldberg were among the leaders of the crowd estimated at 750,000. This weekend marked the end of our time together due to my scruples of having sex with an HIV+ gay man.

I gasped when I saw Bob's name on the Kobacker House roster. In his room, I met an OSU colleague of his who told me that he could not speak and lapsed in and out of consciousness. After she cried her final goodbye, I sat down next to Bob.

Grasping his right hand and gently massaging it, I introduced myself and began reminiscing about our time together in D.C. "You remember when you told me we would meet Derek Jacobi? I doubted you, but we walked right into his dressing room." Bob seemed to recognize me, and his breathing increased slightly. "I still remember my favorite person in The Great March, the single man standing on a corner with one arm around a light pole holding a hand-made 'Corn Fed Iowa Fag' sign." I massaged his hand a while longer and kissed his forehead. I said my final goodbye to Bob when his son,

Seth, arrived. At Bob's memorial service, at his request, a soloist sang "The Impossible Dream" from Man of La Mancha.

> *To Bear With Unbearable Sorrow*
> *Bob*
> *To Reach The Unreachable Star*

***

Dwight and George were a couple. I met them through a mutual friend, Karl, a man whom I was dating. Karl took me to their designer home which they had built on the Cooke Road ravine. George was the architect.

Dwight was admitted to Kobacker with chronic diarrhea and dehydration. With George and Dwight's parents present, I knelt at the right side of his bed, cupped my hands around his ear, and gently spoke, "Dwight, it's Stephen. I'm here with your family. I will miss you, my friend. I will always remember

> *Guardian Angel*
> *Dwight*
> *Son, Brother, Uncle, Partner*

you." I began to cry. Dwight predeceased George.

***

The summer of 1965, after my graduation from St. Edward High School in Lakewood, Ohio, I entered the Holy Cross Brothers, an apostolic Catholic religious order of men who had been my high school teachers. I was sixteen. For the next four years, I lived in community with other Brothers in the Juniorate in Watertown, Wisconsin; the Novitiate in Rolling Prairie, Indiana; and the Scholasticate at the University of Notre Dame in South Bend, Indiana. In July 1969 I left the order, returned home to Cleveland, Ohio, and enrolled at OSU. I kept in contact with several of the Brothers and occasionally visited them at Notre Dame.

The logo for the Holy Cross Order was the cross, symbolizing the suffering of Jesus, and anchors, symbolizing hope, pictured over the motto, Spes Unica or Only Hope, meaning that only through suffering could one hope to attain salvation. Through my Notre Dame contacts I learned how the suffering from AIDS included even these men, one who remained active in the order, and others who, like me, had left the Congregation of Holy Cross.

Bro. Richard, C.S.C., originally from Iowa, lived and worked in the San Francisco Bay area as a social worker. He had a mild ailment for two days. On the second day of his malaise, he left work early and went home to rest. He died that same evening from septic shock.

I knew Lawrence at the scholasticate at Notre Dame. One hot summer day a group of Brothers set out in canoes from the south bend of the St. Joseph River, heading downstream. Brother Lawrence and I shared a canoe, Larry in front. About half-way down river, I noticed that his bare back was getting red, and I suggested, although I was enjoying the view, that he put his shirt back on. After Lawrence left Holy Cross, he worked for the railroad in Chicago where he designed computer chips to track the boxcars. He died several years after his life partner, both from AIDS.

My family and Thomas' family, both from northeast Ohio, became friends and drove together from Cleveland to Rolling Prairie on those weekends when the novitiate welcomed guests.

My mother and sister visited Thomas in the hospital in his final days, noting his wasting syndrome. They assumed he had AIDS. His mother wept about her son dying so young from cancer.

In the summer of 1972, Malcolm and I traveled together for eight weeks in Europe. We used Eurail passes and stayed in youth hostels in ten countries. He taught me the practices of sleeping on trains to save lodging expenses and hanging our washed and wrung underwear, still wet, on the third-class overhead luggage racks to discourage other travelers from using our compartment. We were in Munich for the opening day of the Olympics on August 26 and then traveled to Berlin, where we crossed through Checkpoint Charlie to the drab East. In Portugal we read the news of the massacre of Israeli team hostages. Malcolm suffered from dementia before dying from AIDS.

Requiescat in Pace
Bro. Richard, C.S.C.
Spes Unica

Requiescat in Pace
Lawrence
Spes Unica

SPES UNICA

Requiescat in Pace
Thomas
Spes Unica

Requiescat in Pace
Malcolm
Spes Unica

***

For four years in the early 1990s, I drove to Saco, Maine during the last week of July for GAYLA, a week-long 'Retreat for Men Who Love Men' at the Unitarian Universalist-owned and staffed Ferry Beach Retreat and Conference Center, a thirty-two-acre oceanfront campus. The facilities housed one hundred thirty-five men, with dozens of campsites available a short walk away in the pine wooded Grove. I met other gay men from Unitarian Universalist congregations around the U.S. and Canada. Every year during the opening welcome session one couple from New York introduced themselves by saying, "Hello! We're the Staten Island fairies!"

The week's schedule included morning, afternoon, and evening workshops, programs and classes, all planned and facilitated by the GAYLA men themselves. The planning team ordered a supply of condoms and lubricant for delivery to Ferry Beach and reserved an 'encounter room' upstairs in Rowland Hall dormitory, supplying it with a stack of clean bed sheets. Late in the week when my new GAYLA friend, Tom and I decided to have an encounter, all the sheets had been used and were piled on the floor.

I made new friends and, over the four years, attempted two long-distance relationships with GAYLA men, Tom from Providence and Phil from Boston. My counselor, Rahe Corlis, advised me that these types of relationships were seldom successful unless one person relocated. I did not agree with him, but his advice ultimately proved accurate in both cases.

GAYLA was the summer retreat week that the staff enjoyed most. The GAYLA men produced and performed in an annual, and always outrageous, 'Talent—No Talent Show' and challenged the Ferry Beach staff in volleyball—losers had to wait tables at dinner that same evening, in drag. GAYLA has been a successful retreat week for gay men for over forty years.

Mid-week, the resident chaplain led a remembrance service in the Grove Chapel in the pines where all could speak the names of those GAYLA men or other partners, lovers, friends, or relatives who died during the previous year. By the early 1990s, there was no location in the U.S. or Canada left unscarred by AIDS. We shared the common sadness of funerals and memorial services for our friends and lovers. Standing in a circle in the woods, we mourned together.

The Spirit of Universal Love
GAYLA Brothers
Ferry Beach, Maine

***

Steven was a drop-dead gorgeous prince. He was graced with a melt-your-heart toothsome smile, which lived beneath two wide-set welcoming brown eyes and was surrounded by a medium brown, neatly trimmed full-face beard and mustache. Steven came from a Catholic family. In a private moment, he told me that the other kids at St. James the Less School laughed at him when they saw the cardboard inserts his mother had made to cover the holes in the soles of his shoes. While active military in Vietnam, he learned Vietnamese and was a liaison to local residents. Stateside he assisted Vietnamese refugees who were relocated to Columbus after the 1975 fall of Saigon. He volunteered in the Big Brothers Association and the AIDS Task Force.

During his life, Steven had only one sex partner whom he met in the gay men's social group, Black & White Men Together. His partner infected Steven with HIV, while the partner remained asymptomatic. I took some flowers to him when he was admitted to Riverside Hospital and happened to arrive in his room just as a nurse helped him to change his gown. I was used to seeing a vigorous, strapping man. Because of the wasting syndrome, Steven had lost both massive fat and muscle tissue. He now looked skeleton-like. Formerly muscular and toned, now he was visibly shriveled, his flesh hanging from his bones. Not noticing me at first, he was focused on himself, on his physical deterioration with a mixed expression of desperation and disbelief. I stifled a gasp and willed myself not to cry in his presence. When he saw the flowers he blurted, "You can take those back with you. I'm not dead yet." No smile. No small talk.

With my flowers in hand, I left him soon after I had arrived and cried myself home. The next day his mother phoned me to apologize for Steven's comment, having heard about it from him. She had taken her son home to die, saying to me that she gave him birth and she would be with him in his last moments, and added, "If I ever find the man who put my son through this living hell, I will kill him myself."

At Steven's memorial service, in addition to his family and friends, members of the Columbus Vietnamese community attended and spoke about his kindness toward them. Steven's mother sat in the front row, comforted by her other children. Unknown to her, in the back row sat Steven's sole gay lover, comforted by his friends. Both mother and lover wept bitterly. Both, inconsolable.

> *Diamonds on the Soles*
> *of His Shoes*
> *Steven*
> *Good Night, Sweet Prince*

***

I met Randy Shilts, Paul Monette, and David Wojnarowicz through their writing. Early in the pandemic, they published books (1987, 1988, 1991 respectively) about their personal experiences with AIDS and documented how elected leaders ignored the plight of gay men during this pandemic. They spoke truth to power when so many of us were overwhelmed, trying to survive or laser-focused on aiding those suffering and dying. All three of these gay men died of AIDS-related illnesses, in their prime: Randy Shilts had 42 years, Paul Monette was 49, David Wojnarowicz 37. Paul Monette urges us forward, "Go without hate, but not without rage; heal the world."

And The Band Played On *Randy Shilts* *8.8.1951 – 2.17.1994*	*Borrowed Time: An AIDS* *Memoir* *Paul Monette* *10.16.1945 – 2.10.1995*	*Close to the Knives: A* *Memoir of Disintegration* *David Wojnarowicz* *9.14.1954 – 7.22.1992*

***

After a general Columbus AIDS Task Force meeting for all volunteers and clients, a man about twenty, young enough to be my son, and who had been assigned a new support team, stopped to thank me for a comment I had made. Although I cannot now remember his name, I can still clearly see his face. As he spoke, through his faint smile I sensed his forlornness and longing. He had no job and no money. To his counseling group, he had expressed his desire to see the ocean, once during his life. The group members had encouraged him with the words, "Go for it." "So, I decided to go for it," he beamed. Several months later I learned that he had died from AIDS. I never knew if he had seen the sea.

I Must Down to the Sea Again
Beloved Gay Brother
We Remember You

***

I now live in the Sonoran Desert, beckoned by the southwest sun and mountains. My husband and I set out on that rainy morning thirteen years ago on a four-day journey across the heartland to retire in Tucson. We left the flat glaciated land of the Midwest with its humid summers, its rainbows of autumn hardwood maples, oaks, and sumacs, and overcast slushy winters.

Here, in the blue mornings, I join the palo verde trees along the lower Sabino Creek, its banks adorned with prickly pear cactus, cane cholla, and desert broom. Long-lived multi-trunked velvet mesquites host pendulous witch's broom and parasitic mistletoe, nesting space, and food for a phainopepla, silhouetted overhead against the sunlit sky.

In April, honeybees pollinate the dainty, yellow-flowering creosote bushes, producing fuzzy seed pods, favored by sparrows, lesser goldfinches, and the scurrying white-tailed antelope squirrels. Broken-limbed desert willows lure hummingbirds with their orchid-like blooms. Esteemed elder ironwood presides, marking a bend in the trail.

Quiet, save for the crunch of the eroded sandy, rocky soil beneath my hiking boots. Desert mallow and bunch grass yield and bow to a passing breeze. A vermillion flycatcher darts from its perch on a cottonwood to snatch its prey in midair. Overhead, a pack of Harris's Hawks hiss and circle, jointly hunting a round-tailed ground squirrel. With a rapid, rolling chung-chung-chung-chung-chung from a saguaro, a cactus wren uplifts its head announcing its presence. Coyotes, bobcats, and javelinas assert their birthright of this, their now-shared land. At times, a diamondback slithers onto the trail, tacitly claiming jurisdiction, and goes unchallenged.

With the driving, pounding rains of the summer monsoon season, the creek rushes down from Mt. Lemmon and the Santa Catalina Mountains, awakening the Sonoran Desert toads from the creek bed muck to start their mixed chorus of full-throated croaks, beginning their mating season. From the gentle, soaking rains of winter, the waters again inundate the dry creek bed, promising a spring that will burst with orange desert marigolds, amber brittlebush, and the sorceress white Datura.

When I moved to Arizona from Ohio, the state of my birth, it seemed that I had left behind these hallowed men, of blessed memory, whom I have here named, their justified lives, their afflictions and suffering, their funerals and memorial services, the sadness and the mourning, their grieving families, friends and lovers, the endless tears. Left all of it, all of it, scattered with their ashes or buried with them in their graves.

But on those days when the stream flows, and I stop, listening near the sound of a small waterfall where the creek empties and loses itself, transformed into the Tanque Verde Wash, in my solitude they return. And, I visit with these dead men, my friends and lovers. They are here. With me. Still.

***

Those who have died have never, never left. The dead are not under the earth. They are in the rustling trees, they are in the groaning woods, they are in the crying grass, they are in the moaning rocks. Those who have died have never, never left.....The dead have a pact with the living.

"Breaths" Words: Adapted from poem by Birago Diop
Music: Ysaye M Barnwell as sung by Sweet Honey in the Rock

Stephen C. Kraynak, a native of Cleveland, Ohio, taught for thirty-five years in the Columbus City Schools. He and his husband, Bob Gordon, retired to Tucson, Arizona thirteen years ago. Twice, he has been a finalist in the Tucson Festival of Books Literary Awards Competition. This is his second piece of nonfiction published by The Ohio Writers' Association. Most mornings he quietly walks along the Sabino Creek trail, listening to the birds, admiring the blooming desert and thinking about writing and life.

Memorial Quilt of My Friends and Lovers

Where are you?

JOHN

Are you making it pretty?

Trick   Trick   Trick

JIM

Love in the Time of AIDS

I Love New York

Zack

Give My Regards to Broadway

Columbus Gay Men's Chorus

Robin

Voices Raised. Lives Changed

*Sometimes I Feel
Like A Motherless Child*

Robert

I Am Who I Am

Worth and Dignity of All

Craig

The Whitman Circle

Teacher   Counselor   Guru

Peter Hendrickson

Omega Institute

The Ohio State University

Jack

Columbus AIDS Task Force

Counselor   Pump Fe

Chris

Columbus AIDS Task Force

Columbus Gay Bowling League

James

Metropolitan Community Church

Son, Nephew, Father, Grandfather

David

Love Never Fails

Say His Name

Richie

Newman Men's Support Group

To Bear With Unbearable Sorrow

Bob

To Reach The Unreachable Star

Guardian Angel

Dwight

Son, Brother, Uncle, Partner

Requiescat in Pace

Bro. Richard, C.S.C.

Spes Unica

Requiescat in Pace

Lawrence

Spes Unica

Requiescat in Pace

Thomas

Spes Unica

Requiescat in Pace

Malcolm

Spes Unica

The Spirit of Universal Love

GAYLA Brothers

Ferry Beach, Maine

*Diamonds on the Soles
of His Shoes*

Steven

Good Night, Sweet Prince

And The Band Played On

Randy Shilts

8.8.1951 – 2.17.1994

Borrowed Time: An AIDS Memoir

Paul Monette

10.16.1945 – 2.10.1995

*Close to the Knives: A Memoir of
Disintegration*

David Wojnarowicz

9.14.1954 – 7.22.1992

I Must Down to the Sea Again

Beloved Gay Brother

We Remember You

CHECK OUT OUR OTHER ANTHOLOGIES

HOUSE OF SECRETS: EVERY ROOM HOLDS A STORY

Secrets. They are an integral part of the human experience. They are hidden compartments within each of us where we store our deepest hopes, fears, desires, and vulnerabilities. Secrets also give us a measure of control, allowing us to decide what we reveal to the world and what we reserve for ourselves. If keeping secrets is integral to the human soul, so is the desire to uncover the secrets of others. Our often insatiable curiosity leads us to uncover buried truths, to unravel the mysteries others try to keep to themselves. The delicate balance between preserving, revealing, and discovering secrets is part of our humanity. From these related but conflicting impulses, we develop trust and discretion and learn to cherish the power of knowledge. House of Secrets is a collection of twenty-six short stories related in some manner to guarding or uncovering secrets, written by emerging writers who have significant connections to the State of Ohio. You are sure to find enjoyment within these pages.

METAMORPHOSIS: AN ANTHOLOGY

Change is natural-it's beautiful, it's cathartic, it's necessary. But change is also painful, and ugly, and destructive. It's one of life's only constants. You can either embrace it or struggle against it but it's unlikely you could ever stop it. Inside this anthology we are confronted with many different forms of transformation. Some lift the spirit, some crush the soul, and some show the pathway to the future. It's difficult to capture the essence of a true metamorphosis, but like the chrysalis, this collection contains the "goo of change," so to speak. These 27 Ohio writers have provided touching and ephemeral poems, intelligent and hilarious nonfiction, and fiction that spans from the distant past to the distant future all while being somehow grounded in the present. We hope this collection of stories, poems, and essays manages to take your breath away, break your heart, and even inspire change in your own life-because there's no time like the present to break out of your shell, spread your wings, and embrace your own metamorphosis.

OUTCASTS: AN ANTHOLOGY

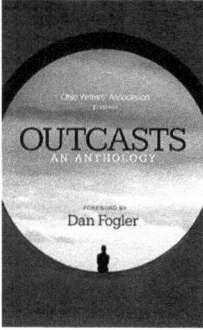

Stories of wizards, prisoners, preachers, and robots. They stick out. They change the conversation. They challenge the traditional narrative. They fascinate us with their ability to act, to dissent, to dare.

ENJOY EIGHTEEN SHORT STORIES that will transport you across a vast range of experiences, realities, and disconnections. Stories of wizards, prisoners, preachers, and robots. They stick out. They change the conversation. They challenge the traditional narrative. They fascinate us with their ability to act, to dissent, to dare. It's rare to find someone who has never experienced the feeling of "otherness"—that isolating feeling of being different and misunderstood. We all are alone in one way or another. We have all felt what it's like to be on the outside looking in. Being an outcast can sometimes mean depravity, sometimes sorrow, and sometimes joy. Being normal is nice, but being an outcast is truly an essential aspect to the human experience.

https://www.ohiowriters.org/publishing

www.ingramcontent.com/pod-product-compliance
Ingram Content Group UK Ltd.
Pitfield, Milton Keynes, MK11 3LW, UK
UKHW021522120225
4563UKWH00028B/424